The Sucker's Kiss

Alan Parker

The Sucker's Kiss

SCEPTRE

First published in Great Britain in 2003
by Hodder and Stoughton
A division of Hodder Headline

A Sceptre Book

1 3 5 7 9 10 8 6 4 2

A CIP catalogue record for this title
is available from the British Library

ISBN 0340 82843 9
ISBN 0340 82844 7

Typeset in Adobe Garamond by Palimpsest Book Production Limited,
Polmont, Stirlingshire
Printed and bound in Great Britain by
Mackays of Chatham plc, Chatham, Kent

Hodder and Stoughton
A division of Hodder Headline
338 Euston Road
London NW1 3BH

For LM

Enormous thanks to Helen Garnons-Williams, Lisa Moran and Ed Victor. Also to the Writers Guild of America and the Screen Actors Guild, whose threatened strikes put me on hiatus and into prose.

Why she loved me, I'll never know.

She always said I had morals that were as unreliable as the Vallejo Ferry and just about as well grounded. I always kidded her that she had hair the color of burnt chestnuts and legs of deepest purple. She wore frocks of printed voile and underwear of crêpe de Chine. *She was beautiful. She was Effie. She was the love of my life.*

My hand stroked the crumpled brown paper bag nestling between my knees, my fingers following the contours of the bottle inside. It was a good wine and I looked forward to pulling the cork and sharing a glass or two with Effie. Out of the rear window of the bus, the San Francisco skyline disappeared behind the hills and I caught myself looking at my reflection in the glass. I wiped away the sweat from my freshly shaved upper lip with my thumb. The snazzy, but seriously phony, Java silk tie looked awkward, out of place and too good for the cream shirt with the fraying collar. I touched the thin cut on my crooked chin; the blunt razor, like my wardrobe, had been courtesy of the Salvation Army. The unstoppable trickle of blood dribbled downwards as I dabbed at the torn skin and hummed to myself the Sally Army anthem: 'Onward Christian soldiers, marching as to war, with the cross of Jesus, going on before.' Such a dumb song, why the heck should I remember it now?

The drizzle outside streaked the bus window like tears. 'The more tears, the greater the magic,' Effie once said. It took me a long time to understand that one.

The police reports on me, of which there are many, say my name is Thomas Patrick Moran. The files always say, 'AKA: Butterfingers.' I was a cannon. A dip. A pit worker. A pickpocket. A thief. And, as immodest as it is shameful to admit, I was the best. Some say they called me Butterfingers because I could slide in and out of a sucker's purse like melted butter. Some say they called me Butterfingers because there were days when my hands shook so badly from needing a drink that I couldn't even hook a wallet from a stiff on a mortuary slab. My job took me to every state in the union, and it's also true that I got pinched in almost every one of them. But I took pride in my work. However humble or pathetic one's labor, you have to take pride in it.

Sure, I admit that there were times when I was lonelier than a lighthouse keeper because I always had to keep my head down for fear of being recognized. Most of the time cracks in the sidewalk, turned-up pant cuffs, worn boots, silver-buckled pumps and pools of piss were more familiar to me than sunshine peeping through a storm cloud. But sometimes I would look at the train wreck of a person in the mirror and realize that I was the same as everyone else trying to make a buck in America. I was no different from the mudsnoots on Wall Street who, like me, had their hands in everyone's pockets. Maybe I even slept a little easier because, gypsy thief that I was, at least I was honest about *my profession. Make no mistake, there's only one map of America, it's green and has an etching of a dead president's face on it.*

I never knew the real world because it was the world of other people. The people I stole from. They had nothing in common with me because, mostly, my only intimate human contact was stroking the lining of a stranger's coat on my way to stealing their pocketbook. I had drifted across America in the company of the abandoned, the dispossessed and the damned, my inner compass taking me east, west, north and south, always guiding me somewhere and mostly leaving me nowhere. But lost, as I always knew I had been, I never realized that I too was one of the damned. That is, until I met Effie, and she taught me that there could be more to a future than just another tomorrow.

They say that in the pocket-picking game the hardest hook to pull is to take something from someone, face to face, staring them straight in the eye. It's called the sucker's kiss and Effie gave it to me – smack on the lips, you might say – right there in a crummy root-and-toot café in San Francisco.

I was seven years old and fast asleep when the earthquake hit San Francisco. It was 5.13 a.m. Wednesday 18 April 1906. My deputy and I were busy chasing Black Bart, the stagecoach robber, and a bunch of cowardly desperadoes out of town when we were interrupted by a massive jolt that woke me and a million others from our slumbers. It seemed that my whole world shook for the longest forty seconds in history. My mom, always prone to instant hysterics, for once had calmly gathered us together – myself, my two sisters, Gracie and Maeve – and walked quietly out of our wooden walk-up on Filbert Street and into the smoke.

Around us, people were yelling and running everywhere, grabbing at their belongings and screaming as if the end of the world had arrived. There were great jagged tears in the road where the cobbles had broken apart like a jigsaw.

But for the four of us, the whole of California could have snapped off and dropped into the sea like a cookie in a cup of coffee and we couldn't have cared less. We just watched with a strange detachment, as if it was meant to be, because, sure as shit, it had nothing to do with us.

I remember we stood there and watched as just a half-block away a gas main exploded and the only home I'd ever known cracked in half and collapsed like pasteboard into the street. Funnily enough, we weren't the least bit afraid or even sad – after all, let's face it, it wasn't *our* house. It was owned by the people who hounded us for our rent the second Tuesday of every month. The same jerks who had threatened to throw us out only the day before. My sisters and I invented names for them: Mr Fatty and Mrs Bones. Odd how we found them funny when their main purpose in life was to bring us misery. Not that they were real villains – they were just ordinary Joes following orders for five bucks a week, scaring little people like my mom and everyone else in our building. There's always something really sad about poor people bullying even poorer people. The real villains were the Nob Hill fat-guts who had sent them. Anyway, the pile of slatboard behind the dust cloud had nothing to do with us. If nothing is all you've got, then nothing is all you can lose.

The four of us just huddled together, kind of resigned to it all as we silently witnessed the panic and madness unfold in the choking smoke that swirled all around us. Whether my mother was in a state of shock or just plain brave, I'll never know – she simply shrugged and waved her hand. I suppose sad people can't get any sadder. Since my dad had died, whatever joy hadn't already been sucked out of her, and whatever morsels of happiness she had scraped up, she had passed on to us three kids.

A cop arrived and started screaming at people who were tossing their belongings out of the top-floor windows. An iron bed landed a foot away from Maeve and bounced up, smacking her in the face. Maeve was bleeding and a woman who said she was a nurse was tearing up bed sheets and using them as bandages.

We sat down on a broken curb and my mom told me to see if I could get Maeve a drink of some kind. I remember walking the streets with shattered glass crunching under my feet and the sound of bells every-where. My handkerchief was pulled up high on my face to keep out the dust and the stench from the broken gas and sewer pipes. All around was chaos, devastation and hysteria and yet I was oddly oblivious to it all. With my handkerchief over my face I felt like some bank robber in a dime novel.

It was as if the whole city had burst every blood vessel in its body. The thick man-made skin of concrete had violently ruptured and the city's guts had vomited onto the pavement. There were gas pipes, water pipes and buckled iron streetcar rails all ripped out of the concrete and left twisted in the air as if they had escaped from some subterranean snake charmer's basket.

A man wearing a butcher's apron and an army helmet was handing out free coffee from the broken window of what used to be Williams' furniture store. He was brewing it in an old tin bathtub, stirring away with a broken broom handle. I nervously asked for four cups. The man in the apron said the first one was free but if I wanted more than one then it would be two cents a mug. And so I walked away with one cup and a lesson: nothing's free in America.

It was then that a huge fireball exploded two streets

away and flames leaped sixty feet high. As everyone else ran away, I did the opposite; I couldn't help myself as I ran towards the free show of a real-life disaster. With morbid curiosity, I stood and watched as dead and injured people were dragged out and laid on the sidewalk. Mesmerized, I gingerly tiptoed through the lines of charred, naked bodies. I was seven years old and had never even seen my sisters undressed, so the sight of these curious, dick-less people with fat, fleshy breasts was beyond my comprehension.

My biology lesson was interrupted as an ambulance wagon almost knocked me down and nurses ran to attend the injured. A man – I guess he was a doctor – took off his coat and handed it to me as he rushed into the building. Suddenly the crazy panic all around me seemed to have vanished in the smoke. I stood staring at the immaculate wool jacket with its silky blue lining. Stroking the smooth satin, I felt a bulge and casually took a peek inside. It was a wallet stuffed with bills. Now, surely I couldn't take this man's wallet – after all, he was selflessly helping others. He was probably, at that very moment, even as I stood there, tearing at his own shirt to make a tourniquet to save some poor soul's life. But it was there and then that I realized that nothing's free in America because everything belongs to someone. And from my brief experience in life I noticed that the problem was that everything generally belonged to someone else. I concluded, standing there in the smoke and the wailing, choking grief of the great 1906 San Francisco earthquake, that this was how things were and probably always have been. What stuck in my throat was that even though it was surely wrong, it didn't matter two bits because that was the way of the world and right then that world had come tumbling down all around us. My mom, a little out of touch with the principles of capitalism, had always told us that Jesus said, 'Everything belongs to everybody,' and so I took it upon myself there and then to start sharing things around. It was as though I was being given a sign from heaven. The sign said, 'sucker', and I felt not even a teeny twinge of guilt or the slightest sense of wrongdoing. No, to tell the truth, I felt . . . well, just great. I deftly pocketed the doctor's wallet and, taking care to smooth the blue satin lining, I hung the coat neatly on the ambulance door handle. Let's face it, I could have filched the guy's coat as well, but you have to have certain principles in life.

With the crisp bills I managed to buy a loaf of bread, coffee for my mom and sodas for Maeve, Gracie and myself. The cops were telling everyone to move on and head towards the Embarcadero. There must have been thousands of us being frog-marched down Filbert Street as the fire-steamer engines raced past us – the firemen frantically roping their bells for us to get out of the way. People walked with their personal belongings stacked high on their heads and mothers clutched babies to their breasts. It was an odd, funereal procession as everyone ambled along in tongue-tied shock.

Suddenly the somber march was interrupted as people began to scream and run in all directions. A giant tawny bull came charging down Stockton Street, pursued by a gang of about thirty people. Without thinking, I joined in the chase after the terrified animal.

At the crossroads on Jackson a Chinese guy ran out into the street and threw a huge machete, which sank deep into the fleshy flank of the unfortunate beast. This slowed the animal down a little but still it galloped bravely onward. There was a trail of blood that must have bled the wretched animal dry because in Portsmouth Square it stopped running and turned to face us all. Suddenly the mob became very quiet, as mobs do when faced with imminent danger. The bull stared straight at *me* as it stood there scraping its hoof in a puddle of its own blood. What could I do? Say sorry, it wasn't *my* machete? The Chinese guys were defiantly strolling up to the exhausted, wounded animal like they were matadors in Spain or someplace. Just then a shot rang out and a mounted cop killed the bull stone-dead with a bullet to the side of the head. Our collective oohs and aahs were short-lived as the very same cop galloped towards us, firing his revolver into the air. The mob split in all directions and I ran down Clay until my lungs gave out and I collapsed onto my knees, coughing up soot and dust into the gutter. A soldier gave me a swig from his flask, which tasted like the water from the rusty barrel in our yard. It made me feel a whole lot better except for one thing: I realized I had lost my mom and sisters. I was on my own.

I chased up Telegraph Hill and climbed down the Filbert Street steps to the Embarcadero. The Ferry Building tower was still standing, although a little wobbly, and it was a beacon for the thousands of families elbowing their way to the ferries, hoping to get across to the safety of the East Bay. It was hopeless and there was no way I could find my mom for now. I decided to make the most of my predicament and as I was pushed around in the crush my hand slipped into places where it didn't belong.

For the rest of that day I dashed all over San Francisco, helping out wherever I could by holding people's coats. With a handkerchief over my face to keep out the dust and smoke and the stink of the shattered sewers, I wasn't just a kid, I was Billy the Kid – I was Dick Turpin, Robin Hood, Jesse James, Black Bart – I was Terrible Tommy Moran, the human coat-hanger. I had so many wallets that I couldn't stuff them all in my pockets. It was as if somehow old God up there had given me permission.

The army had pitched thirty rows of tents in Jefferson Square and that night I billeted with a battalion of the 22nd Infantry who had come in from Fort Dowell on Angel Island.

The winds blowing in from the ocean had suddenly picked up, sending the red-hot cinders high in the air as the heat from the fires created its own gusts and the scorching draughts of air whipped the flames into a frenzy. That first night was so bright with flames that it seemed like day. I fell asleep wrapped in a smelly, mildewed army blanket. In one day I had lost my innocence and gained enough dubious self-confidence to last a lifetime.

2

The next day, the fires were raging out of control. I headed to our old church of Saints Peter and Paul on Filbert to see if anyone I knew was there, but the flames from Chinatown had licked along Powell and sadly the church was no more.

It was no surprise that Chinatown had gone first, after all, it was a tinderbox of jumbled slat and board and didn't even have a fire station of its own. There were eighty fire stations in all of San Francisco and someone in City Hall joked that the twenty thousand Chinamen who lived there could piss the fire out, for all they cared. Chinatown survived for barely six hours before everyone was evacuated to the army barracks out at the Presidio, including a line of gaunt-faced hopheads who had puffed their pipes of opium on their way to heaven and awoken to the madness of hell.

The National Guardsmen were the worst for looting. They were foraging amongst the Chinatown ashes with gunnysacks full of melted jewelry as they systematically ransacked the place, or what was left of it. Mayor Schmitz had issued a proclamation that the police and army should shoot on sight anyone found looting, which was a joke because these guys with the gunnysacks *were* the army.

I saw a bunch of kids who had been caught stealing on Powell. They were roped together and being hauled down to the wharf. Around their necks they had cardboard signs saying, 'I am a thief.' Can you believe that? It was a pitiful sight but it didn't put me off for a moment. After all, I was taking wallets from people's live bodies so you couldn't call that looting, and let's face it, if anyone was going to wear a cardboard sign saying, 'I am a thief,' how about the National Guard and most of the Board of Supervisors at City Hall?

There was another guy hanging out of a broken jewelry store window who had been bayoneted to death and the soldiers had just left him there as a warning to others. He still had a silver coffee pot in his hand. By sunup, that too would be stolen.

The firestorm was now engulfing half the city and the firemen, police and military were helpless because the quake had ruptured all the city's main water lines and the central supply pipes from San Andreas Lake and Crystal Springs had been shattered in a thousand places. A navy unit was desperately hooking up a mile of hose to bring water from the bay at Meigg's Wharf to Jackson Square.

I remember the air being full of smells: smoke, dust, gas, sewer shit, dynamite and the worst smell of all, which the soldiers said was rotting and charred flesh. The army had started to blow up buildings to try to create a firebreak on Van Ness and they had even brought in artillery to shell the buildings across the street. I loved watching that, it was like being slap in the middle of a real war, except there was no one firing back. I helped a guy to calm the horses that were getting real spooked by all the hot cinders floating in the air. Everyone said that the army seemed to be creating more problems than they were solving.

At the Palace Hotel they were trying to save the building but the top ten floors were already in flames, which seemed kind of dumb to me. Down below they had been emptying the kitchen larders. Originally they had offered up their famous fruit flans but as the flames crept down the building they decided to give away the contents of their wine cellar, which attracted a good deal larger crowd. I managed to grab a bottle, which apparently was kind of special, and a guy gave me a dollar for it. To be accurate, he gave me five dollars because I had my hand in his back pocket a second after he put away his wallet.

On the third day I attached myself to a column of soldiers from Fort Mason who had been sent to guard the old US Mint building on Fifth and Mission. They said there were rumors that it was about to be attacked by an armed gang and I was really looking forward to that.

A few soldiers in the column were also detailed to guard a whole bunch of convicts from the city jail. Once the flames had reached the building next door, the jailers had promptly quit for Oakland, leaving the prisoners locked in their cells to await their own barbecue. The prisoners were now sitting manacled in the street, waiting for an army truck to arrive. There were only four troopers to guard them, so the sergeant handed me a carbine and told me to point it in the direction of the convicts. As I could hardly lift the rifle, I think the prisoners were more concerned that I'd pull the trigger by mistake – which is what very nearly happened when an explosion on Market whooshed a giant cloud of hot embers in our direction. I dropped the rifle as one hit me in the eye and I fell to the ground clutching my face. Boy, did it hurt. But the convicts didn't run away. Instead they all ran towards this screaming kid wriggling on the sidewalk. A soldier and two convicts put ointment on my eye and bandages around my head.

A mounted cop galloped me down to a refugee camp on Valencia, where he dumped me at the front of a soup-kitchen line that was six blocks long. The people standing there were rich and poor, all mixed together, hoping for a handout. That was the crazy thing about the quake – it was a great equalizer because just about everything had tumbled down or burned, whether it was a swanky hotel or a slatboard slum. But right then I couldn't give a heck because I thought my entire eye was on fire.

A pushy Salvation Army woman grabbed my arm and dragged me to a tent where they were relocating people and lost children.

'Where's your family?'

'Don't know.'

'Are you lost?'

'No, my mom and sisters are.' I let out a yell as the pain pierced my eyeball.

'Does your eye hurt?' she asked.

I nodded.

'How much does it hurt?'

'Like fuck, lady,' I answered. No one said that word at home, but for the last three days it was the only word I ever heard. I think I shocked the Sally Army lady.

'Like what?'

'A lot,' I shouted.

'We're going to have to get you to the hospital in Oakland.'

She led me to another tent and told me to lie down on a cot. A friendly nurse put dollops of fresh ointment on my eye and gently wrapped a new bandage around my head. She also gave me a spoonful of something from a tiny blue bottle to make me sleep. That night my whole head started to burn and I thought that the fire in my eye had spread to my whole body just like it had in the city. I dreamed I was on my own in the streets and the fires had subsided. It was scary being alone out in the dark because the cops said that a lot of the graves in the cemeteries had been disturbed in the quake, releasing the dead bodies. A guy at the Palace Hotel told me that people had even seen skeletons walking down Market Street. In my nightmare I kept running and running. Just like I did for the rest of my life.

At sunup I was helped down to the Ferry Building along with a whole bunch of kids from the Protestant Orphanage Asylum and put on a boat to Oakland. I looked back at the charred remains of the city that seemed to be almost completely destroyed. The air was full of black smoke and the stench of water on smoldering wood. As I looked across the bay I could see the last fire as it was being put out. It was a little after 7 a.m. and I looked up at the dark sky with my good eye. It had started to rain.

3

What was left of San Francisco after the 1906 quake and fire was a great place for a kid growing up because it seemed that the entire city was a construction site. They said that five hundred blocks of thirty thousand buildings were destroyed in the fire and every week a brand new building popped up.

My burns healed pretty good but it left me with a slightly droopy left eye, which people said was kind of cute – like a perpetual wink.

My mom got us a new apartment in a patched-up building in an alley off Filbert Street. After the fire they knocked together a makeshift wooden staircase that zig-zagged up the outside of the building and as you climbed the steps you could hear it groan. My mom was a great seamstress and worked for Mr Kittleman, who owned the Madison Modes dress shop over in Fillmore. Old Mr Kittleman loved my mom and helped her with the first month's rent. He used to bring stacks of fabric to the apartment because my mom could make anything from a wedding dress to a three-piece suit. Kittleman would leave the two-inch thick mail-order fashion catalogs and circle the things he wanted her to copy. I loved those catalogs; I would sit on the wooden stairs for hours flicking through the pages with Gracie, memorizing every suit, sock, frock and shoe. It became a lifelong obsession.

It took three months to rebuild my old school – even then, it was just a slat-board shack that they'd thrown up on Filbert and Powell among the debris of the old Saints Peter and Paul Church.

I was free to roam the streets and sharpen my new-found talents. All those guys bending over their saws, hammers and monkey wrenches, showing the cracks in their butts, were easy pickings for me as I honed my pickpocketing skills.

I went all over the city, but my favorite place was Chinatown. After 1906 it was suggested that Chinatown, or *Tangrenbu*, which is its old name, be relocated out to the mudflats at Hunter's Point in San Mateo County. The Chinese elders got wind of this plan and so they started rebuilding in the same five square city blocks where they had always been. The bricks were still warm from the fire and they were tossing them around like hot muffins. A lot of palms must have been greased for permits because Chinatown went up so fast that it was rebuilt in less than two years – a whole year ahead of the rest of the city.

I first met Sammy Liu in the summer of 1908. I must have been about nine and I was working the crowd at a ceremony in Chinatown to change the name of the old Dupont Street to Grant. All the City Hall dignitaries were there – well, the ones that weren't in jail – all lined up and cutting the ribbon. There was a small crowd of mostly Chinese watching with detached amusement – probably because they had no intention of changing the name of the street that bisected Chinatown. Twenty years later they still called it *Dupon Gai.*

Usually I had no trouble lifting from Chinamen. Although they were a little sensitive to the touch, they had those baggy jackets and giant pockets that you could practically climb into and they wouldn't feel a thing. All over Chinatown they used to paste their newspapers on the walls and as they stood there, deep in thought while reading the small print, I would be working away. That day at the ceremony I had my hand in this guy's burlap haversack and took out what felt like a large bundle of dollar bills. Without looking, I slipped the roll into my pocket and backed away from the crowd. In a side alley by the Nin Yang Candle factory I took out the stash only to discover that the neat roll of paper was just that – paper – all roughly the size of dollar bills with Chinese writing on them. It was then that I was startled by a high-pitched giggle. I looked up and there was a skinny Chinese kid. He was probably the same age as me, but a lot taller.

'I watched you pick that guy's pocket,' he said.

'So?'

'You're pretty good.'

I shrugged immodestly. It was the first time that anyone had ever actually praised me for my curious antisocial skills.

'You know what you have there?'

'No.' I looked down at the meaningless paper bundle.

'*Wenhuashe.*'

'Huh?'

'The guy who collects all pieces of paper thrown away in Chinatown with writing on it.'

That seemed crazy to me, but over a plate of beef porridge at the Yoot Hong basement on Clay, the skinny kid called Sammy Liu explained. The guy I had rolled was the paper gatherer because in Chinatown it was considered disrespectful to toss away any piece of paper with Chinese writing on it.

'It's mostly Chinese horseshit,' said Sammy. 'It's really a way of keeping the streets clean and every so often the *Wenhuashe* picks up delicate information that someone in Chinatown would buy with real money. So it makes people . . . careful.'

Sammy lit up a cigar that was at least eight inches long. He said that it had been rolled on the thighs of Chinese virgins deep in Chinatown, where white guys didn't dare to tread. I asked if that was also Chinese horseshit but he insisted it was true. I looked around to see if anyone would tell this ten-year-old kid to put out a cigar as big as his arm. But curiously, no one said a word. More than that, as we walked out, the lady behind the counter waved her hand as Sammy tried to pay. He said thank you and she bowed, nodded and smiled most nervously.

'We ate for free?' I said as we climbed the steps to the street.

'Yeah, but it's not really me. It's my uncle.' He didn't want to explain further and so he swiftly changed the subject.

'You wanna play stickball?'

4

We played stickball in *Ohn Nu Hong* Alley, which Sammy translated roughly into English as 'Piss Alley' because that was where everyone in Chinatown urinated; hence it was always available for stickball. Over the next few years Sammy and I played a hundred Stickball World Series, as we became best friends. We were the San Francisco Seals, we were the Oakland Oaks, we were Frank and Jesse James, we were the Katzenjammer Kids, we were Wild Bill Hickok and Bronco Billy, we were Cochise and every Apache that ever lived. When Geronimo died in 1909, Sammy and I went into mourning for a whole week and when we launched one last daring raid on Fosco's pastry shop on behalf of the Apaches, we got chased all the way down Columbus by a cop on horseback.

Sammy and I were also the undisputed, if unofficial, American champions at rat catching. All over the city they had posted these notices that said:

REWARD FOR RATS:
A REWARD OF 5 CENTS WILL BE PAID
FOR EVERY RAT DEAD OR ALIVE
DELIVERED TO DESIGNATED HEALTH
DEPARTMENT RECEIVING STATIONS.

There was always a bubonic plague scare going on in San Francisco. Usually they blamed it on the Chinese – all those rat-infested steamers arriving from Hong Kong and Shanghai. Every so often they would fish some unfortunate Chinese stowaway out of the bay who was supposedly carrying some kind of God-awful disease that could possibly wipe out half of California.

Some smart guy figured out that the plague wasn't spread by the rats, but by the fleas on the rats. Apparently the fleas then take a shine to, and a bite at, humans. Sammy borrowed an old dog called Poo Shoo that could sniff out a rat from twenty yards. We caught black rats, brown rats, red rats and gray rats – rats as big as your hand and rats as big as tomcats. We made these great wooden tongs so that we didn't have to touch them before dumping them into buckets full of kerosene. After weeks of chasing Poo Shoo into every gutter in San Francisco we turned in over fifty rats to the receiving station and had to share the grand sum of two dollars-fifty. After that we both got a little disillusioned with honest labor, so I reluctantly decided that my pickpocketing was probably more lucrative and Sammy went to work for his uncle.

Chin Ju Bing was the meanest sonofabitch gangster in Chinatown. He ran the *San Yi* who, along with their main rivals, the *Si Yi*, owned just about everything from laundries to whorehouses and the *fan tan* gambling joints to the *pak kop piu*: the white pigeon lottery. They called it that because you always lost and everyone would tear up their tickets and throw them in the air like a flock of pigeons and then scramble to pick up the pieces for good luck. Chin Ju Bing was also known as Little Joe. But to Sammy he was Uncle Joe, surrogate father and protector ever since Sammy's dad was found with a .38 bullet in his head in Grocery Alley. Wherever Sammy went in Chinatown, I basked in his sunshine.

Sammy used to work for a nickel a pipe, in one of his uncle's hoodoo joints in Mah Fong Alley behind the stables. They said that the smell of horse dung disguised the sweet smell of opium in the barn beyond. Sammy's job was to scrape out the bowls of the pipes and mix the ashes, the *yen-shee*, with the new opium. He used to make me go down there to keep him company. I used to help by sprinkling water onto the blankets on the floor, which helped to suck up the fumes. Occasionally I would relieve the hophead suckers of whatever dough they had left after paying their money to 'kick the gong around', chasing the sweet blue smoke into oblivion. In the dim light of the Chinese nut oil lamps the hopped-up saps, lying helpless on the wooden bunks, were pushovers as I stripped their pockets. I felt bad, but Sammy said that these people had already lost their souls, so they certainly wouldn't miss their wallets.

My favorite place of all was this great Chinese theater on Jackson. Friday nights were the best – all those waiters out of their heads on cheap rice wine, or whatever else took their fancy. I remember there was this great comedian called Ah Soon who used to make jokes about the rival tong gangs. The audience used to laugh till the tears ran down their faces and their dollar bills practically dropped out of their pockets. I never understood one word of any of the Chinese jokes but I used to laugh along with them like I was from Shanghai or someplace.

One night, some guy called Big Mike Abrahams came crashing in. He jumped right through the back curtain and took a bread knife to Ah Soon on stage and cut the guy's throat right there in front of us all. The audience kept on laughing until the blood squirted as far back as the tenth row and then they finally figured it was for real and started to scream. Some kind of drug thing, they said it was, or maybe he just didn't care for Ah Soon's act. I've heard of comics dying on stage but, frankly, Big Mike probably understood the jokes less than I did.

Big Mike used to hole up at this flophouse on Union, which is where the Chinese guys eventually caught up with him. One night they sealed up his room with burlap sacks, stuck a rubber tube through the keyhole and gassed the poor guy while he was sleeping off a bottle of Happy Jack. I guess you could say that he went to his maker a little more peacefully than poor Ah Soon did. Sammy said the *Hip Sing Tong* guys did it. Mind you, they always said that. Mostly because they usually did.

5

My mom always made me sit outside on the stairs when Maeve and Gracie were having their weekly bath, so my knowledge of the opposite sex was somewhat limited. I consequently relied on Sammy's experience and my own research at the Mansion on Jackson Street near Kearny. I know that 'The Mansion' sounds fancy, but actually it was the crummiest and biggest brothel in San Francisco. This guy McCarthy had got elected as mayor on a promise of making San Francisco 'the Paris of America', and the first thing he did when he took office was to take graft from a guy called Gerry McGlane, who was allowed to open a 'Parisian' brothel.

Inside there were over a hundred tiny curtained-off cubicles where for a couple of dollars guys could take their pleasures with a South American beauty or, for a dollar more, they could get a genuine 'Frenchie' all the way from Paris or Warsaw or some place not around here. Not that Sammy and I were very much involved. The girls liked us and we would pour their drinks, and if it was a slow night they would show us a thing or two.

As fate would have it, I was there with Sammy the night the police raided the place. When the cops saw so many spotty kids getting their two dollars-worth, they immediately closed the place down and made us all line up outside in the freezing cold. We stood there, ten skinny kids, shivering on Jackson Street with nothing but our underpants and a skin full of goose bumps between us and pneumonia.

'My mom will kill me,' I said.

'Forget it. Your mom won't know,' said Sammy. He was freezing too, but he was completely unafraid.

'But they're taking our names.'

'Don't worry, they're bluffing.'

'They look serious to me. What makes you so sure?'

The cops were taking their time getting to us as they took the details of each of the kids standing there in the street catching their deaths.

'My uncle says these cops have had more grease than the Van Ness streetcar wheels. And you know what happened to Police Chief Biggy.'

'No. What happened?'

'Big Bill closed down the Municipal brothel a few years back and . . .'

Sammy shook his head as if that was sufficient to finish his sentence. We both clutched ourselves, trembling from the cold. But I wanted to know more.

'What?'

'He mysteriously disappeared.' Sammy's lips were now blue and his teeth were chattering. 'From his police launch. They fished him out of the bay the next day.'

'Murdered?'

'No one knows.'

'S-s-suicide?' I chattered. I was now beyond cold and

had a problem putting my words together. Sammy shook his head, no.

'Strict Catholic.'

'How about the guy piloting the boat? Didn't he see anything?'

'Amnesia.'

'Amnesia?'

'Couldn't remember a thing. My Uncle Joe said the rumor was that when they fished Biggy out of the water he'd had his dick chopped off – they found it in his coat pocket with his watch. That's enough to give anyone amnesia.'

Sure enough, the cops took down our particulars and told us all to scram. We grabbed our clothes and ran home splashing through the puddles, shivering and laughing in the rain.

Two days later, the Mansion was open for business again.

6

I have to say right now that my mom was never pleased with my chosen profession. Let's just say that she strongly disapproved of my associations with rats, be they dead or alive, four- or two-legged, and certainly not Chinamen. I guess I was a problem for her and it was more than she deserved. My mom was a big woman with arms like ham hocks and although she never seemed to say much, on the occasions when she was driven to shouting, you could hear her three blocks away. She wore thick glasses from too many years of sewing by dim light and had three vertical creases etched into her forehead which gave the appearance of a permanent frown. The funny thing about my mom was that even though she made those beautiful dresses for Mr Kittleman, I never saw her in anything but a brown smock and an apron. And a hat. She always wore a hat when she was sewing, because she said she didn't have time to fix her hair.

The day she got her new sewing machine was the first time that I had seen her truly happy since my dad died. Mr Kittleman had helped her with the payments; I guess my mom was a good investment. He only paid her two dollars-fifty a dress and they always took pride of place in his window. Mr Huber, who lived upstairs, helped the deliveryman carry the sewing machine up the wobbly staircase as Maeve and I guided the way. The machine had curly iron legs and a shiny mahogany top, and it was my job to keep it polished. It had pride of place in the corner of the apartment and my mom seemed to spend her every waking hour rocking back and forth as her feet worked the iron treadle and she yanked the material under the foot of the needle. She was a good woman and certainly didn't deserve a son who made her so mad. And boy, did I make her mad. It was not so much that I kept putting my hands into other people's pockets. I think she could live with that, because she never ever mentioned the dollar bills I used to slip into her sewing basket. Most particularly, I think she got mad because I got caught a lot and what was a secret family embarrassment mushroomed into a neighborhood scandal.

Being nabbed is an occupational hazard when you're serving such a tough apprenticeship. Frankly, I learned very early that it's more the law of averages than it is the law of the land. The police got to know me pretty well, and mostly they used to smile at the thought of me relieving a Nob Hill fat-gut of a wallet that was bigger than I was. True, I got collared many times, but more often than not they let me go with a finger wagging and an Irish wink that made me feel that I was one of them. I learned early on that thieves and cops were really one and the same – chipped from the same block of St Patrick street granite and separated by a blue uniform, a pension, and not much else.

When things became really bad, the cops would threaten my mom that if I were caught just one more time they'd lock me up for good. They said that I could be sent to a special prison they'd recently built for juvenile offenders in San Jose where you had to wear a strait-jacket and were fed from the municipal garbage dump – and crazy priests played with your dooley.

So at those times when it seemed like a good idea to keep my head down for a while I would be forced to stay in the apartment, and when mom went over to Fillmore to take her finished dresses to Mr Kittleman, I would be guarded by my elder sister Maeve. I used to try bribing her with all sorts of trinkets from my stash, but she was incorruptible and didn't hesitate to smack me if I dared shift out of the armchair. Maeve had a mean streak that I thought was above and beyond the call of duty for the way older sisters usually mistreat bratty little brothers. She had never felt the childish happiness of not knowing and not caring. Maeve never knew the pleasure of breaking a vase and hiding it in the trash, of kicking the plug out of the rain barrel and flooding the yard. Poor Maeve, she had no childhood at all. She was born old.

I loved my little sister Gracie, who was two years younger than me but, as Mr Huber upstairs pointed out, she hadn't been given a full deck of cards to play with. My mom said that God hadn't finished working on her when the angels brought her into the world just a little too quickly. I never could figure that one out – I guess God must have been on a coffee break or something.

Not that Gracie was crazy or anything; let's just say she was a little slow. She would scream like a madman if she saw a cockroach and I would bat the insect with a broom and hug Gracie as we watched the bug wriggle across the floor in its silent death throes.

The two of us would go all over the neighborhood together as we climbed the steep hills and dodged the Mason Street cable cars.

'Eskimos, Tommy!' she used to shout to me and I'd rub her nose with mine like they say they do in Canada and she would laugh like a corked-up barroom drunk. Sure, Gracie had a head that was emptier than a Cuban rattle but she had the prettiest face with the weirdest green eyes and a way of looking at you that made you think that she was looking at someone standing behind you. She had these big black pupils that bobbed around inside those green eyes like drunken nickels. But she sure could turn people's heads. Complete strangers would stop to pinch her cheek and stroke her yellow hair and meanwhile I would take the opportunity to dip their purse or take the loose change from their pockets.

At Mr Rizzola's corner store, Gracie and I were world champion consumers of snowball cones and peppermint stick candy. He would always shake his head, wondering where these two poor kids ever got their money. When we arrived home my mom used to ask where all of Gracie's new toys had come from and I'd say people thought she was so cute they just gave them to her. Fortunately my mom never visited Posnick's Five & Dime on Kearny, where they probably would have had a word to say about the droopy-eyed kid they were forever chasing out of their store as he dragged his blond-haired sister behind him.

At the end of the day, Mr Huber would step over Gracie and me as we sat on the steps flicking through mom's catalogs. He worked at the brick factory at Corona Heights and I used to have fun creeping behind him as he dragged his tired body up the wooden stairs. I would swipe his wallet and he never used to feel a thing, but I always gave it back to him at the top of the stairs. It used to really make him laugh – sometimes he even gave me a dime. He used to shake his head and say, 'You're some kid, Tommy. And a good-looking boy. The way you take my wallet . . . oh my . . . I hope I live long enough for you to be President.'

Mr Huber was a hell of a nice guy, but I have to say that he and Mrs Huber were a curious couple. He was a shy, kind of dull man who worked all the hours God sent so that Mrs Huber could dress up in her ridiculous rose-pink taffeta dresses. She was loud, gaudy and dripping with cheap jewelry – 'pig meat strutting around as lamb chops,' as my mom used to say.

In the daytime, Mrs Huber used to have a lot of guys coming by, which I never could figure out at the time. Every other month it was a new chump and she was real friendly with them. My mom called them Mrs Huber's 'gentlemen'. She used to pass me on the stairs and tickle me under the chin and, sometimes, I got a wet, crimson kiss on the cheek and a quick peek at her breasts. Her face was powdered as thick as cement and she stank of *eau de cologne* and gin. At the time I could never understand the sham and lies of their attachment. I often wondered if old Mr Huber knew about his wife's shenanigans or was that how all married people behaved? It sure confused the hell out of me and put me off that 'love, cherish and obey' stuff for a long time to come.

7

One time, after a midday visit by one of Mrs Huber's 'gentlemen', I followed him down the Filbert hill, and while he waited for the cable car on Mason, I made my move. As my hand fished around his jacket pocket I screamed in agony as a police nightstick dug deep into my kidneys. I remember my mom's face as the cop brought me back to our rooms and tossed me through the door. He introduced himself as Officer Horgan and before he had even caught his breath from the steep walk-up, he politely asked where my mother had originally hailed from in beautiful Ireland. His Irish accent was so thick that you'd swear he'd got off the boat only last Tuesday. Funny, it didn't matter how many years these crusty bog-hoppers had been here, they still kept their brogue, just like the Italians kept their language, I guess – more for protection than anything else. But this particular fish-eater sure didn't believe in special treatment, because instead of staying for a nip of Irish whiskey left over from Christmas and a verse or two of 'The Rose of Tralee', he suddenly turned nasty and snapped at my mom, 'Where is the boy's father?'

'He's no longer with us,' said my mom.

'Is he in San Francisco?'

'No, I believe in heaven.'

'I'm sorry, ma'am. May God look after him.'

The cop removed his hat as if the very act of doing so would bring my dad back, but it also seemed to take the lid off of his angry side. My dad always said that if you put an Irishman on a spit there would always be another Irishman handy to baste him, which never seemed more relevant to me than now. As I stood in the doorway of the apartment, my head contorted upwards, his giant fist viciously gripped my hand and my collar at the same time. His knuckles dug into my windpipe and he stooped down until his eyes were inches from mine. He had a face like a mildewed bath sponge and a nose bigger than a horse's dick.

'Now listen to me, and listen well. If you get caught thieving again you're definitely going to the kids' prison in San Jose, you hear me?'

I nodded, finding it hard to breathe so I couldn't say anything even if I wanted to, which I didn't.

'Or we'll be sending you and your mother back to Sligo, do you hear me?'

I nodded again as he lifted me on to my toes. It really hurt as Horgan kept twisting and I had no choice but to roll the bastard, slipping my hand into his pocket and lifting his notebook and whistle.

He let me go and put his hat back on.

'I'm sorry, ma'am, but with no father, this kid needs discipline. He's a menace to the streets. You should be thinking seriously as to what you're going to be doing with him.'

'I will, officer,' said my mom, 'I will.'

'Good day, now, ma'am. I should be booking him, but my brother's wife is from Sligo.'

Yeah, sure she was. Everyone knows that no one from Sligo ever married anyone who wasn't from Sligo, that's why we're all crazy.

He tipped his hat, made for the door, and my mom slumped over her sewing machine and began to cry.

I walked out and sat on the wooden step as the self-important, shanty Irish cop loudly clumped down the stairs below me like he was treading through molasses. I rubbed my reddened hand and this made me think of my dad, whose hands were always red. He worked at the Thatcher Ice House at Meigg's Wharf and when he came home after a long day of hauling and hacking at ice blocks his hands were perpetually frozen and raw. After work he would stand by the stove in the corner of our old apartment rubbing his fingers and saying that he couldn't get the blood back into them. My mom used to pour hot water into a china basin and he'd slip in his hands and sit there in silence, kicking off his boots as Maeve and I tried to rub life back into his rock-hard feet. He died of bronchitis the Christmas before the earthquake.

I stood up and with all my strength angrily pitched Horgan's stupid police whistle deep into the shadows of the alley. He briefly turned around as he heard the clanking of metal on the cobbles. He shrugged, rubbed his horse-dick nose and walked on.

Inside, my mom was still sobbing in the corner, stooped

over her sewing machine. I walked over to her and put my hand on her shoulder.

'I'm sorry.'

She wiped her face with her apron and looked up at me. 'We're going to have to go to the priest.'

The cop was bluffing about Sligo, of course, but that had done it for my mother. She could handle me being locked up in a reformatory in San Jose, but she would most certainly not entertain the possibility of going back to Sligo.

8

My school was attached to the church of Saints Peter and Paul. Well, it had been until it burned down in the fire. Now the Salesian School shared the same makeshift wooden building with the church. The scary dark-robed priest was called Father Imielinski, who had a thick Polish accent and smelled of wet socks. He lectured me, graphically pointing out that even at my tender age the prospect of eternal damnation was not beyond the realms of possibility. But what were they to do with me? He repeated from the catechism, 'God has to keep your hands from picking and stealing . . . picking and stealing . . .' After the fourth time, I was beginning to get the message.

The next stop was St Mary's Cathedral on Van Ness. I was hauled off to meet with Father Ramm. Father Ramm had become something of a hero of the Catholic Church in San Francisco ever since he risked his life after the quake by courageously climbing the spire of St Mary's at the height of the great fire, thus saving the cathedral by putting out the flames with his cassock.

The inherent goodness of this kindly priest exuded from him as profusely as his rancid tobacco breath, which was so hideous that it made my eyes water. But as daunting as this man was, I was not afraid. After all, next to Black Bart, the stagecoach robber, Father Ramm was everyone's hero in Catholic school.

'Were you naked, Father?' I suddenly blurted out the question that had bothered me since 1906.

'When was I naked?' he asked, rather defensively.

'When you climbed St Mary's spire during the Great Fire.'

'No, I wasn't naked.'

I furrowed my brow, a little disappointed. 'So how did you put the fire out with your cassock, Father?'

With a sigh, Father Ramm neatly stepped away from this curveball.

'I just did.'

'Was it a spare cassock?'

'No, it wasn't.'

'Was it the one you were wearing?'

'Yes, it was.'

'So you were naked?'

'I was not.'

'Were you wearing a vest and underpants?'

'I was wearing a coat.'

'A coat?'

'It was with the coat that I extinguished the flames.'

'A coat?'

'A coat.'

There was a short silence. Father Ramm seemed grateful that the interrogation by adolescent had ended. He looked at me. I looked at him. I smiled.

'It's a better story if you were naked,' I said. His hand

smacked the side of my head like an oak mallet and knocked me off the chair.

He picked me up from the floor, clasped me tightly to his chest, stroked my hair and mumbled a Latin prayer. His cassock stank of incense smoke, body odor and Prince Albert rum-and-maple pipe tobacco. I distracted myself from the impending possibility of being suffocated at his navel by lifting his tobacco pouch and a very nice briar pipe from his deep cassock pocket. I promptly put them back. Never ever roll a priest.

After long deliberations between the reverend fathers they concluded that I was unhealthily contumacious and would therefore have to be sent to a special Catholic home for recalcitrant boys in Sacramento. I hated the sound of 'contumacious' and 'recalcitrant' because what the fuck did that mean? I also hated the sound of Sacramento. Even Sligo sounded better than Sacramento. Personally, I always loved the sound of Sligo. Whenever my mother had partaken of a glass or two of Mrs Huber's gin she would always speak lovingly of her birthplace and our ancestral home. Consequently my sisters and I knew Sligo well, with its hanging gardens, its sunny beaches where you could buy three Coca-Colas for a penny and where on each St Patrick's Day small guys jumped out of the long green grass giving away handfuls of Irish dollar bills. Just why my mother ever left Ireland was always a mystery to Maeve and me.

And so, quite terrified at the prospect of what my future held, I sat silently on the hard wooden bench in the small anteroom at St Mary's. In the inner sanctum my mother wept, grabbing the priest's arm and clasping it to her head. Interspersed with Hail Marys and Glory Bes she kept saying over and over how grateful she was that the church was taking me off her hands. As I sat there I thought that she was rather too grateful and so I decided I would put them all out of their misery – and at no expense to the church or the state of California.

I pulled my bandanna over my face – as much to emulate Black Bart as to block out the nasty sweet smell of incense. I made a gun with my two forefingers and thumb and edged backwards – and anyone who tried to stop me was a dead man. I climbed the shelves full of sacramental wine jugs and squeezed through the small window at the back of the sacristy. Dropping onto the lead roof of the adjacent seminary, I slid down the drainpipe and ran as fast as I could through the horsemeat shop in the yard behind.

I felt guilty not saying goodbye to my mom, but frankly she was probably relieved to find me gone. One way or another, I was off her hands. In the years that followed I often wondered if she worried about me and how I was – or whether she, Maeve and Gracie would have ever come to visit me at the home in Sacramento. Who knows? I always wanted to ask her and, perhaps, say sorry for leaving that day. After all, she was my mom and I loved her. Although at times it felt that the feeling wasn't entirely mutual – it's easy to see why. The same goes for Maeve and Gracie. I really loved them, especially little Gracie. I left on 12 February 1913 – two days before my fourteenth birthday on Valentine's Day. I told myself that maybe one day I'd get the chance to explain things to them and they'd understand. Perhaps one day we'd all be able to meet for a reunion hooley and dance like dervishes, get drunk and sing those sad Irish songs about Sligo and Donegal that always make you cry. But most of all, perhaps we could laugh out loud till our sides ached and, simplest of all, be happy just like other people.

9

I grew up on the road and, as the freelance nature of my occupation demanded, I went all over by riding the rods, hopping the freight trains from Cheyenne, Wyoming to Duluth, Minnesota; from Hastings, Nebraska to Fayette, Missouri. I lost half the skin on my back to the railroad cinders and had a scar from my neck to my butt to prove it.

If you stayed in one place too often the whiz cops – who specialize in making life difficult for cannons – pickpockets, like me – start to think they're related to you. I always worked alone and, as I've pointed out, I always had principles. I never took from anyone who didn't look as if they could stand the loss and always left a dime for the guy's trolley fare home. Most of all I never took more than I needed to live, just like they do in the real jungle. And month by month, year by year, I became pretty good at what I did. I had the instincts of a bat in a crowd. I could collide without touching. I could sip coffee in a two-bit diner and listen to six different conversations at once. My eyes became trained so that I could spot a silk scarf fluttering in the wind like a hunter spots a white-winged dove.

I had nothing and needed even less: just a new suit

every so often to make me look older and a quart or two of good bourbon, which I admit I had become fond of at too early an age. You could say that it wasn't much of a life, but it was a living. Those weren't the best of times for anyone, and at least I always had a job, which is more than a lot of poor souls could boast about. Also, I never took from cripples – even rich ones. Or priests. I definitely wouldn't roll a priest, on account of superstitious reasons. They say an honest buck is the only one that doesn't dance on your pillow at night, but personally I slept easy. You've got to think of the sucker the same way a fisherman thinks of a bass – you can't get sentimental. As I saw it, I had a rare and magical gift because I could take money from any place on the body – and I'd put you off your sandwich if I told you *all* the places.

I had given my young life to the shadows and the dust of my profession and day by day, year after year, I adjusted to the loneliness of a life amongst strangers. Along the way there were a few girls who kept me company and sometimes I even remembered their names. I never thought for a second that I would ever settle down – not with one person and not in one place. Over the years I had known too many so-called happily in love people and I'd also rolled the very same suckers – fishing through their wallets and purses stuffed full of deceit and betrayal. Honestly, you'd be surprised at what respectable people get up to in their spare time. In a way, you could say that I've had a privileged look into other people's secrets by virtue of stealing stuff they kept close to their chests – but never so close that I, or some other pit worker, couldn't lift it off them to take a peek. For me, falling in love was what other people did – not that I didn't think about it, but there just wasn't room for such distractions in the life that I led. I traveled with a light bag. When it came to attachments, give me a stranger anytime. You don't know them and they don't know you. There's no room for history. No room for pride. No room for expectations. No room for disappointments. No room for lies.

I kept my hands smooth and silky like a baby's butt – powdered them four times a day and filed, shaped and buffed my immaculate nails morning, noon and night. And so I kept on moving – every week it was a different town and every month a different state. I always avoided banks because there are too many professional snoops on the lookout for you. I spent my time at racetracks, on streetcars, subways and at labor meetings. I particularly liked labor meetings because everyone's a brother there and they're usually talking about money, so I always felt I was personally participating in my own way.

Political meetings always intrigued me. It seems only natural to lift someone's wallet there – after all, isn't that just what the guy up on the stump is fixing to do, once he gets elected?

I knew some carnivals and circuses that had their own whiz mobs working the crowd. Even the ringmaster was in on it. He'd say, in a kind of grand and self-righteous way, 'Ladies and Gentlemen, please beware of pickpockets.' This was a great help to us cannons. The moment he said it, any poor sap with a roll on him immediately checked his wallet with a tap of the hand. This was like a road map for me because it showed exactly which pocket to go for, making it real easy. In five minutes I could hook a few fat ones and then sit back and enjoy the show.

Except, of course, that one day in Erwin, Tennessee, when an elephant called Skippy ran amok and stampeded the crowd, trampling some poor guy to death. That was the last circus I ever did. The people got so mad that they rioted. Apparently the circus owner refused to shoot the animal, which was understandable, because Skippy was his bread and butter. I was helping the circus hands haul the unfortunate creature onto its truck when a mob of about a hundred people arrived. These weren't crazy people, just ordinary local folks, they even had their kids in tow. They were screaming and jeering hysterically and pushing the circus minders out of the way. I wouldn't have believed what happened next if I hadn't seen it with my own eyes. The frenzied mob attacked the giant elephant, hacked at her throat, wrapped ropes around her and strung her up from a railroad derrick. I mean, an elephant, can you imagine that? That's a considerable feat of human ingenuity, let alone human cruelty. I just thought to myself, boy, if they're hanging elephants now, then this is certainly no place for me. I haven't been back to Tennessee since.

It was then that I started 'catching out' – hopping on freight trains for a free ride all over the country. That's where I met Hoagie.

10

In 1906, *as the earthquake ripped inland from the ocean, it completely destroyed Agnew's Insane Asylum out at Santa Clara. The local sheriff and twenty deputies surrounded the devastated building as thousands of inmates escaped their cells and vanished into the night. Some were caught and roped to trees, but many went free. A few of them went on to become successful businessmen and one guy even ran for political office.*

Moral: Who's to know who's crazy?

I was in a barbershop in Cincinnati and had taken my place in a line of ten chairs as the army of barbers clicked their scissors and slapped their razors on the wall straps. As I got my chin and cheeks oiled I checked out the guy next to me who had a white marble face as pale and cold as a cathedral statue and a comical moustache that was as phony as a swipe from a charcoaled cork. But to my eye, for a skinny guy he seemed to have a money belt on him that looked like he was about to deliver twins. As the barber covered the guy's face in a hot towel I slipped my hand into his side pocket. Sure enough, he was loaded.

'Where you from, neighbor?' he suddenly said to me from under the steaming towel.

'Me?' I asked, kind of surprised. 'All over, mostly . . . originally from San Francisco.'

'What line of business are you in?' he said.

'Oh, this and that. I'm thinking of going to Salinas to get some work there.'

'Salinas? You into pulling lettuce?'

'Yep, or whatever I can get,' I answered.

'You don't look like a farm boy.'

'Oh yeah, I'll take the work wherever I can get it.' I closed my eyes as the barber brushed my face with a thick soapy lather and wiped away a small hole for me to speak through.

'Are you into advice?' the stranger said.

'You need advice?' I replied, but then he took me by surprise.

'No, fella, you do.' He stood up, wiped his face with the hot towel and cleverly spun two quarters, which came to rest on the marble counter.

'Firstly, always know what time of day it is. It's simple, but important.'

'Yep, always do.'

He leaned towards me. 'The name's Hoagie, pleased to meet you.'

'Hoagie?'

'It's short for Illyich.'

'Yeah, right, pleased to meet you, Hoagie.' I looked in the mirror and saw an advertisement on the back wall for Adcock's Shaving Soap. 'Tommy . . . Tommy Adcock,'

I said as I stretched out my hand. He took it firmly and I could feel his touch. He knew that my smooth, soft hands had never pulled a lettuce or picked a string bean.

'And the other advice?' I asked. For some strange reason, this guy was beginning to intrigue me.

'You can't make a crab walk straight.'

'No, you can't.'

'Bread always falls on the buttered side.'

'Yep.'

'And never go with a girl from Peoria, Illinois. Ever been to Peoria, Tommy?'

'Just passed through.'

'Cute as they are, you'll only end up pissing pins and needles.'

I laughed and he finally stopped shaking my hand. I was sure that this guy was crazier than a summer beet-fly, but as I looked at the ceiling and the barber started to scrape the open razor up my neck, I was in no position to philosophize.

'And greed has very long arms,' he added.

'Yep, ain't that the truth,' I said to the tin ceiling.

'Say, have you got the time?' he asked.

'Yeah, sure do. It's . . .'

The barber stood back to strop the razor on the leather and I lifted my hand from beneath the smock.

'It's . . .' I couldn't give this guy the time because I had no watch. I had fifty watches and my favorite gold beauty with the silver and gold linked chain and the fancy new luminescent face was no longer on my wrist.

The pale-faced guy polished his shoes with a brush

hanging on a hook in the wall and said, 'It's twenty after two,' and handed me back my favorite gold watch with the luminescent face.

'And maybe you'll need this too, if you're gonna pay for that shave.' He handed me my wallet. He also waved the wad I had taken from him only seconds earlier.

'You have to hang on to these, fella. There's a lot of goddam thieves about.'

'Ain't that the truth,' I said in complete disbelief. This guy had rolled *me*. Me! He had taken my watch, taken my wallet and even taken back the wad I'd stolen from him. For the first time in my life *I* was the one who had been rolled. What's more, he had given them back. I paid for my shave and ran down the street after the stranger called Hoagie. It was raining pitchforks and lightning was striking, but I wasn't about to take cover.

In the corner of a bar on Sycamore Street, Hoagie explained that I should never use my left hand when doing a right-hand cross.

'If you're trapped in a barber's chair, you can't move your body. If you can't move your body, you can't make the fake. All is fake. All of pickpocketing is an illusion, just as the whole of life is an illusion.'

To make his point he gave me back my penknife. Boy, was there no end to my humiliation? I loved that penknife. It had a mother-of-pearl handle and was inlaid in silver with my initials: TM.

'You sonofa . . . you took my penknife?'

'I did. Were you attached to it?'

'I was, it has my initials on it.'

'Did you have it engraved?'

'No, it belonged to someone else,' I answered, with a degree of embarrassment. Heck, I'd never talked to a thief before. I'd always thought myself a notch above my fellow piker dips and usually avoided them. I never thought they were as good as me, and even if they were, it was like looking at an unwelcome reflection in a mirror. But Hoagie was different.

'The person had the same initials as me . . . TM,' I said with no real assurance.

'I thought you said your name was Tommy Adcock?'

'That's not my real name . . . it's Tommy Moran.' Boy, this guy was wiping the floor with me.

'To be a good liar, you have to have a good memory. You see, that's also why *I* am attached to the knife,' said Hoagie.

'You are?'

'Yes, I have the same initials, because my real name is Tiekhorad Miczislaus.'

Whatever his name was, he was making a point.

'Tommy, when you steal something, it doesn't belong to you. The reason it doesn't belong to you is because it doesn't belong to the person you took it from either. Nothing belongs to anyone. Everything is stolen, one way or another.'

I nodded in agreement. I never thought I ever had a guardian angel. I always thought that if I did, he had got distracted at some roadside gin joint. But I listened to Hoagie like he had white-feathered wings sprouting from his shoulder blades. He ordered two more beers and continued.

'It's a fact of life,' he said, 'basic economics, pure and simple. It's been that way ever since the world began, and no one's going to change it because, sadly, greed is in every plug-ugly one of us.'

'In my whole life I never met anyone who didn't prefer a fast buck to a slow one,' I contributed.

'Exactly,' said Hoagie. 'It's human nature, because the whole world is trying to finagle a dollar out of the other guy one way or another. They say embezzlers steal three times as much as bank robbers and that's a fact, because I read it in *The New York Times*. I mean, look at all those bankers who took the little guys' savings and lost them in business failures – that's still stealing, in my book.'

'Someone once said if you yelled, "Stop, thief!" at the New York Stock Exchange, the bodies would be piled twenty-deep making for the exit door,' I added as I sipped my beer. I was beginning to enjoy myself.

Hoagie laughed and leaned forward. 'There's no doubt that behind every great fortune is a great crime. To my mind, the great American thieves weren't Jesse James and Billy the Kid, but guys like Carnegie, Rockefeller . . .'

'Dupont and Vanderbilt?'

'Crocker, Morgan, Havemeyer – all of them. Those guys smoking their Cuban stogies had their hands in the whole country's pockets and they not only got away with it, but people have made them into goddam heroes. Make no mistake, Tommy, you can bet a dollar to a doughnut that those fortunes were all built on the pain and suffering of others, I have no doubt.'

Boy, did I like my new friend Hoagie. He wasn't much older than me, maybe in his mid-twenties, but Hoagie knew everything. He was the smartest person I ever met. Maybe clever enough to run for president, but he never would, of course – as he was too smart for that job.

'Tommy, stealing someone's wallet is just a cookie dipped in coffee in the great big scheme of things.' He shook his head. 'But ignorance . . .'

'Ignorance?'

'Do you read?' he asked.

'Read? I read the newspapers a lot.'

'No, books. Do you read books?'

I shook my head, slightly embarrassed. My childhood and my education had ended the day I climbed out of the sacristy window.

'Tommy, just because you're uneducated doesn't mean you have to be stupid. Do you know why President Wilson is so dumb?'

'No.'

'Because he can't read.'

'He can't?'

'Nope.'

'But he's the president.'

'It's a fact,' Hoagie shrugged.

He put his hand in his pocket and took out a small, dog-eared, leather-bound book and slid it across the table. I picked it up and read aloud, '*Mr Peter's Bijou Literary Compendium.*'

'Read it all, Tommy, every word, especially the stuff by the Shakespeare guy.'

'You're giving me this?'

'It's not mine to give, Tommy. And it's not yours to own. Remember, nothing belongs to anyone – not a book, a gold watch, or a peanut farm. For the short time that we're on this earth, we're all just borrowing things for a while.'

At the Mill Creek Marshaling Yards, Hoagie and I hopped a freight. He showed me how to catch the grab rail on the fly by running level with the train.

'Always grab at the front of the car, not the back, because it can swing out and throw you into the wheels,' he shouted, and then leaped six feet onto the train. Hoagie could run faster and jump higher than Jim Thorpe at the Olympics.

For a while we followed the harvest girls as they traveled the country looking for work. These girls picked peaches in Oregon, broomcorn in New Mexico, grapefruits in Kansas, cherries in Michigan, string beans in New Jersey and topped beets in Idaho. Some of those girls were real cute, too. They were also lonely, tired, far from home and far from fussy. Not that I was some kind of ice block in the emotional department, I have to say. I had my moments and with my droopy-eyed wink I only had to look at a girl to get a smile back. But when it came to attachment, I was always on the next train to somewhere else. Anywhere else.

It was on a freight from Kansas City to Joplin, Missouri when tragedy struck. There must have been two hundred 'bos on that train, some of them clinging to the side like barnacles on a Hackensack River tugboat. The cinder bulls – the railroad cops – were just supposed to eject you from the cars, but in some states they were real mean and would randomly empty the barrels of their shotguns into the night, like they were shooting rabbits in their yards.

I had caught some shot in my rear end in Kansas, and couldn't sit down. These slugs didn't kill you, but they stung like hell. We all carried them around like a badge of honor. Under a pile of empty sacks in the corner of a boxcar full of sweet potatoes, an obliging young farm girl called Dolly was digging out the pellets from my cheeks with her teeth. Dolly's teeth were sharper than a surgeon's knife as she captured each one, spat it out and poured whiskey on the tiny wounds.

There was a scream of steel on steel as the train slowed and word came down that the bulls had boarded and were shaking down the boxcars. Hoagie was curled up asleep with another farm girl and suddenly jumped up and danced around like a wet hen.

'Get up!' he shouted. 'We have to get off the train. I know these kinds of stops. These bulls out here are crazy. Grab your stuff! We have to go.'

Maybe he knew something we didn't, because he usually did. We heard the sounds of gunfire as an army of bulls stalked the cars. Hoagie and I helped the girls climb down from the train and they ran off into the night.

We scrambled our belongings together as the train once more took on speed. Above us, on the roof of the boxcar, we could hear a hundred barrels going off as the bulls took potshots at the train's illegal cargo. I had heard that they did this every so often. It never made the papers but you'd see a lot of unremembered dead bodies left rotting by the tracks in the middle of nowhere.

Hoagie yanked on his pants and climbed out onto the running board of the boxcar as the train gathered speed. I handed him my bundle and he helped me out when suddenly the wind took off my hat and as I grabbed it I lost my footing. Hoagie caught my arm as the train dragged me through the cinders at the side of the tracks, ripping my jacket and shirt off my back and most of the skin down to the bone. With all his strength, Hoagie hauled me up into the safety of the car but the train lurched again like a drunken fairground switchback and Hoagie pitched forwards and disappeared.

I leaned over and looked into the darkness, my eyes smarting from the grit and the smoke, but could see nothing. Rolling back into the car, I passed out on the splintered boards.

As we crossed the state line, half of Hoagie stayed in Kansas and the other half was dumped in Missouri as he was sliced in two and dragged along by the giant steel wheels. Hoagie, or Illyich, or Tiekhorad Miczislaus or whatever his name was – he was my guardian angel and he was always special. He's the only person in America with a grave in two different states.

12

In the weeks that it took for my back to heal, I took Hoagie's advice and read his little compendium from cover to cover. It became my bible. A dance-hall madam called Beckie in Kenosha gave me some more books. I had that *Moby-Dick* in my bag for months – it weighed a ton and so I finally gave it to a barkeep in Minnesota. He told me that he was once a deckhand on a tugboat and always fancied chasing a whale some day. *Gulliver's Travels* kept me from freezing to death on a cold winter's night in Bismarck, North Dakota as I burned it one page at a time.

I learned arithmetic at the racetracks and knew more about American geography than a college professor.

'Just because you're uneducated, doesn't mean you have to be stupid,' Hoagie had said, 'although the world might try to tell you that you are.'

I took his advice to heart. There were seven wonders of the world, twenty-two religions, five senses, four thousand languages, seven deadly sins, sixty-six books in the Bible, thirty-eight Shakespeare plays, a hundred and fifty-four sonnets, three musketeers, four deuces, twelve labors of Hercules, ten Commandments, nine planets and one Galileo. All these numbers add up to one thing: your own stupidity. They only mean shit if you don't know this stuff and someone else does. The very fact that you have no education means that you have to start using your brains. 'There is no darkness but ignorance,' it said in Hoagie's book and, a day at a time, from Boston to Brobdingnag, a little light began to filter through to me.

I thought of Gracie, my mom and Maeve a lot during those years. If I found a wallet with a sizable wad inside I would always send money home. The same goes for a quality necklace or a ring with a good ruby. I even had my picture taken for them by this guy in Winooski, Vermont. The photographer was a real artist and took great care with his giant camera.

'You work in the quarry business?' he asked.

'Yep, stonecutter.'

'Which quarry?'

'Barre.' This guy was nosier than a cop. I had been over at Barre only a couple of days before. Those Scottish, Italian and Swedish stonecutters went into town on a Saturday night to get loaded and I had enjoyed their company as I emptied a few glasses – and a few pockets.

'How's the pay?'

'Just great. Can't complain.' I guess fifty cents an hour was pretty good. But it had to be, considering that most of those guys would be dead from inhaling granite dust before they were thirty. Pretty ironic when you think about it – considering they were carving headstones for most of the cemeteries in America.

'This picture for your sweetheart?'

'No, my mom.'

'Then you'd better manage a better smile than that one, and try and keep both your eyes open wide.'

The eye thing was beyond my control, but many a farm girl had said I had a nice smile and I beamed away like the giant clown outside the House of Fun on Coney Island. The photographer ignited some powder on a stick and I thought I had gone blind. A week later I picked up my picture.

Over a beer at Geraghty's Saloon, I stared at the photograph as if I was looking at a complete stranger. That photographer was good, because the guy in the picture looked a whole lot better than the one in my shaving mirror. I kidded myself that I even looked kind of handsome. Sure, I had grown tall and slim and if I were a boxer, at 145 pounds, I would have made a decent welterweight. I had my dad's narrow face, black Irish eyes, one of them droopy, and the beginning of my mom's frown. My nose, sharp and slightly bent, was not as noble as Geronimo's, but close. My hair, always cut neat and short, was pomaded, slicked back and as shiny as an eight ball. I folded two hundred bills into an envelope and slipped in the photograph. I had written on the back, 'For Mom, Maeve and little Gracie. Your devoted son and brother.' What a joke. It sounded like something you'd read on a funeral wreath.

My book said men shut their doors against a setting sun, but I had no house, and no door, so from state to state I just walked towards the horizon. I always had enough money for a sit-down meal of corn beef hash, beans and gravy at whatever town was waiting up ahead, and after I switched off the lights, sure as shit, at sunup another new day was sure to dawn. That's about all I could rely on in those days.

As I walked amongst the tumbleweed, sagebrush and bleached cattle skulls I'd occasionally come across an old, sole-less boot sticking out of the sand atop a skeleton shinbone – hobo headstones, we used to call them. I had this poem in my book by a lady called Emily Dickinson. I used to shout it out loud as I was walking, 'I'm nobody! Who are you? Are you nobody too?'

That's when I got to discuss things with Him up there. Not in a religious way, you understand, but as accomplices – brothers of the road, you could say. I always took the position that *He* was working for us, not that *we* were working for Him. As far as I was concerned, I was the archbishop and sole congregation of my own religion – a tax-free charitable organization solely for the benefit of one Thomas Patrick Moran of Easy Street, America. In many ways, the more I looked around me the more I could count myself as fortunate. Mind you, I have to say that living the life I did, I had rubbed myself up against Lady Luck so often I had probably given her a rash.

But I have no doubt that trouble definitely followed me around. Like the time I rolled this guy in Chicago. To be honest, I never met anyone who was a big fan of Chicago – except gangsters or crooked politicians. It was too cold, too damp and too damned corrupt for my taste. You never knew whose pocket you were dipping into, and in a city where every pocket is lined with dirty money, it's a risk that no sensible person in my profession needs to take.

I was working the Chicago and North-Western railroad station on West Madison when I saw this big guy at the shoeshine. I waited for him to pay his three cents and as he moved away from the bootblack and joined the crowd I bumped him. Fanning my hands across his vest I felt a roll as thick as a triple tuna melt. As always, I quickly checked out his clothes: extra long Chesterfield, twenty-four-ounce wool mixed serge, satin lining, three outside pockets, one inner, eight button-vest, but no jacket, Java silk shirt.

It was an easy lift because he had a belly on him as big as a truck, so I figured he was used to bumping into people and would never even notice me. The back of his head was completely square – whether he had a clumsy barber or bad genes, it was hard to tell. He didn't smell too good either; in fact, he could have done with a little Lysol disinfectant for personal use. I deliberately showboated a sneeze over his left shoulder, which forced him to shift the weight of his body ever so slightly to his other side, so that I could slip under his jacket and get closer to the wad bulging in his right inside pocket. With my forehead I slowly lifted the rear of his split-straw boater just enough for him to be conscious of it and so he raised his hand to adjust the front brim. In the tiny, infinitesimal seconds when his beefy arm moved away from guarding his stash, I had my fingers – just my fingers, never my hand – tightly around the wad inside his pocket.

Then it was away – spiraling through sunlight for the briefest of moments before vanishing into the darkness of my pocket.

Rule one in the sticky finger trade is to strip the contents and dump the leather as soon as possible, so I took his bundle into the men's washroom to clean it out. To my surprise, it wasn't a wallet at all. I slipped it out of the leather case and my jaw dropped lower than my pant cuffs. I was holding a beautiful bible. It was really old – so old that it had gold leaf on the front and thick yellow parchment pages that crackled as I opened them. It was covered with fancy, ornamented letters, probably painted by a bunch of Italian monks a thousand years ago. It sure wasn't your ordinary everyday bible, and Big Belly who I hooked it from sure didn't look like some Vatican missionary to me. This bible was so delicate, so exquisite and yet, as I soon found out, so lethal.

13

At a pawnshop on Michigan Avenue the fence guy carefully slid the book out of its leather case and flicked through the pages.

'Jesus Christ!' he said.

'What is it?'

'It's the bible of the *Unione Siciliana*.'

'Italian?' I shrugged innocently.

'Oh yeah, very. This here bible is the one the Mob swear their allegiance on.'

I looked upward and offered a quiet prayer to anyone who was home in the clouds above the swinging ceiling lamp. I figured St Peter and the guys were busting a gut laughing at my predicament. I tried to keep a brave face on the proceedings. 'So what's it worth?'

'It's thirteenth century.'

'Thirteenth?'

He nodded. 'Probably Flemish, I'd have to look it up.'

'That's old.'

'Very.' Somehow I knew where this was headed.

'Belongs in a museum, which is probably where it came from in the first place. The initial letters are liquid gold.'

'Gold? How much?'

'How much what?'

'What's it worth?'

'A fortune. A king's ransom. More money than *you'll* ever see in a lifetime.' He looked up. 'That's if you ever see a lifetime.' He then promptly slid it back across the counter like it was a stick of dynamite with a lit fuse.

For a while I thought the smartest thing would be to toss the bible into Lake Michigan, but I felt a little uneasy doing that, it being a religious book and all. And anyway, it was too precious to rot away in the Michigan mud. I looked up to Hoagie and his Boss and asked them squarely what I should do with the damned, excuse me, thing. I thought I heard Hoagie's voice say, 'Give it back and apologize.' I figured, sure, I'll just walk down to Colosimo's or the Four Deuces Café on South Wabash, hand it over to the first person called Sal or Vinnie, and say, 'Sorry, guys, big misunderstanding. I'm sorry I stole the most valuable item in your brotherhood – I was really after your wallet. Please give my apologies to Mr Colosimo and Johnny Torrio. I'll just rest the back of my head on the tablecloth next to this plate of meatballs while you cut my throat.' Even Tommy Moran's not that dumb. I can only put this down as one of Hoagie's less inspired ideas. As I mulled this over, walking towards the lake I thought that nothing is ever as bad as you think it is, but sure as shit, the more you think about it, the worse it gets.

The wooden buttresses along the shoreline were draped with six-inch-thick ice and, considering I was doomed to the fires of hell, it felt like the coldest place on earth.

Maybe I should go back to my rooming house and take a shower – undertakers appreciate a clean corpse. I sat on an iron bench with the wind ripping into my face as it whistled across Lake Michigan sounding like a bunch of hot-joint, slapper sirens drowned beneath the surface of the water.

'Tommy,' the sirens said, 'it's not *their* bible anyway. They stole it. It belonged to the church, you dumb cluck.' This seemed to me to be the better advice of the day. When lightning strikes it's better to grasp it than to become a charcoaled stump – and so I took heed.

I walked back from the shore for two blocks and slipped into a gray stone pile called St Clare's. Dipping my hand in the holy water, I crossed myself and waited for the confessional box to be free; I must admit that I got kind of chills. After all, I hadn't been in a church since I was a kid, when I jumped out of the sacristy window at St Mary's all those years ago. Up on the wall was one of those wooden Jesus statues: the kind that it's hard to look at for more than a second or so – the ones with blood seeping out of His hands and feet. I always found those creepy. It wasn't some vague effigy but 'Jerusalem Jim' Himself, hanging there in all His agony for all eternity – a period of time I had a hard job coming to terms with. 'INRI' it said. 'Iesus Nazarenus Rex Iudaeorum,' I whispered to myself, repeating a childhood memory – Jesus of Nazareth, King of the Jews. I stared at the statue and noticed something that has always bothered me. Jesus is supposed to have His eyes closed but – maybe it's me – if you look long enough, He's always peeping under the lids at you . . . no one else in the church, just *you*. At that moment an old lady shuffled out of the confessional and I nervously took her place in the box.

The priest had a voice like a motorized log-saw with a thick accent that reminded me of Father Imielinski back at Saints Peter and Paul. He also had a loud, wet cough, the kind that makes you grab for your handkerchief. Maybe it was the surroundings, but I suddenly had an attack of Catholic guilt and found myself blurting out not only the dumb story of me stealing the Mob's bible but, while I was about it, I also asked for about seven thousand other offenses to be taken into consideration for forgiveness. I explained that I didn't get to confession very often, but I think he'd already got the gist of that. I was sure he was going to condemn me to eternal damnation because his coughing grew more and more violent. I made it easy for him, pouring out my lousy life, sin by sin, state by state. I even kept it alphabetical from Alabama to Wyoming, like he was reading the telephone book or something. Even then, I missed out a lot of good stuff – maybe some other time and some other priest. Through the mesh I could see the guy thrashing around in the semi-darkness, seemingly drowning in his own phlegm. I just assumed that he was having a bad asthma attack or something, so I continued my litany of misdeeds. To tell you the truth, I was getting to enjoy it when suddenly the priest stopped coughing and I heard a terrible thud as he fell off his seat.

'Father? Father, are you there?' I pressed my face to the grille but couldn't see him. 'Father?'

Still there was no answer. I got up and pulled back the red curtain on his side of the confessional. He was slumped on the floor, hand still at his throat, his milky eyes staring toward heaven. I undid the buttons of his cassock, slipped my hand inside and tried to find his heartbeat. I could hear my own pounding loudly, but nothing from him, so I concluded he'd had a heart attack after his coughing fit – possibly brought on by having to listen to my shabby life story. I knelt down and placed the handsome black and gold *Unione Siciliana* bible in the poor guy's hand and tiptoed to the door. That wooden statue of Jesus still stared down at me and I noticed there was a sign underneath that said, 'Jesus died for *your* sins.' The *your* was painted in red, so I felt immediately responsible for His demise up there on the cross as well as the misfortune of the Polish priest slumped in the confession box clutching the gold Mafia bible.

I got out of town fast – while I could still breathe fresh air and with a neck smooth enough to put my tie around. What the heck was I doing in Chicago in the first place? Needless to say, I never returned.

14

In April of 1917, that lard-head President Wilson declared war on Germany. I remember hearing about it at a doughnut and coffee stand at the Kentucky Derby. Germany? Where the heck was that? I had spent time in Germantown, Philadelphia and Germantown in Tennessee. Most of the beer in America was made by Germans. The only language I ever heard in Cincinnati was German, and they couldn't all be agents of the Kaiser, could they? And now we were going to war with these people? Go figure it.

Every year since I was fourteen, I'd work my way down to Louisville and take in the races. Kentucky and Churchill Downs, where they hold the Derby, is a great place and I knew that we were taking this war stuff seriously because they had plowed up the lush green infield and planted potatoes. Potatoes? Can you believe that, on Churchill Downs? Apparently they had a crop failure up in Idaho so Louisville decided to help with the war effort by digging up the hallowed turf at Churchill as a goodwill gesture. Mind you, they didn't take the war so seriously as to actually cancel the racing. They were too smart for that, because business is business.

I was fishing for suckers at the payout window just

after a nag called Omar Khayyam had romped away with the big race, beating the flea-bag I myself had backed by half a block. I never had much luck at playing the horses – not that it mattered, because I always reasoned that if I didn't win with my two-dollar bets I could always roll some guy who had won some real money.

A southern-looking guy with a straw Milan brim hat and a face that looked like a pig's intestines made his way to the down ramp. He walked with a brisk, cocky gait as he flipped through a sizable bundle of scratch. Boy, was he a happy winner – somehow you knew that he would be naming his firstborn 'Omar'. I could have clipped him there and then in front of the booths but I felt uneasy – almost as if I was being watched.

I tailed Mr Pig down the ramp all the way to the grandstand and carefully checked the way he walked and the fabric of his clothes: his percale shirt, artificial silk batwing necktie, worsted navy blazer – two button, double-breasted, single back vent, slanting slash pockets. Was he wearing a vest, suspenders? What about his pants? They were cotton duck, loose fitting with tunnel belt loops, two baggy side pockets and one tightly buttoned right rear pocket. His shoes were side-laced albert oxfords – but even I couldn't roll the guy if that's where he stashed his bills.

I quickened my step and pulled level with his left elbow. I could see that his inside pocket held his winnings for sure, but what was that on the right side? There was a slight bulge, which only I could see. A pistol? No, Mr Pig surely didn't have the eyes for that line of work. What was it? My palms were itching and I rubbed my talc-umed smooth hands down the sides of my pants.

I had my chance when the guy stopped to buy a sar-saparilla and I joined him in the line. I had swiftly lifted the hem of his jacket when immediately in front of him a freckle-faced blind girl with stunning, red curly hair falling over her shoulders turned and smiled at us both. Mr Pig and I politely doffed our hats in a way that folks do to the blind. It's almost as if to say, 'Sorry, ma'am, that you're blind and I'm not.' People are funny that way. What the hell was a blind girl doing at the races, anyway? Maybe it was the atmosphere; it can really bowl you over. And let's face it, who's to say she couldn't pick a winner as well as the rest of us boneheads at Churchill?

Once again I gently lifted the hem of Mr Pig's jacket and fanned the inside. It was a good jacket, as I had thought – expensive, worsted, with a fine quality lining that felt like Venetian silk. Stiffening my body, I shifted my weight onto my left leg and slid my hand across him to slowly and painstakingly reef the inside of his jacket as, inch by inch, my fingers tucked up tiny pleats of the silk lining. I was now so close that I could feel him breathing – the beat of his heart ever so slightly unsyn-chronized with my own – and I could see a trickle of sweat running from his dyed eggplant-colored hair down the back of his scarlet sunburned neck. I smiled as I realized that Mr Pig was rubbing himself up against the red-haired girl. I waited for her to scream, which from my experience would have been fine by me, because there's nothing like a noisy distraction to enable an easy walk-away. I felt my way closer to his inside pocket towards what was obviously a large roll of bills. By massaging the lining I gradually edged them up to the mouth of the pocket and deftly dropped the bills into my left hand. Mr Pig was really rubbing now; probably he had a hard-on and at any minute the poor girl in front of him would be screaming. He would then jump back in embarrassment and I would be able to make an easy hook. But that's not what happened. Curiously, as he rubbed away, for some reason she didn't scream. Was she enjoying it as much as he was?

With my heart thumping like a Salvation Army drum, I slid my right hand slowly and smoothly past the damp shirt, across his breasts, over his nipples, past his tight suspenders towards his other pocket and then, suddenly, I stopped dead. I had found some weird things inside people's jackets before, but this one really shook me. Keeping my body as stiff as a mine-shaft stanchion, I sucked much needed air through my nose. It was my turn to sweat and the beads slithered down my forehead, itching like crazy – but with two hands up a guy's jacket I had no hope of scratching. For the first time in my entire career as a cannon I was holding not a wallet, a wad, a watch, a pen, a checkbook, a comb, a gun or a bible. I was holding another human hand.

For a good five seconds my heart stopped beating because it wasn't Mr Pig's hand but a slender female hand, and I suddenly realized why young dead-eyes with the stunning red hair hadn't screamed. She was in the same game as me. He was rubbing her because she had been pratting up against him. The poor guy was being corkscrewed from either end. I kept my nerve but she didn't, and suddenly withdrew her hand rather too fast and then it was Mr Pig's turn to scream. As the guy popped his cork, I grabbed the blind girl's hand and ran.

Mr Pig, strong and athletic as he was, caught up to us after five yards. With one hand he grabbed my shoulder and with the other, a handful of the blind girl's hair and yanked so hard it must have torn the skin on her scalp. We were nailed, and I was already imagining what the inside of a Louisville jail looked like when remarkably, Mr Pig fell headlong onto the cement floor. It seemed the blind girl had an accomplice – another blind girl – a sister maybe, with the same pretty face, the same red hair and, most of all, the same blind eyes. She had managed to thrust her white stick into the genitals of our pig-faced pursuer, who was consequently rolling in agony on the floor with a broken kneecap or some other more personal injury.

I grabbed both girls and continued through the crowd. Looking back, I could see that maybe five or six Pinkertons were already on our tails. We reached the bottom of the ramp and ran through the bookies' enclosure, which was filled with thousands of punters placing their bets on the next race. As people started to grab at us I threw Mr Pig's roll of bills into the air. It was an old, if somewhat expensive, ploy, but it always works and suddenly the crowd was scrambling for the free greenbacks – and we were away.

*　　*　　*

Three miles from the track, on the soft green grass at the side of a quiet road, the three of us lay exhausted and laughing. I had heard of the blind Mackintosh twins, Ada and Honey, but until now our paths – or, more accurately our hands – had never crossed. We were united by a rare camaraderie because we three were members of an honorable and ancient profession and, for a moment, it was great not to feel as I always did: totally alone.

I liked the sisters immediately. Sure, they were blind, but most of the time you would never have known it. Not that they were cheating. There were a lot of people on the road pulling the blinko scam – pretending to be blind – but these girls were sadly the genuine article. To be precise, Ada was completely blind but Honey wore thick spectacles like the bottoms of liquor glasses, which helped her see a little. You had the feeling that all their lives these two funny, spunky girls had never let their handicaps bother them for a second. And they were no dog biscuits either, if you half closed your eyes they were, well, attractive – with nice figures, although they hid that with their baggy clothes. Whereas Ada let her red hair fall loosely over her shoulders, Honey wore hers in a more sophisticated French twist. They were nicely dressed, but not excessively gaudy – what they called 'presentable' – fitting in, as they had to, with most social groups and situations. The three of us decided to stick together for a while.

15

We hitched a ride as far as a town called Glasgow. The Mackintosh girls were keen on their Scottish roots, so the name appealed to them. I guess we were about ninety miles south of Louisville when the guy in the hay truck dropped us off. A bookie I knew at Churchill told me that there were these mammoth caves down there with over three hundred miles of mapped passageways. The guy said you wouldn't believe how many people came from all over the country to witness this natural phenomenon. Now, I wouldn't want to give you the impression that I was at all interested, geologically speaking, in this subterranean freak of nature – for me, it was strictly business. Also, I have to say that Ada and Honey thought it was kind of amusing that we would all be down there in the dark tunnels where no one could see but them.

We each paid our ten-cent admission fee and began climbing deep into the hillside. The guides carried giant kerosene lamps, which they held aloft on broomsticks as they led us through the winding underground trails. The eerie, smoky shadows that danced across the cave walls were ideal working conditions for someone in my profession; a hundred tourists an hour walking along in semi-darkness looking up at the ceiling? It was really all

75

too easy. The sisters and I glided in and out of that crowd like we were on rails as the guides pointed out the wonders of Mother Nature's handiwork. A million years ago, the insides had been sucked out of this mountain and we were doing the same as we sucked out the cave watchers' wallets. Before noon we had made three trips, which were so successful that the lining of my coat visibly bulged with more than three dozen wallets and purses. It was while we were paying our ten cents for a fourth trip that Ada threw back her head and sniffed the air.

'Uh-uh! Don't think so,' Honey said. 'Smells bad.'

I was about to put down my ten cents when Honey pointed over her shoulder. 'We smell a cop.'

They were right. At the entry gate, the local Glasgow sheriff was patiently listening to a hysterical woman who was waving her arms around and pointing into her haversack.

'Ain't that the truth,' I said. 'Grab hold.' With the Mackintosh sisters on each arm, I slowly walked past the sheriff, who politely tipped his hat at the sight of Ada's white stick. As we reached the end of the curving dusty road, I looked back to check that the sheriff's car was no longer in sight.

'Okay. Let's go,' I whispered.

I helped the twins through a gap in the wooden fence and we ran like hell.

Two hours later, Honey, Ada and I sat in the middle of a vast strawberry field just north of a small town called Red Boiling Springs and way south of Glasgow. We flipped through the leathers and emptied the contents on the ground. We had twenty-seven dollars and thirty-six cents, which, after some deliberation, we divided three ways. Honey scraped a hole in the dirt with her shoe and buried the telltale wallets and purses. There were a few pieces of cheap jewelry, which I insisted the sisters keep, and a decent gold fob and chain, which I pocketed for myself.

We had stopped in Scottsville at a coffin maker called Guppie Tate, who, apart from the manufacture of wooden overcoats, had a couple of sidelines, the lesser known of which was making walking sticks. Honey's stick had been snapped in half back at Churchill when she stabbed Mr Pig in the whirligigs. We had to wait a while for the white paint to dry and so Guppie invited the three of us out to his backyard to introduce us to his more notorious sideline. There amongst the rows of polished black coffin lids was a liquor still cooking away. He uncorked a jug and gave us all a shot of his home brew that he called Sneaky Pete.

'Best whiskey in Kentucky,' he said proudly.

'Sure is strong,' I said with some difficulty. The back of my throat was already on fire from less than a sip.

'Liquor with a kicker gets you drunk a whole lot quicker,' he said, and who were we to argue?

Guppie gave us a good price on a large bottle of Sneaky Pete and, to save him having to go to church that week, he threw in Honey's new stick for free.

Back at the strawberry field in the balmy spring after-noon, the scent from the fruit wafted past us and I inhaled deeply as it mingled with the smells of sweat and cheap cologne. I guess we were all getting a little pie-eyed as we took our turns swigging from the bottle of Sneaky Pete. Ada had gathered a whole skirt full of straw-berries, which to my eyes at least, didn't seem ripe enough for picking – but her sensitive fingers had found the soft and juicy early crop.

I pulled off my shirt and Honey gently stroked my back.

'Wow. That's some scar you have there, Tommy. How'd you get that?'

'Cinder burns. Riding the railroad.' It was something I had to live with. The cinders had healed inside the stripped skin, leaving a thick, blue scar and now it gath-ered curiosity. It didn't bother me because even though I had to live with it, at least I didn't have to look at it.

'Jeez,' said Ada, whose fingers gently followed the welts. 'Feels like a map of Texas.' They both laughed and Ada kissed me gently, somewhere down around Laredo.

I lay there as Honey popped strawberries into my mouth – as though she was dropping logs into a sawdust hopper. She was singing that song, 'Let Me Call You Sweetheart'. I was thinking what a nice voice she had when she inter-rupted herself to lick a stray line of strawberry juice that had dribbled down my cheek. Through my half-closed eyes I couldn't help noticing that she had a tongue that could lick the paint off a house. Ada took off her jacket and unbuttoned her silk blouse down to her waist. Honey pulled off her top, and in one smooth move stepped out of her gingham skirt and began to unbutton my pants. Boy, were these two a great team. Maybe they couldn't see too well, but they knew their way around a guy's body as if they had their own private road map. Honey couldn't get my pants over my boots, so she pulled her hair up on top of her head, readjusted the tortoiseshell hair comb, took off her glasses and went straight to work with that long tongue of hers licking my bat and balls. Ada worked at the other end, lifting her skirt to reveal surprisingly pretty underwear. She yanked off her baggy French lace drawers, placed a knee on either side of my face and squatted down. Maybe it was because I was tight as a goat, but it sure was a great afternoon. I'm not much of a muff diver, but I can strongly recommend that Kentucky cocktail of Sneaky Pete and strawberry juice. Further down my body, Honey Mackintosh bobbed up and down between my legs, her big soft lips locked around my hootchee and, true to her Scottish roots, she sucked away like she was the last person left on earth to play the bagpipes on Robbie Burns' birthday.

16

The sun slowly dropped to the horizon, throwing long shadows across the fields. We were walking along the straight, dirt road with thick clumps of red huckleberry on either side when we heard a car behind us. Honey immediately knew it was a cop wagon and sure enough, it was. Most people would have run, but our instincts were to keep on walking. After all, no one knew us down here and anyway, once people saw those two cute girls with their sad disabilities, who the hell was going to give them a hard time? The wagon got closer and we three held our breath as it passed. I tipped my hat, but the young, skinny deputy sheriff on the driver's side seemed not to notice. We walked maybe another mile when we were suddenly swatting at hundreds of flies buzzing all around us.

'Smells bad,' said Honey.

'Dead meat,' said Ada.

I saw a sign on a wooden pole that said, 'Kroeger', as we walked over an old wooden bridge, that stretched across a narrow creek running through the property.

As we got closer to the farm I could see the first animal that lay dead, the poor creature's blood still pumping from its throat. We walked up the track to the old slat-board farmhouse.

'What can you see?' asked Ada as she swatted at the flies.

'A dead cow,' I said. 'Three dead cows, maybe more . . . and a mule.'

'Dead? How did they die?'

'Can't tell. Throats cut, it seems.'

'And chickens?' said Honey. She pointed to a chicken's head that she had trod on.

'Yeah, chickens,' I said as I saw dozens of them strewn around the farmyard with their chopped-off heads separated from their still twitching bodies.

The spotty young beanpole sheriff seemed to be in as much shock as we were. He should have told us to mind our own business, or wonder what the hell we were doing there in the first place, but he didn't. He seemed almost glad of our company. A Mexican guy, a farm worker maybe, sat on the front porch of the house, weeping uncontrollably. He was being comforted by another sheriff who patted his back. The deputy sheriff saw us approaching and started talking nervously, like we were from the newspaper or demanding an explanation.

'They're all dead,' he said, taking off his hat and revealing a thin, small face with a sideways-looking eye and a white forehead where his Stetson ended. He seemed just plain scared, not knowing how to cope with the sight of the carnage all around us. And brother, who could blame him?

'Old man Kroeger hanged himself in the barn. Must have drowned his wife first.' He nodded to the side of the house where a woman's legs dangled from a rainwater barrel. He then pointed towards the yard. 'The mulatto's over there.'

We walked to the wooden pen where I noticed that the pigs were strangely splattered with blood.

'Who is it?' said Ada.

'Young girl. Someone shot her. A lot of blood.' I didn't describe what I really saw. Lying in the pig trough was a young girl – a beautiful, light-skinned black girl, aged about eighteen. Her stomach had been shot away and she had been almost cut in half. Her young breasts were clearly visible and I followed the line of her long neck to a pretty face, oddly at peace.

I walked down to the creek that passed behind the barn and noticed four white crosses, in a neat row on a knoll. I leaned over into the water and vomited. Ada joined me.

Honey just stared ahead, her out-of-focus eyes squinting at something in the distance.

'What is it?' she said. I looked to where she was pointing. Shocked. I felt my senses being chewed up and spat out as I tried to assemble my words into an order that might present some kind of meaning.

'It's a . . . g-goddam b-b-baby,' I stammered. In the creek, tangled amongst the long grass growing from a mud bank, was the drowned body of a small infant. I waded into the water and pulled the baby from the coarse grass that clutched at its body. The corpse was so small – barely a week old – and its tiny head flopped in my hands. Ada sobbed and pulled her collar over her mouth. Honey held out her arms and I placed the baby gently into her hands. I walked back, treading carefully through the bodies of headless chickens, past the cows floating in blood, past the mule whose giant, watery eyes stared upwards saying, 'Why me?' The deputy sheriff and his sidekick scribbled notes as they vainly tried to record this incomprehensible scene. The sidekick, scarcely twenty years old, was more officious than his nervous boss.

'You going somewhere?'

'Just walking.'

'Walking?'

'Kind of hard to take, ain't it?'

The deputy nodded. 'Just don't wander too far. We'll be needing witnesses' statements and stuff. That kind of thing.'

'Sure, I'll be right over there.' I pointed to the dirt road. After walking a yard or two, I turned back to the deputy. 'By the way, I think you should look down by the creek.' I looked at my boots and shook my head to avoid having to give a full description of what we'd found.

I walked down the dusty road for five minutes, maybe ten. When I finally looked back towards the Kroeger farm it was a good half-mile in the distance. The flies still buzzed around me and as I swatted them, for some reason I started to run. I ran faster than that nag Star Hawk last year at the Derby, chasing George Smith in the home stretch. I ran as though the Grim Reaper himself was chasing me. I ran because I was being chased by the typhoid bugs that buzzed around my face. But most of all, I ran because I was being chased by the creepy shadows of old man Kroeger's madness.

Running faster and faster, I gasped for breath and my mouth filled with flies. I took off my coat and swung it around like a madman with St Vitus's dance as my mind jumped through the hoops of someone else's life. Say old man Kroeger had a lover – the young girl with the smooth coffee and cream skin that lay there in the pig trough with her insides on the outside and her blood splattered over the bodies of fifteen pigs. Not a nice way to die. Okay, so she was his secret cuddle bunny that he snuck off to whilst old lady Kroeger prayed for the four children she had lost to diphtheria and so turned her back on him in bed, night after night. Coffee Cream filled old Kroeger's void until she told old man Kroeger that she was pregnant and he dropped her quicker than a bellyful of mule shit.

I stopped to catch my breath. Across the road was a shack that seemed to have been crushed by some long departed giant's foot. The roof and the front wall had toppled into the yard and no one seemed to have noticed. Rainwater from the swollen ditch gushed out of what would have been a front door. With no money for food, Coffee Cream had scooped up her white man's offspring and walked to the Kroeger place. Old lady Kroeger wasn't pleased as she looked at the black woman standing there in her front yard, holding her husband's child. She had buried four children of her own and couldn't understand why this grubby-faced, colored infant had survived to punish them all. She snatched up the ancient single shot carbine that was always kept loaded by the front door, walked out into the yard, aimed it at Coffee Cream and pulled the trigger. Half of Coffee Cream's stomach exploded in the direction of the pigpen and the rest of her body crumpled into the feeding trough as she dropped her baby into the mud. Old lady Kroeger picked up the screaming, terrified child and walked to the creek. Kroeger ran after her but watched helplessly as she tossed the infant into the water. The old man was beside himself with grief as he dragged his wife by the legs back to the muddy yard. He thrust her head into the rainwater barrel. She kicked for a while, but in less than a minute her body was still and Kroeger finally let go his grip on her neck. He went back into the house, returned with a butcher's knife and a revolver and proceeded to slaughter every sadsack animal he had kept alive through all these difficult years.

I kept on running. In the distance I thought I could see a truck, but maybe it was a mirage, like those Arab guys get in the desert from smoking too much camel poop. Maybe I'd had a terrible nightmare after too pleasurable an afternoon topped up with rotgut Sneaky Pete liquor. Maybe I dreamed the whole thing. But then again, maybe old Kroeger had walked to his barn, sliced the throat of his trusty mule on the way and thrown the rope over the highest beam. And if this was true, the rope would have come back from its loop over the rafter, Kroeger would have grabbed it, walked up the wooden slatted stairs to the hay store, put the noose around his neck – and jumped.

17

I couldn't run anymore. I vomited again and staggered like a rum-pot drunk into the road, as a tobacco truck screeched to a halt barely three feet from me.

'You okay, fella?' asked the gaunt-faced driver as he jumped out of his cab and helped me up. He had strong farmer's hands and I thanked him by throwing up once more. He jumped back to save his shoes. 'Hey! Fella, what you been drinking?'

'I'm sorry. Strawberries and Sneaky Pete sure don't agree.' I wiped the spittle from my face and Gaunt Face smiled kindly and understandingly.

'Which way you headed?' he asked.

I shielded my eyes from the low sun as I looked ahead at the long straight road. 'I don't know.'

'I'm going as far as Cynthiana. You're welcome to a ride.'

'Cynthiana sounds good,' I said. After what I'd just seen, anywhere sounded better than where we were.

I jumped into the cab and tried to clear my head of the carnage in the Kroeger yard. I felt bad that I hadn't said goodbye to the Mackintosh girls. But I was sure that I'd meet up with them again one day over a plate of strawberries washed down with something a little less potent than Sneaky Pete. A single last fly buzzed around the cab and landed on the dash right in front of me. I smacked it dead with my hand.

The driver was a tobacco farmer by the name of Isaac. He told me that he was on his on his way to a labor meeting in Cynthiana.

'We're thinking of forming an alliance,' he said.

'You are? Who's that?'

'Us small farmers. It's the only way to stop the big tobacco growers from squeezing the life out of us.'

I nodded in agreement but stared at the straight road, still trying to shake the images of the Kroeger bloodshed out of my head. He droned on about the price of tobacco and I was sympathetic, but frankly, I never met a farmer who didn't complain.

'The prices are shameful. You can't make a living.'

'That's definitely not right,' I offered.

'We're going to have this guy from North Dakota come down and talk to us.'

'I.W.W.?'

'Huh?'

'Wobblies?'

'No. None of that socialist shit.'

'The Non-Partisan League?' I surprised Isaac with my knowledge.

'That's it. You know them?'

'I was in North Dakota once at one of their meetings.' He smiled at me like I was a brother-in-arms.

Cynthiana was an unusual town with cast-iron façades on the buildings. In a feed barn at the end of Main Street a guy called Shelby from the Non-Partisan League stirred up the assembled farmers from a makeshift stage with fiery talk of brotherhood and how the little guy can stuff those rich guys. Fat chance, I thought, as they cheered him to the rafters. I swiped a tobacco pouch for later, but mostly all these guys had in their overalls were nickels and dimes. I have to say I admired the spunk of these hayseeds. I'd heard Shelby talk before and he pretty well sang from my hymnbook from a social point of view, even though the very thought of organized anything went against the grain for me. They closed the meeting by singing 'John Brown's Body':

> He captured Harper's Ferry with his nineteen men
> so true
> He frightened old Virginia till she trembled through
> and through
> They hung him for a traitor, themselves the traitor
> crew
> His soul is marching on . . .

That's when all hell let loose.

Suddenly, in burst maybe twenty National Guardsmen with fixed bayonets on their rifles and it was obvious that although they were a little out of practice they seemed intent on using them. A bull-necked sergeant manhandled Shelby off the stage and announced that they were rounding us all up in the name of the Selective Service Act, whereby we all had to register for the draft. As most of them had a week to do so anyway, the assembled farmers were convinced that it was a nifty ploy to break up their meeting. The government had been really nervous lately – they had the Anarchists up there in Minneapolis, the Communists in Toledo, the Socialists in Detroit and the I.W.W. in Cleveland – it made you wonder if it was the Germans who the government saw as the real enemy. It stank, but at that moment in time it wasn't worth risking a bayonet in the butt.

The army meat wagon they threw me into was already half-full of guys that they'd picked up locally. I sat next to a young kid with a bright red scurvy face whose hair had been falling out in clumps. He was rubbing his shoulder and seemed in pain.

'You okay?' I asked.

'Kind of rough, these army guys,' he answered. I put my hand over my mouth to avoid his fetid breath.

'It's always the same when you put a guy in uniform,' I said. He nodded in agreement, clutching his shoulder and letting out a deep sigh that filled the truck with a smell not dissimilar to rotten cabbage.

'I guess they've got us,' I murmured through my fingers.

'Not me,' he answered.

'Not you?'

'Uh-uh. Nope. They grabbed the wrong Kentucky boy here.'

With some difficulty he fished into his back pocket and came up with a cloth pouch holding a bundle of papers, including an army registration form.

'Seventeen,' he said proudly, waving his papers in front of me before returning them safely to his pocket. 'A whole thirteen months before I'm even old enough to register.'

This apple-knocker was so smug that it made me want to punch him, except he suddenly smiled, presenting a mouthful of brown rotting teeth that you really wouldn't want to come into contact with your knuckles. He said he had been singing hymns at a Boonesboro church when the army guys interrupted the service and hauled off all the young conscription-age men. He was still holding his hymnbook and proudly showed me the inside cover. There was an ornately engraved color panel with his name in elegant calligraphy, signed by someone called the Bishop of Jesus' Tabernacle of the Assembly of the Righteous. At the bottom of the page, beneath his brown and yellow fingernail, I read, 'Reuben Hickey, date of birth: Dec. 3 1901.'

'Boy, are you lucky. I guess you miss the draft by a whole year. You sonofagun.'

Reuben nodded and smiled once more, revealing his piano key teeth. I began to feel sorry for this chronically ugly kid until he started talking about his church and how it was devoted to the hidden teachings of Jesus, and that all the country's troubles were because of all the colored people in the world. I could have argued the point, but what was the use? Some southern gospel grinder had filled his head full of shit and that was probably what had rotted his teeth.

* * *

The wagon drove through the iron gates of Fort Dantonville and through the rear window I could see the long lines of conscripts that snaked in all directions across the dusty parade ground. The National Guard corporal yelled at us to get out of the wagon:

'Out! Out! Out! Registration forms at the ready. Move it! Out! Out!'

Reuben Hickey's shoulder was still bothering him and so I put my arm around his waist.

'Here, let me help you. Just put your weight on me.'

The poor guy winced with pain and I felt bad as I slipped my hand inside his baggy coat and relieved him of his cloth pouch and hymnbook. The National Guardsmen screamed at us to join the long lines. Another soldier picked on poor Reuben and ordered him to run at the double to join the farthest line. The Bishop of Jesus' Tabernacle of the Assembly of the Righteous couldn't help him now.

The smell of nervous sweat filled the air as we all stood in jagged single file staring at our feet. In the newspapers they kept showing these patriotic pictures of healthy young men with wide apple-pie smiles, climbing off tractors and kissing goodbye to their perfectly understanding mothers, wives and happy children. But frankly, I couldn't see too many happy smiles from where I was standing. We just stared at our boots and shuffled forwards, kicking up dust. I didn't take a vote on it, of course, but I figured that no one in that yard was overly keen to join the slaughter over there in France. I looked at their faces – they were the ordinary Joes from any small town in

America: the guy in the feed store, the barkeep, the black-smith, the migrant farm worker and the kid who pumps gas. It sure didn't seem a fight that was much to do with any of us.

At a wooden table in front of the yard a sergeant looked at my borrowed papers, checked the age, crooked his head and eyed me most suspiciously.

'How old are you, Hickey?'

'Seventeen, Sir.'

'You ain't aging too well, are you, Hickey?' I thought he was right, but I also thought he was being sarcastic.

'Hard times, Sir. I had the scurvy and been sleeping rough. But I ain't complaining, 'cause it's God's way, Sir.'

I could see that he was still unconvinced. I swiftly shoved the hymnbook onto the table, spun it around and tapped at where it said, 'Date of birth: Dec. 3 1901.' He wasn't about to argue with the signature of a bishop. 'I'd look a lot younger if I could get a shave,' I added for good measure.

He hammered my form twice with a large red stamp and handed it back to me.

'Re-register December, 1918. Dismissed. Next!'

I scooped up my papers and winked at the guy behind me.

'Don't worry, buddy. With luck, the war will be over by Christmas.'

I walked back past the poor saps clutching their reg-istration slips and I started to feel a little guilty until I reminded myself that it was the government's fault. The only reason the US didn't have a big enough regular army was because they'd spent the last couple of years chasing that crazy Pancho Villa all over Mexico for no good reason. At least Mexico was the backyard closest to us, unlike France. Where the hell was that? The only Paris young Reuben Hickey had ever heard of was a town somewhere south of Cincinnati.

I met this guy on a truck to Lexington who explained it all to me. He said he was a schoolteacher from Pikeville in east Kentucky. He said he had a wooden leg and so had been excused from duty. I was about to congratulate him, but he said he was real sore about it and so had forced the army guy to register him anyway. He really couldn't wait to get over there and start shooting people. More out of making conversation than real interest, I let it slip that I didn't understand what the hell the US was doing over there in France anyway.

'We're righting the wrongs of selfish despotism,' he snapped back at me.

'We are?'

'Oh, yeah. Without a doubt. I'm telling you, those goddam people are eee-vil, evil bastards. Worse than . . . animals.'

'The French?'

'No, the Germans.'

'Oh, sure, the Germans?'

'Are you stupid or something?' he snarled.

Some people really amaze me. Here was a guy who was actually volunteering to be shelled, machine-gunned, gassed or gutted by a German bayonet five thousand miles from his home in Pikeville, Kentucky, and he was calling *me* stupid? He made me mad, so I snapped back at him, 'No, I'm not stupid, Long John Silver, but maybe you are. What the hell good do you think you can do with that peg-leg anyway? Sow cabbage seeds in no-man's-land?'

Peg-Leg showed me exactly what he could do when, with incredible agility, he swung his wooden stump high and smacked it against the side of my head. I think I blacked out after the third stomp, after which he must have rolled me out of the truck.

When I came to, I was lying in a paddock ditch covered in horse manure. I pulled myself up and walked in the direction of Lexington. My head ached like hell and I was certain that my shoulder had come out of its socket. I was limping and I stank of shit – but at least I wasn't as bad off as those poor bastards in the trenches over there in Europe.

18

My friend Howie Papp raised horses in Kentucky for the Tsar's cavalry. He was so proud of his magnificent animals, which he claimed were the best in the world. Then someone told him that they'd had a revolution over in Russia and they'd murdered the Tsar, the Tsarina and all the kids in July of 1918. Howie said whatever was going on over there sure had nothing to do with him, and that whatever side his horses were fighting on, they would certainly give a good account of themselves. But later he heard that when the animals were unloaded from the steamer in Petrograd they were immediately slaughtered for food because everyone there was starving.

    Moral: Once you start eating horses, the only thing left is to chew on one another.

The war wasn't over by Christmas, but it was by the following November, though most of the guys didn't get home until a year later. Some of them even got sent to Russia.

Whilst the war ground on and the brave doughboys were routing the Germans at Meuse-Argonne, I crisscrossed America, adding a dozen states to my travels.

I had been working the crowd at Niagara Falls, where

some crazy Englishman was attempting to swim the whirlpool rapids. He had drowned and been washed up on the beach and although no one else was in the mood to celebrate, I still ended up blind drunk in a back-alley guzzle joint off Fourth Street.

I hitched a ride to Buffalo and spent the night at the Salvation Army Calvary Mission on Oneida Street. They had these spindle-back oak benches where they let you sleep for one night only. The benches were comforting enough when you were numbed from a skinful and hard enough for you not to sleep in too late the following morning when you sobered up. Not that you'd want to hang around for too long. Ever since the general strike in Seattle, the government was rounding up any suspicious-looking guy without a job but with a head full of opinions. If you didn't agree with the war they called you a 'Socialist'. Worse still, if you didn't agree with being unemployed or badly paid and had a name that ended with an 'itch' or an 'ovsky', they called you a 'Bolshevik' and deported you even if you were born in Poughkeepsie. Sometimes these guys were being unloaded from the boat in Vladivostok before their families even read about it in the papers. No, it sure didn't pay to hang around too long.

At 6 a.m. a Sally Army sergeant snapped up the green canvas blinds and the sun burned into the room. Through my bleary, bloodshot eyes I started to read the quotations that were beautifully and painstakingly painted on the mission's walls. 'Intoxicating liquors come forth like the Egyptian angel of death slaying the fairest born in every family,' said one, and, 'There are three things that last: Faith, Hope and Love. And the greatest of these is Love.' I smiled because everyone knows that there are four things that last: Faith, Hope, Love and a good serge suit. Another sign said, 'How long since you wrote Mother?' For some reason that one really woke me up and a month later, in the summer of 1919, I found myself back in San Francisco.

After so many years on the road I wanted to offer a few explanations. Sounds crazy, I know, but deep down I always believed I was a good son and hated the thought that my mom might have felt badly about me climbing out of that window at St Mary's. Somehow I always had this idea that if I could just get to talk to her for five minutes, she'd understand. Probably sounds kind of foolish, I know, but it always nagged at me that I'd left so abruptly without even saying goodbye or even giving her my opinions on Sacramento. By the way, I've since been to Sacramento many times and although I was quite right not to spend my educational years there, it's not a bad town.

I arrived back in the city on the day that they were having a parade to welcome home San Francisco's own. It goes without saying that it wasn't yours truly they were having the parade for, but to celebrate the 363rd and 347th Divisions of the American Expeditionary Force returning from France.

Those doughboys were full of piss and vinegar, marching along to a tremendous reception. There were the sounds of military bands and Stars and Stripes flags and bunting draped everywhere. The young soldiers who had escaped the slaughter at Cantigny and St-Mihiel were linked arm in arm with their moms, dads, sisters, wives and girlfriends as they proudly marched down Market Street singing, 'Inky dinky parlez-vous'.

There was a column of soldiers who had been blinded from the German gas bombs. They had bandages over their eyes – each of them shuffling along, clutching the shoulder of the guy in front of him, never again to see City Hall, Union Square or the fog drifting into the bay.

After the parade, people in the bars were laughing and slapping one another on the back. I was looking at the rows of army rifles stacked against the walls, which looked kind of dangerous to me, when a guy grabbed me and said, 'Nate! It's you! Nate Raginsky.'

'No, you must be mistaken, I'm not Nate,' I answered.

The soldier laughed and gently slapped my face and ruffled my hair. 'Same old Nate. Always kidding.'

He turned me around to face the rest of the bar. 'Folks, this here is Nate Raginsky, who threw the Mills bomb at the German machine-gunners at Fère-en-Tardenois. They gave him the Medal of Honor. The guy's a goddam hero.'

Everyone cheered as he hugged and kissed me. I tried to say that I was never posted. In fact, I'd never had my name pulled out of the big glass bowl of the draft lottery. I had never even left the country. I never saw a Mills bomb, or the trenches of Fère-en-Tardenois. I didn't even believe in the war and, worse than that, I had lied to get out of going. But what kind of a shit-heel was I to have any opinions about the war anyway? I'd only read about it in the newspapers. By all rights I should have been there, coughing with the gas and dragging my maimed buddies through the mud. Where was Reuben Hickey, the kid with piano teeth from Kentucky, who went instead of me? Did he ever make it home to Boonesboro, to his Tabernacle of the Righteous? Or was he left in France somewhere in an unmarked, quicklime grave with nothing left of him but his rotten teeth?

The soldier continued to ignore my protestations and it was easier to accept his offer of a drink and meet his brave buddies, not to mention his entire family. Sometimes it helps to have little regard for self-respect. It makes it easier to live lies and accommodate the shabby humiliation that such occasions present.

After the third drink I started to enjoy being a war hero and although my own courage had been somewhat wanting, it was impossible not to be humbled by these gutsy kids who against all the odds would now live to have gray hair. We all agreed that it was time to call 'sauer-kraut' sauerkraut again, and not 'liberty cabbage', and it was just too darned silly continuing the ban on the word 'hamburger'. Anyway, no one had ever called it a 'liberty sandwich', as the papers had told us to. Yep, we all agreed that the Germans were brave soldiers and we ought to be nice to them now we had licked them. They made it sound like an Army vs Notre Dame football game, as though no one had been killed, gassed, blinded, or maimed. But at least they had been there. I hadn't.

19

I made a few inquiries at the place where we used to live on Filbert. My feet clanged on the new iron stair-case, a great improvement on the rickety old wooden one they had so hastily built after the quake. I took a deep breath and knocked on our old apartment door. After a minute or two it was opened by a stubby stranger with suspenders over his long johns.

'Hi, I'm Tommy.'

'Yeah?'

'I used to live here.'

'You did?'

'Yeah, is my mom there?'

'Mom?'

'Mrs Moran? Slany Moran? Maeve? Gracie?'

'Can't help, fella, never knew them. They must have moved out a while ago.'

Upstairs, Mr Huber still lived on the third floor. He greeted me with a hug when I told him who I was.

'Tommy! Little Tommy Moran!' he shouted. 'Come in, come in. Well, I'll be . . .'

I sat at his kitchen table as he poured coffee. He told me that he'd retired from the brick works in Corona

Heights but still had a lot of back trouble.

'And Mrs Huber, how's she?'

'No idea. The bitch left me.'

'I'm sorry to hear that.' I could have told him I saw that one coming when I was eight years old, but I didn't want to appear a smart-ass.

'Now I'm on my own.'

'That's too bad.'

'They went up north.'

'Mrs Huber?'

'No, your mom and the girls.'

'Where?'

'Don't know. Old Mr Kittleman had a heart attack.'

'He did?'

'When he died, they closed his dress store and so the Singer people took back your mom's sewing machine and she couldn't work. That was tough for her.'

'I bet.'

'They came one day and carted it down the stairs. She was kicking and screaming after them so much, they had to call the cops.'

'Oh, boy.'

That was hard to hear. What had she done with the money and stuff that I had sent her over the years? There was enough to buy ten sewing machines.

'So little Gracie knocked on my door one day and said they were off grape picking.'

'Grape picking?'

'Napa or Sonoma way, it was.'

'Did you have an address?'

'Nope. Got a Christmas card from Gracie one year. I always had a soft spot for that kid.'

'Me too.' I picked up my hat and as we hugged I slipped a twenty into his vest pocket.

'Thanks, Mr Huber, I hope your back feels a lot better.' For fun I swiped his wristwatch and when I gave it back he laughed so hard I thought I was going to have to call an ambulance. As I ran down the stairs he leaned over the rail and shouted after me, 'When you gonna run for President, Tommy?'

'Any day now, Mr Huber.'

'I look forward to that.'

Good old Mr Huber, always the optimist.

I walked down Kearny and took the streetcar at Lotta's Fountain on Market to the loop in front of the Ferry Building, bought a ticket and climbed the gangway to the Vallejo Ferry.

It was a nice day, the water on the bay was smooth and there were a few passengers braving the salty wind and seagull droppings on the top deck. I sat on a wooden bench at the stern and lifted my head to breathe in the ocean air. From the middle of the bay I looked back and thought how fresh, new and magnificent the city looked. Tall buildings had sprung up all over so that the new skyline was a complete stranger to me.

I thought of Maeve and Gracie making their way up to the wine country where the vineyards had flourished. Now that the Chinese had been pushed out, there was plenty of work for folks from all over to take their place

– as long as they had strong backs, nimble hands, uncomplaining dispositions and were willing to pick grapes for a nickel a box.

I shielded my eyes as the sun burned through the silver fog on the bay and followed the new buildings and the line of the waterfront to Meigg's Wharf at the bottom of Taylor Street. That's where the Thatcher Ice House used to be, where my dad worked. I remembered the day he announced to us all that Gracie would have to be sent to the California Home for Feebleminded Children. As fate would have it, my dad died the following Christmas, just before the quake, and the Home for the Feebleminded burned down in the great fire, so my little sister got a reprieve. Just as well, because if you ask me, it sounded worse than the home for recalcitrant boys in Sacramento where they were going to send me. I thought of my dad stooped over the stove in the corner of our apartment warming his red raw, perpetually cold hands and Maeve and me rubbing his rock-hard feet. Boy, that sure put me off ever working for a living.

I looked down into the waters of the bay and watched as the ferry spat out oil into the white frothy wake. My dad's funeral was a small affair, just my mom, Maeve, Gracie, Mr and Mrs Huber and my dad's best buddy, Félim. As the undertakers lowered the coffin into the ground, Félim whispered out of the side of his mouth towards my mother, 'Pat owed me eighty bucks, Slany.'

'He did?' she whimpered through her damp handkerchief.

'He does,' stressing the present tense to emphasize that

the debt still stood, but this was lost on my mom.

'But we don't have eighty dollars, Félim.'

'How much do you have?'

'Nothing. The funeral took all but seven dollars and we owe twenty-eight dollars in rent. As a matter of fact, we were wondering, as you were his best friend, if you could see your way clear to lending us the money.'

'But Pat owed me eighty dollars!' he insisted.

'And I guess he always will, Félim.' And with that she walked forward to throw dirt on the coffin.

I always loved my mom for that.

Next to me on the ferry an old sweaty guy with a soup-strainer moustache was fanning himself with his Panama. Further along sat the guy's wife with a haughty manner and carrying a good quality, hand-laced cowhide purse with one of those easy-lift locks. She was wearing a baggy velour coat with tricotine collar and cuffs, and had a hat on her that looked like it had cost the lives of ten birds. I closed my eyes and let the sun warm my face; I had no intention of going to work. Suddenly the sweaty guy thought he saw a fish and leaned right across me. I couldn't believe my good fortune.

'Wow, will you look at that sturgeon? That baby must weigh seventy pounds.'

The lady with the ten-bird hat looked over the edge of the ferryboat and smiled.

'Come and see, Betty,' he called over to his skinny daughter, but she seemed even less interested in the marine life than her mother. She had barley sugar drop-curls and was wearing one of those fashionable Junior Miss apron frock uniforms that made you want to give her your ticket to punch. Old Sweaty leaned over further to get a better view of his sturgeon when all at once he let out a violent gasp. I had both my hands inside his jacket when he suddenly toppled forwards, stone-dead, into my arms. As I already had his wallet in my hand, it was a few minutes before I dared say anything. I couldn't move – the guy was dead weight and I felt his cold, clammy face on my cheek.

'Ma'am? I think your husband has had a heart attack.'

Mrs Ten Birds gave me another haughty look and then, when what I had said penetrated the mountain of feathers, she screamed. I was helpless with the dead man propped in my arms and his wallet tight between my fingers.

It seemed liked a week before we docked at Vallejo. The police climbed onto the boat, took the dead man from my arms and tried to calm the hysterical Mrs Ten Birds. Betty, the Junior Miss, stared at me as if I had been solely responsible for her father's demise and, probably because I was still holding his wallet, she began to wail even louder than her mother. I leaped over the side of the boat and ran.

20

There used to be this circus act called Zacchini, 'the human cannonball'. Idelbrando Zacchini would climb into a cannon and with a loud bang was propelled at a hundred miles an hour for thirty yards, to great applause. The act was such a success that circuses all over the world began to copy Zacchini, resulting in thirty dead human cannonballs who sadly didn't have old Idelbrando's skills.

    Moral: Flying is easy. Landing in the net is the hard part.

The police were crawling all over the electric railway depot and so I got a ride on a wagon pulled by a six-horse team of Percheron grays delivering French oak barrels to a local winery. I jumped off at the crossroads in a place called Yountville, and as I had no idea where my mom lived, I just started to walk the narrow trails between the vines. There was a clear blue sky and the vineyards were full of orange and yellow poppies and overhead I could see a flock of white-throated sparrows.

The workers in the fields seemed to have come from all over and for an hour I couldn't even find anyone who spoke English, let alone remembered if they'd seen a plump Irish woman called Slany Moran with two daughters in tow. How did I even know if they were still together? Maybe sweet Gracie had been sent away by the nuns to Albuquerque? Maeve could be in a monastery in Donegal or Uruguay or someplace. When I was a kid I used to imagine her being shanghaied onto some schooner bound for New Zealand, Australia, or some other country at the butt-end of the world. But at that moment I hoped that she was over the next hill.

What I will say is that it was certainly beautiful country up there. It seemed that I had spent my whole life working crowds in busy cities where the fetid stench of street dirt, rot-gut breath, body odor and back alley dog shit were all I knew. It smelled so sweet and clean here that it was almost like I was breathing fresh air for the first time in my life. I had to light a cigarette to remind my lungs I was still living on the same planet that I had previously inhabited.

Across the fields I could hear music – a jangling, foreign sound – and treading carefully through the vine rows, I headed toward it. In the distance I could see some kind of party in progress. People were all dressed up in their Sunday best and dancing to this bouzouki-type band that sounded even more foreign than Greek. To be honest, I was never big on parties because I usually got so drunk I couldn't see a hole in a ladder. But these people looked like they were having a hell of a time and to be completely frank, it was the long line of jackets hanging on posts that really caught my eye. But then I got distracted. No, that's an understatement. I'm kind of familiar with earthquakes, and this one was a number ten on the Rossi-Forel Scale – bigger than the 1906 shimmy, as far as my heart was concerned.

The first time I saw Effie, she was surrounded by at least four guys who were all dancing with her. She had dark chestnut hair, tied in a chignon behind her neck and was wearing a printed voile frock that fluttered upwards as she spun around. From where I was standing she looked about as beautiful as a girl could be – or maybe the mustachioed pumpkin-heads dancing with her were so plug-ugly, she just looked beautiful by comparison – but I don't think so.

Now, as I've said before, I'm a loner by profession – my idea of a good party is a few drinks – sometimes too many – three or four fat wallets and maybe a good quality gold watch. To me, a social life was what other people had while I went about my business. So I can't describe how much I surprised myself, when suddenly my coat was off and I was out there jumping and jigging around like I was a late arrival from some crazy-house bouzouki dance troupe.

I didn't dance with Effie at first because it seemed that everyone was paying attention to her, even the lanky local priest – and you know my feelings about priests. But soon it was my turn and we danced together for an hour. Probably it was just a couple of minutes, but as you've no doubt gathered, she had quite an effect on me.

The band took a well-earned rest and Effie introduced me to her mom, who was a handsome woman with a nice smile. She shook my hand warmly even though she was somewhat preoccupied with the state of her husband, who appeared to be as drunk as a wheelbarrow. The old man had a small head, a face like red Kenosha granite, graying hair and huge, bushy eyebrows so thick that they looked like they were nesting birds. Effie's mom was anxious to get him home and that they should say their goodbyes. After a lot of pleading, and to my great relief, Effie was allowed to stay a little longer, having been promised a ride from her friend Irène. Her dad shook my hand, thinking I was a member of the band, and complimented me on my bouzouki playing.

Effie and I walked along the creek by the side of the winery. As dumb as it might seem, I held out my hand and introduced myself.

'Tommy Moran.'

She took my hand, shook it and smiled sweetly. I think she appreciated my gentlemanly gesture.

'Effie Kazarian . . . Effie's short for Euphemia.'

'That's pretty. Your folks are . . . ?'

'Armenian.'

Boy, I felt stupid. Ignorance is the greatest sin, Hoagie said. *He* certainly would have known Armenian – probably even a few choice words from the language, but *I* sure didn't, I mean, Armenia? Where the heck is Armenia? I had read *Gulliver's Travels* from cover to cover, from ocean to ocean, and I knew Lilliput and Glubbdubdrib and even the Land of Houyhnhnms, but I didn't know Armenia from Milk of Magnesia. I had taken Hoagie's advice on the avoidance of stupidity, but there's the rub: the more you know, the more you realize how much you don't. Have you ever noticed that? It's why clever people are always in so much agony. They're bright enough to know that they can never be clever enough. I tell you, being stupid is a faster route to contentment.

'Well, my dad's Armenian, my mom's Italian,' Effie helped me out.

Italian was easier for me. I knew Colosimo's Café, Florestano's Famous Fettuccini and even clever stuff like Michelangelo, Rossini and a few lines from *Romeo and Juliet*, which possibly might have impressed her at that moment, but I let it slide. They say that people who say nothing are the smartest ones, and so I bit my tongue and nodded.

'So, do you live around here?' she asked.

'No, I'm just visiting. I've been looking for my family . . . my mom and sisters.'

'Do they live here in the valley?'

'Maybe. I don't really know, to be honest, I haven't seen them for some time. I left home a while ago, and we kind of lost touch.'

'Did you quarrel?'

'Not exactly . . . I left six years ago.'

'What are their names? Maybe I know them.'

'Slany Moran . . . that's my mom. My sisters are Gracie and Maeve.'

Effie shook her head.

'So, do you live in San Francisco?'

'Oh, no, I've lived all over . . . it's my job.' Jeez, how

much dumber could I appear? I sounded like I was a salesman for Pepsi-Cola or J L Kraft.

'So what kind of job is that?'

I knew that was coming, and for a split second I nearly told the truth, 'Picking . . .'

What was I saying? Picking pockets? Why not picking peaches in Hood River, Oregon?

'Picking the sunshine from a butterfly's wings . . .'

She smiled and I thought I had impressed her because for the first time in an hour I had the feeling that, in her eyes, I didn't look like some nut that had escaped from a bouzouki asylum. I had no evidence of this, of course, except that she held her smile for a second longer than was necessary and her hand was suddenly resting on mine.

'I'm a magician,' I found myself saying.

'A magician?'

'Yep, a magician.' For some inexplicable reason she was intrigued, and so there was no going back.

'Like at a circus?'

'Sometimes circuses.'

'Vaudeville?'

I nodded. 'Vaudeville. And baseball games, political rallies, racetracks.' I tried to think of places where I hadn't stolen a wallet. I shrugged, 'Wherever there's people.'

She was mildly impressed though not entirely con-vinced. 'I don't believe you.'

Out of her ear I produced her watch, which I had hooked from her wrist and as she looked down in com-plete amazement I took the opportunity to kiss her cheek. As my lips touched her smooth skin, so close to her lips, my heart sounded like a mule in a tin barn. As for Effie, she didn't seem to notice, she just stared at her watch.

'How did you do that?'

I took a silver dollar from my pocket and gave it to her. 'One newly minted silver dollar.' I looked at it closely, 'Dated 1919. I'll get this back by the end of the evening. So hide it.'

'Hide it?'

'Not in the barn, on *you*. Anywhere. But please, not in your shoe, because that's difficult, even for me.'

We returned to the party and I continued to impress Effie with my suspicious sleight of hand. Hard to think why, but I suppose she had spent her life on this hillside, surrounded by decent people and all that God can give in the way of kindness, earthly beauty and stuff I once thought was a crock of shit. The darker side of human beings, which I undoubtedly represented, seemed remote and curious, if not a little amusing, to this pretty eighteen-year-old.

As it grew dark, Effie's cloth bag contained at least six wallets as I showed off and she giggled at the outright nerve of it all. It never occurred to her for a moment that it was dishonest. She probably thought it was a cute party trick and that I was planning to give them back and so I watched, powerless, as she proceeded to do just that.

Irène was from a well-off, local family and had her own Model T coupe. Effie held on to me as the eccentric Irène and her sister Edith screamed loudly as we barreled down the narrow tracks between the vines, kicking up the red dust. It's an understatement to say that the three girls were a little tanked up from the wine.

The sisters dropped us at the gates of a small winery. A sign on the fence post said, 'Eichelberger-Monticule Proprietor A.G. Kazarian'. I climbed out of the coupe, glad to be alive. Effie, more used to Irène's driving, crossed herself as she waved goodbye to the crazy giggling sisters. As the Ford coupe disappeared in the red dust, Effie took my hand and led me to a narrow corkscrew path that spiraled up to the top of the hillside.

We lay down amongst the hyacinths and yellow poppies and kissed. My hand slowly reefed up the tiny pleats her chemise of *crêpe de Chine*. Except it wasn't a chemise, it was one of those one-piece, silk union suits that even I found hard to get inside. I moved my hand up the inside of her thigh and she stopped kissing and pulled my hand away.

'Uh-uh. You can't rush these things, Tommy.'

'I know,' I said. 'It takes six months to build a Pierce-Arrow.' It was a dumb thing to say. Why a line from an advertisement for a fancy automobile should stick in my head was a mystery to me, except for notions of Cupid. Frankly, I could have said I'd walk a mile for a Camel and it still would have made her laugh.

I held up the silver dollar she had hidden in the top of her stocking and flipped it between my fingers to catch the moonlight. Effie smiled and looked at me as if to say, 'Is nothing safe with you around?' Well, that's what I hoped that she was thinking, considering my hand had been so far up her thigh.

I was beginning to have thoughts of steep hills and a long walk home when she suddenly came back at me with her mouth open and yanked off her dress. I pulled off her union suit and she undid my pants. I looked up at the sky and felt woozy staring into that pitch-black ocean, bottomless and endless, sparkling with mysterious, untouchable galaxies.

Effie hurried home and I began the walk down the hill. She had said that she would meet me the next afternoon by the gas station at the Yountville crossroads. The red slatted bench, she said. How could I miss it? At five o'clock. How could I be a second late?

As I walked down the steep hill I looked across at the leafy vines in the hazy gray light of dusk. As Effie and I made love in the vineyard we didn't know it, but the coming harvest and grape crush would be the last before Prohibition. I crunched onwards down the red dirt road to the valley floor.

21

I had been away from San Francisco for six years and five months and I was one day late.

Effie had given me the name of a labor fixer in Sonoma who might be able to locate my mom and sisters. The guy had given me an address in Agua Caliente and I walked up a dusty road, which had the pretty name of Sunnyside. There were blooming pear orchards on either side.

At the house, Gracie ran up and hugged me tightly. She had grown into an attractive young woman, skinny as a pickax handle, her yellow hair now neatly bobbed and with those green eyes that I had always remembered – the kind of eyes that seemed to be permanently focused in the distance, as if she had been smoking banana skins or something. As I had expected, my sister Maeve was as welcoming as an armored car with a moveable machine-gun turret. She was big like my mom and greeted me cordially, without any surfeit of affection, brushing her cheek against mine as if a kiss would be too good for me. She gave me a handkerchief to cover my mouth and showed me to the front parlor, where my mom lay in an open coffin in the corner of the room, dead from the Spanish flu.

I knelt down and started to shake like a plate of Jell-O as I stuttered my pathetic apologies.

'I'm truly sorry, Mom. I'm sorry I couldn't get here in time.' Boy, did I sound stupid. 'I'm sorry you had to work so hard. I'm sorry I wasn't there to grow up and bring money home like I was supposed to. I'm sorry I was such a bad son. I'm sorry I was such a shitty brother to Maeve and Gracie. I'm sorry I turned out to be such a shit-heel that you couldn't wait to get rid of me.'

I was shaking even more now, and I nervously reached out and took my mom's arm to steady myself. The ham hocks I remembered were now broomstick thin and as cold as a spade left out in the snow. Her stiff, bony fingers were bent around a rosary that sprinkled into the folds of her starched cotton smock. I stared at her pale, dead face. Was she listening? Or was she far from here on her way to where good Catholics are supposed to go on their pre-paid ticket to paradise? I looked at her closed eyes and thin, purple lips. Her sewing days had long been over and so she wasn't wearing her thick glasses. The three vertical lines on her forehead that I always remembered had been joined by many others, but somehow, she wasn't frowning anymore. Her wispy hair was gently brushed over her almost bald head, which she had always covered with a hat.

I knew that face so well. I knew that face as well as my own. We shared the same sharp Geronimo nose and curled ears, but now her face was dead. For some reason I had stopped shaking.

No words, of course, were adequate or of any use

anyway. It might have made *me* feel a little better, but it sure wouldn't have helped my mom much. Any conversation with her would have to wait until I joined her in the hereafter – assuming, that is, the unlikely event that I would end up in the same good guys' place where she undoubtedly was headed.

Kneeling there, I felt suddenly calm. I whispered one more thing: 'I'm sorry I never told you I loved you.'

I stared at my feet as we crunched along the gravel on the way to the graveyard on a hillside looking down into the Valley of the Moon. I walked behind my two sisters who had linked arms. Just a few feet separated me from them but right then it seemed like five miles. I wanted to walk next to them. I wanted to hold them close and share their grief, but it was as if it was only *their* mother we were burying.

Boy, it's sad when you only see your relatives at funerals. I found myself staring at my mom's coffin because it wasn't crafted like the polished wooden caskets that I'd seen in Guppie Tate's yard. Those had been lovingly fashioned from the finest black Kentucky cherry. In contrast, my mom's coffin looked like something they'd box tomatoes in – you could almost hear the nails tearing from the wood as the funeral guys lifted the box from their shoulders. They cautiously felt for a handhold, avoiding the splinters in the roughly-planed Oregon pine.

The priest mumbled away in Latin. They say the reason

that prayers are in Latin is so that the whole world can say them, whatever language you speak. Truth is, it's so that the whole world won't understand them. Now, I'm not big on praying, but I always felt that, if I needed to, I could really get something going with God, in a conversational way. Boy, was I mad at Him, but I needed a prayer – any prayer – words from the scriptures to say out loud to accompany my mom up there to somewhere nice. That's what sons are supposed to do, aren't they? I waited until the priest had finished his prayer, cleared my throat and stepped forward, avoiding Maeve's eye. But I couldn't for the life of me remember any words that made sense. Mother Mary, Matthew, Mark, Luke, John, Moses and St Paul – what the heck did St Paul say? He said so darned much that was jammed into my head at the Salesian Catholic School. Why had it deserted me now? I knew that my mom would have expected a few good words because she knew her prayers, dozens of them, a mile long. I looked at Gracie and smiled as I remembered. Mom must have memorized half of the gosh-darn Bible. Shouldn't a couple of lines have perched on a shelf inside my head? Instead I found myself saying the words of one of the poems by that Emily lady: 'And then I heard them lift a box, and creak across my soul.'

I suddenly raised my voice like I was Pope Benedict himself in St Peter's Square or someplace:

'Creak across my soul,
Creak across my soul,
Creak across my soul.'

Maeve and Gracie looked at me as if I was crazy. I balled my hands into tight, white-knuckled fists as they lowered the coffin into the ground on that dusty hillside. A hand stroked mine. It was Gracie's. She dug into my fist, opening it and entwining her fingers in mine. I lifted my head and looked at her. Such a pretty girl, with the same wide-open eyes that seemed to have traveled with me all my life. My face crumpled in tears. Gracie stroked the side of my face and whispered, 'Where have you been, Tommy? It's been so long.'

'I don't know what to say, Gracie. How are you? Are you well? I love you.' I wiped the corners of my eyes with my cuff as I stammered like a rum-bag drunk. 'Gracie, don't make me feel bad. I know you needed me. I wasn't here. I wasn't anywhere.'

She leaned across and rubbed her nose against mine.

'Eskimos,' she whispered.

'Eskimos,' I replied.

'And thanks for the jewelry and the money you sent.'

I shrugged my shoulders as if to say, 'You're welcome,' distracted by the loud thuds as the shovels of dirt buried my mom's coffin.

'Are you rich, Tommy?'

I shook my head and held up my frayed cuffs.

'Mom wouldn't let us keep any of it. She said you'd probably stolen it. Had you?'

I nodded.

'Mom made me take it to confession at Peter and Paul's. I used to say, "Father, my brother keeps sending us all this jewelry and money. He's rich 'cause he's a big shot back east." They knew all about you, of course. The father used to tell me to leave the stuff behind in the box on the shelf and said he would pray for you.'

I can imagine the priest not asking any questions. They thought our whole family was nuts, and anyway, they were probably grateful for the donations, wherever they came from. I kept staring at Gracie, who took out a handkerchief and dabbed my cheeks.

'That was probably the right thing to do,' I said.

Gracie smiled. 'Oh, but I didn't give it all back. I used to keep some stuff and not tell Mom.'

'Oh, Gracie.'

She pulled up her sleeve, revealing a pretty gold watch. 'Do you remember you sent me this?'

I nodded and smiled. 'Yeah, I remember.' I remembered sending it, but I sure didn't remember stealing it – I'd swiped so many that they all became blurred in my coal cellar of a memory.

I pulled her towards me and hugged her. Over Gracie's shoulder I could see Maeve watching us. I gave her a smile and she returned it with an iceberg stare, so big and cold it could have sunk an ocean liner. Good old Maeve, she never did fail to let me down. She turned her head away and looked back at the diggers who had almost filled the grave. Suddenly they stopped their work and began pointing to the top of the ridge, where, emerging from a cloud of red dust, a convoy of cars was being followed by a police meat wagon. For one frozen minute the graveyard crew leaned on their spades as the vehicles screeched to a halt not twenty feet from my mother's grave and out climbed six cops followed by Betty, the Junior Miss, and her mother in the hat, Mrs Ten Birds, whose recently deceased husband I had held in my arms. Betty pointed in my direction and began to shriek.

I ran. I didn't stop to think how they knew I was there – maybe they weren't even pointing at me, the thief with the droopy eye, but I ran anyway. It was second nature, as I guess it would be to a lot of people who have lived the life I have, with their picture on a wall someplace in every cop shop in America.

I looked over my shoulder as the police wagon plowed into the vineyards behind me. The rows of vines grew narrower and the wagon ground to a halt. Maybe the precious vines were too valuable to risk damaging, or maybe they didn't want to get their boots dusty. When I reached the top of the second hill my lungs gave out on me. I threw up in the ditch and looked back. Goodbye, Mom. Goodbye, Maeve. I'm sorry I turned out to be such a gutbucket loser. Goodbye, sweet Gracie. I looked up towards the ridge of the Sonoma-Napa Mountains where Effie would have been waiting on the other side.

When you run from something, the walk back is a whole lot longer.

22

I thought maybe I could hop a train and get out of town for a day or two until the smoke cleared and then I could come back. But I didn't count on what would happen next. 'When sorrows come, they don't come in ones and twos,' the Shakespeare guy said, 'they come in shitloads.' Maybe he said it better, I can't remember exactly.

At the freight marshaling yards at the Oakland depot there was one of those Southern Pacific 'Big Boy' double-header engines taking on water. There were a dozen scrabble-ass poor 'bos catching out like me, crouching in the darkness, keeping out of sight of the railroad bulls. A young couple and a big black guy huddled close to me. The big guy introduced himself as Mose and the rattle-boned, white kid was called Dexter. The country kid was permanently stooped and smelled worse than a vase of dead lilies in a funeral chapel. Kneeling next to him was his young wife, who must have been about seventeen, clutching a tiny baby in a blanket. Dexter didn't seem to want to introduce her and she sure didn't seem too interested in conversation. She had one of those faces that suggested that her mom had married her first cousin – the kind of face that, from a very early age, had been fed nothing but pignuts from a hickory tree. Big Mose gently stroked the baby's head to keep it hushed.

'Where you headed?' I whispered.

'Fresno. Hope to get some potato work down there,' said Mose. 'How about you?'

'Yeah, Fresno. Fresno sounds fine. I'm not that fussy, to tell you the truth.' Mose smiled at me like he knew I was running from something. In my double-breasted suit, even with the frayed cuffs, I sure didn't look like I was dressed for digging potatoes.

The train shuddered; its giant steel wheels clanked into motion, steam hissed through the spokes and suddenly a dozen shadows ran towards the boxcars. I helped Dexter with his bundles as Mose slipped the lock with his knife and lifted Dexter's wife and baby up into a car. As the loco picked up speed, the boxcar began to pull away from us and we snatched at the grab rail of the following car. Dexter climbed to the roof as I held my arm out for Mose, who hauled himself up by getting a toehold on the bottom rung of the steel ladder. As we pulled out of the depot the three of us clung to the wooden slats that ran the length of the roof. The train lurched as it took the bend and I looped my belt around a slat and re-buckled it to stop myself being tossed off the side. The three of us crouched there on the roof for ten minutes without moving, then Mose pulled himself to his knees.

'Oh shit,' he said. 'It's a goddam bull.'

I looked behind me and saw the railroad cop coming

towards us along the roof of the next car. He was carrying
one of those Browning twelve gauge shotguns under one
arm, and with the other he hung onto the catwalk as he
crawled towards us through the engine smoke.

'Dex, no! Put that away!' Big Mose screamed.

I turned around to see that the skinny kid had drawn
a knife. The dumb putty-head was standing there, his
skinny body taut and arched like a cat's back. What was
he thinking? Maybe it was instinct – an animal thing, a
shit in the pants reaction – with his wife and baby huddled in the boxcar below? He might as well have got his
pecker out and pissed at the cop for all the good his
dopey knife could do. The bull fired and the kid took a
barrel at full choke, which took away half of his stomach
before he disappeared from the roof of the train. I desperately tried to unbuckle my belt, but the bull leaped
across the two cars and smacked me across the face with
the butt of his shotgun, shattering my jawbone and ripping my mouth apart. It was then that Mose hooked his
fat arms around the bull's head and in a second snapped
the guy's neck like a two-cent Hershey bar and tossed
him clean off the roof.

Mose helped me into the boxcar and I collapsed like
an empty gunnysack on top of the bags of Spreckel's
sugar. Dexter's wife sat opposite, huddled in the corner.
She had wrapped herself in the cardboard lining that she
had torn from the walls of the empty freight car. You
might have expected her to say something. 'Where's Dex?
What was that shot? Is Dex okay?' But not a single word
– she just clutched her baby in its blanket and said

nothing. She stared at me with those terrified, pignut eyes. Mose pulled the cork from a bottle of cheap liquor he had in his bundle and gently dribbled the hooch into my newly enlarged mouth. It hurt like hell and tasted like coffin varnish. I tried to say thank you, but my bottom lip appeared to be dangling down on my chin somewhere and it came out like I was talking Cherokee, 'Ayer-k-e-e-w.'

'Just drink it all. You gonna be all right, fella,' said Mose.

I coughed and spluttered as the hooch burned my throat. I sure hoped he was right, because at that moment a pauper's grave in Potter's Field looked a lot closer than Fresno.

Effie, what were you thinking when you were waiting there at five o'clock on the red slatted bench at the Yountville crossroads? What were you thinking when I didn't show? For a brief moment in time I had held her between my fingers like a wallet on a chain – gently, slowly, almost there, almost mine, almost a life . . . butter-fingers. She was suddenly gone in a puff of magician's smoke. I had followed a lot of rainbows in my time on the road, and if there was anything good at the end of one, I hadn't found it yet. It seemed that I could never walk fast enough.

The twin Southern Pacific Big Boy locomotives hit their stride as they chewed up the miles in the California night. The click of the rails held no romance for me. My broken jaw rearranged itself as the boxcar filled with the smell of soot; my head reeled from bad liquor and my hill of horseshit dreams was fast disappearing once more into the crowd of life. Soot, smoke, black.

I woke up a year later in a field in Paducah, or Wapello or Thunderbolt or someplace. I was a loner once more.

23

In September 1923, at the Polo Grounds in New York, Jack Dempsey faced Argentina's Luis Angel Firpo, 'The Wild Bull of the Pampas'. Dempsey knocked down Firpo seven times in the first round only to catch a punch that knocked Jack clean out of the ring. Dempsey climbed back in, beat the count and went on to knock out Firpo in the second round.

    Moral: Sometimes it doesn't matter if you get knocked out of the ring. What matters is that you have the courage to climb back in again.

The following years for me vanished into a haze of highway gasoline fumes, railroad smoke and White Snake gin. It seemed that I was either being hit in the face by a shovelful of dirt in some Kansas dust storm or washing my face with a handful of snow in Wisconsin. I just kept moving.

Prohibition, that noble experiment, that victory for Christendom, which was meant to rid us of the evils of the poisoned cup, had just plain imploded. It screwed up people's dreams and mangled their values so that no one cared or knew what was right or wrong anymore. It turned good men into criminals, mothers into whores and the whole country into copper-nosed drunks – and I was right up there with them. Suddenly I had a hundred million brothers in arms because *everyone* was breaking the law.

But we Americans were lucky; we had only fun over here. In Europe they had all those crazy guys like Mussolini and Stalin bumping everybody off. Over here we had Jelly Roll Morton, the Turkey Trot and the Hootchy-Kootchy. Sure, we had gangsters too, but a few bodies full of bullets in a Yonkers ditch were a small price to pay for a plentiful supply of illegal booze. And anyway, our gangsters mostly killed one another.

Happy Sally, Old Stingo and Dixie Bell liquor were the country's new heroes – just as much as Jack Dempsey, Knute Rockne and Babe Ruth.

When that jerk Senator Volstead from Minnesota brought in his dumb Act, the whole country was meant to go teetotal. Sure, like hell it did. They might have had better luck drying up the Atlantic with a post office blotter.

> Who'd care to be a bee and sip
> Sweet honey from a flower's lip
> When he might be a fly and sail
> Headfirst into a good cocktail

Tell people they can't have something and they'll want it all the more as the whole country dived 'headfirst into a good cocktail'. Women got the vote and promptly shingled their hair, flattened their bosoms, lowered their waistlines, lifted their hems and dropped their panties. Boy, they were wild times, but to be honest, they kind of passed me by like a Wyoming freight train because I was more often too sozzled in the sawdust of some gut-bucket backdoor saloon. I hadn't even learned the Charleston, for heaven's sake. 'Up on your toes and down on your heels,' the whole country sang. Everyone threw off their jackets and danced the night away, flapping their fannies, shaking their knees and smiling like a Pepsodent billboard. It was the 'throwing off of the jackets' that most interested me because as the party hit the roof, I hit the jackets. If only my hands would stop shaking.

Like a lot of people during those times, I traveled from city to city, in my case one pocket ahead of the other guy and one doorway behind the cops as I followed in the tracks of a migrant population. I was a one-toothed shark playing in a school of herring. I'd wake up in some hayseed town, shower, powder my hands, file and polish my nails. I'd take my pants – always neatly pressed – from under my mattress, breakfast on cold coffee and a cigarette and be out looking to hook a money clip to get me to the next blind-pig speakeasy. There I could get drunk enough to be able to fall asleep in yet another fleabag flophouse where a room cost twenty-five cents or with a bed, an extra ten. I spent years drinking coffee in jerkwater towns and sipping 'genuine French champagne' made in Cincinnati.

I shared the freight cars, followed the rail tracks and walked endless dusty roads that reached into the far horizons of this vast, jumping, but oddly troubled country. To me happiness was just a rest stop in life – a short respite on the way to an ambush up ahead. Maybe I thought that my cockamamie life had some purpose, but in truth I was drifting from ocean to ocean, place to place, from here to nowhere, like a mosquito in a stagnant pond. I didn't belong because, somehow, it wasn't my country and, opinionated as I was about the boneheads in Washington, it was really the fault of the boneheads who *voted* for the boneheads. That sure wasn't me, because I never voted, never had a paycheck stub in my pocket and, sure as shit, never paid taxes. I didn't own a jalopy, a tin bath or a fishing pole. I had no wife, no children, not even a steady girl. Why? Why did I run away from Effie, whose face never left me? I saw that face in every crowd, on every billboard, in every shadow, in every cloud. What life would she have made for herself while I was drifting? She sure wasn't going to be waiting for me on that red slatted bench for the rest of her life. And every time I thought of Effie I was reminded of my two sisters, who I had left behind on that hillside in California. How were they? Gracie's wild eyes stared back at me each time I closed my own. Up in Canada I even rubbed noses with a real Eskimo. Gracie would have liked that. Every blond kid reminded me of her whenever I stopped to give one a dime or a penny candy. Like that time I was in Coney Island.

I first visited Coney Island before the war, when it was full of rich people at Luna Park peeling off their dollars as they lined up for the 'Trip to the Moon'. Now everything had changed. They'd torn down the swanky bathhouses

along the shore and built a new boardwalk so that everyone could get to the beach. They'd even built a subway
from Manhattan so that half a million working people
from the tenements and sweatshops could now escape
the city, splash in the ocean and sunbathe on the trucked-
in, phony brown sand. Half of the people out there could
barely speak English: first stop, Ellis Island, next stop,
Coney Island.

I walked along Surf Avenue, bought a root beer at
Paddy Shea's and put a nickel into the mechanical piano.
Those days, everything cost a nickel at Coney Island,
whether it was a ride on the Thunderbolt Switchback
Railway or going to see Laurello, the only man in the
world with a revolving head. After walking for a while
along the Riegelmann Boardwalk, I realized that I was
paddling the wrong canoe. What was I doing here, putting my hand into poor people's pockets where I'd find
nothing but small change?

I sat on a bench with my root beer, took off my jacket,
unbuttoned my shirt and looked across the beach at the
giant crowd of New Yorkers enjoying themselves. I closed
my eyes to the sun.

'You on your own, mister?'

I opened my eyes and saw this little blond kid in a
red and white striped bathing suit staring at me.

'Excuse me?' I said to her.

'Are you on your own?' she repeated.

'I am.'

'Why are you on your own?'

'I don't know. I guess I don't know anybody here.'

'Nobody?'

'Nope.'

'Don't you have a mom and dad?'

'Nope.'

'That's a shame.' She stared at me like I was an attraction at the Foolish House.

'You want to come and play with me and my brothers?'

'Nope, I'm fine.'

'Did you have a hot dog even?' When this kid grew up, she'd probably join the Salvation Army.

'Not yet. Maybe later. Did *you* have a hot dog yet?' I asked her.

'Nope. They cost a nickel and my mom makes me and my brothers take it in turns. I had one last week.'

'You did?'

'It's my little brother's turn this week.'

'How many brothers do you have?'

'Four.'

'So you don't get a hot dog for a while.'

'Three more Sundays and then it's my turn again.'

'You wanna hot dog?'

'Yep.'

'Feltman's or Nathan's?'

'Nathan's, theirs are a nickel. Feltman's are ten cents.'

'They say Feltman's are better.'

'Nathan's are good, too,' she said.

'Can I buy you a hot dog?' I offered.

'Yep, if you like.'

I undid my laces, took off my shoe and pulled up the insole. She still stared at me like I was a madman.

'You ever seen Laurello, the guy with the revolving head?' I asked.

'Nope. But I heard about him.'

'You ever seen the tattooed man, or Bonita and her fighting lions?'

'Nope.'

Out of my shoe I took fifty dollars and gave her the whole lot. 'Here, give this to your mom.' She looked at me, now certain that I was crazy.

'I think that's too much for a hot dog,' she said.

'That's okay. Just give it all to your mom.'

'Thanks, mister. Are you gonna have a hot dog?'

'Yep.'

'Bye, mister.'

'Bye, Gracie.'

'My name's Lily.'

'Oh, yeah, 'bye, Lily.'

She ran down the wooden steps to the beach like she was on the US Olympic track team.

I walked over to Steeplechase Park and took a ride on the mechanical horses. At the subway station I bought a newspaper, a ticket to New York and finished my hot dog. Lily was right; Nathan's do taste good – and they're only a nickel.

On the train I opened the paper and there was this big bold headline, 'VALENTINO IS DEAD.' Poor old Rudolph, I used to like that guy. A girl in Calipatria once told me that I looked a little like him, but I think she was just yanking my yam. The paper said there were rumors that Rudy might have been poisoned by a jealous lover or shot by gangsters, but most probably it was peritonitis and pneumonia that got him. It said that Rudy's fans were numb with grief. I liked the sound of that. 'Numb' is good for my business and so I decided to take a look.

There must have been thirty thousand people lined up outside Campbell's Funeral Chapel on Broadway, waiting for their chance to walk by the coffin. The morticians had spiffed up Valentino's corpse so that the fans could get a last glimpse. He was laid out in the casket dressed in full evening clothes and his face looked about as real as a ventriloquist's dummy. I remember reading in the *Chicago Tribune* that Rudy was a homosexual – 'a pink powder-puff', the *Trib* called him. Try telling that to all those hysterical women sobbing into their handkerchiefs.

The wreaths were all lined up against the wall and I noticed one that said, '*Ciao, Rudy. Il suo amico, Giuseppe Masseria*'. That name would make anyone fill their pants. Masseria was Joe 'The Boss' – the city's Mafia big cheese. Maybe they did shoot Rudy after all? Masseria was famous for dodging bullets in his early days, but since he'd taken over every racket from New York to Pittsburgh he had become better known for the bullets going in the opposite direction. He was also called Joe 'The Glutton' by his enemies: murder and food being his principal passions. He once had a guy stabbed while he was eating dinner with him. The dead man sat slumped in his chair, bleeding from the knife still in his belly, while Joe 'The Boss' took his time finishing his calamari.

Inside the funeral chapel there were a dozen blackshirt heavies guarding Rudy's coffin as people filed past. At the side there was a giant wreath from Mussolini saying, 'All the best – Benito'. This struck me to be as phony as a three-dollar bill – who the heck would believe that? Can you imagine Mussolini saying, 'All the best'? I mean, whatever he said, it would have been in Italian, don't you think? Anyway, a hundred or so anti-Fascist people turned up in the street, booing and stuff, which was all too much for Rudy's fans, who didn't know Fascism from a baptism. As it started to pour with rain there was suddenly one hell of a riot.

I waded into the crowd to hook some leathers when the mounted cops decided to charge. There were women lying screaming all over the sidewalk, and those who weren't trampled underfoot were crushed together. Campbell's plate glass window shattered and huge shards fell into the crowd. There was blood everywhere. I helped a couple of terrified women pull free as people were piling up three deep in the rain.

How crazy is it when women are being crushed to death, anti-Fascists are beating up Fascists and the police are beating on everyone? All because of a wax dummy who once was a goddam movie star. What the hell was happening to this country?

24

I was lost among millions of other desperate souls. For too many years everyone had rushed around blindly, like headless chickens, pecking at the elusive bucks tossed in their direction. But now, as a people, we had lost our way and didn't know where to turn. The country was guzzling so fast from the prosperity cup that it had begun to choke. Money was all that mattered, and the pursuit of it became the new religion as people went down on their knees to worship the great god, Greed.

It seemed that everyone was onto some scam or another. I once saw a guy pull a Studebaker along by his hair, and another guy who used to bounce down stairs on his head. He could do twelve up but only nine down. He must have needed a bottle of Bromo-Quinine to get rid of that headache. People would do just about anything to make a buck. Take my friend, Soapy Marx, for example.

For a short while I made a good living working with Soapy, who I had met in Minneapolis. He was a really smart guy, with diplomas, who had invented a wonder cure called Marmello. Just what it cured so wonderfully depended on which month or which season it was and which town we were hitting. Originally he said it cured obesity, and you'd never imagine how easy it was to get these Fatty Arbuckles to part with their money. In truth, Marmello was just a concoction of bicarbonate of soda, a little grape juice and some secret ingredient that Soapy swore was given to him by a blind gypsy woman from Minsk.

After one particularly libidinous night with a girl called Romola in a whorehouse in Jefferson, Missouri, Soapy had an epiphany. By chance – and don't ask me how he found out – he discovered that Marmello could also improve your sex drive if you rubbed it on your private parts. Soapy promptly renamed the elixir Romola after his bedmate and would stand up on a table in these bathtub gin joints proclaiming, 'Romola will provide once more with gusto the joyful satisfaction, the pulse and the throb of physical pleasure.' And who's to say it didn't?

As a matter of fact, I tried it once myself the night I met this girl in Wetumpka, Alabama. I was lying there with her legs over my shoulders, thinking maybe old Soapy was really onto something, when the door burst open and this gorilla of a guy was at my throat with a foot-long Navajo hunting knife. He said he was her husband and unless I handed over my money he'd cut off every limb – starting with my private part that, courtesy of Soapy's Romola, was embarrassingly prominent. It was a flim-flam trick, of course, and the lady was in on it, even though she was overacting all surprised and screaming her lungs out like she was Florence Lawrence in the movies. I'd heard of the old badger scam before, but that was the only time it had happened to me. I gladly parted with the contents of my wallet as the irate 'husband' dragged his 'wife' out of the room. Somehow it seemed like a fair exchange to me. I'd got caught with my pants down, just like all the suckers who had bought Soapy's elixir.

I'm telling you, everyone was at it. It was the only way people could behave when it seemed like the whole world had gone crazy and no one believed in anything or anyone anymore. Except for perhaps the price of stock in Bethlehem Steel or American Can. Everyone was playing the stock market – every bellhop, cabbie, seamstress, secretary and cop on the beat looked forward to their dividend checks. You'd go for a five-cent shave and the barber would be yapping on about the price of General Motors and Texaco.

When Wall Street went belly-up, it didn't surprise me for one minute.

I would routinely fan these guys in their hundred-dollar cashmere suits and their fancy Paris shirts, but the contents of their wallets wouldn't buy you a shoeshine. It started to worry me that these swells knew something that us clunk-heads didn't, because they had stopped carrying US banknotes.

So for a while I started collecting cravat stickpins – probably the easiest hook of all. I would flutter my hand ever so gently across a guy's chest and, using only my nails, I'd tweak out his gem-head stickpin – sometimes a diamond, sometimes a ruby, but always a winner.

Giacomo Facciola, who ran the biggest hock shop in Philadelphia, was my favorite fence. One day early in '29, I untied a silk handkerchief to reveal a dozen or so pins and he picked them up one by one, looking at them closely against the naked electric lightbulb dangling over his counter. He had a magnifying loupe permanently screwed into his right eye and it kind of unbalanced him so that he would look at you with his left eye at an angle, like a pigeon, which made you do the same. He shook his head, his face registering disapproval. 'Glass,' he said.

'Giacomo, don't kid me.'

'My name's Jack,' he said.

Like shit it was. I knew he hated being called Giacomo. I had teased him about it for years. 'But Giacomo's your name,' I reminded him.

'It makes me feel like a wop. I don't want to be a wop anymore or a meatball or a spaghetti-head. I want to be a Jack, okay?'

'Okay.' There was a short pause. 'But whatever your name, you're still a wop.'

'Yeah, and these are still glass.'

'That's not possible.'

'What I see through here is what's possible.' He tapped the loupe.

'What do you mean, glass?'

'Glass, like you get in windows.'

'Why?'

'Why? Because of shit.'

'Shit?'

'This country's going to shit, Tommy. In the shitter. Didn't you hear the splash? I did. We're always the first to know. That's the privilege and curse of our crummy professions. You have your hands in the back pockets of

America, Tommy – it gives you a unique perspective. Maybe we should both retire now.'

'What do you mean?'

'It's not new to me, Tommy, I'm a pawnbroker. I make a living out of people who are dumb enough to spend more than they earn. But sooner or later, the whole country's gonna be lining up outside my store.'

'Why?'

'Because everyone's living on crazy money. Even Babe Ruth makes more than the president. The truth is, the country is in a recession, and no one's taking any notice.'

'That stinks, Giacomo.'

'It's Jack. And you'd better believe it, Tommy, because you have it firsthand. Don't believe the newspapers. Don't believe the crap you hear sitting around in big leather chairs, sipping bootleg martinis in those spiffy men's clubs you steal from. Don't believe the latest dumb dance craze, just believe in what you *don't* find inside the sucker's wallet.'

Giacomo Facciola should have been an advisor to that doughnut in the White House, because from his dusty store in Philly he saw the whole catastrophe coming long before the shit hit the Wall Street fan in October of '29.

When the bosses and stockbroker fat cats started writing goodbye notes to their sweethearts and pumping .38 slugs deep into their own brains I wasn't surprised and it didn't bother me for one minute. But, when these guys' clerks and the elevator jockeys joined them in hell by jumping out of windows forty floors up, their heads smacking against a slab of downtown granite and their brains splattering twenty feet in all directions, I got concerned. I realized that Jack, formerly known as Giacomo, was prophetically accurate. But if the rich guys, whose greed had caused all this trouble in the first place, were cashing in their chips and their lives, then what hope was there for us yo-yos down on the street? It was then that I had this thought that kept me going: okay, avoiding falling bodies might be hazardous, but down here from my viewpoint looking up, the odds of survival are a shitload better than the poor schmuck who jumped from the forty-sixth floor. It doesn't matter who you are, the bread always falls on the buttered side.

That's when I sobered up.

25

Things got so bad that mostly the price of a cup of coffee was all I could find in most suckers' pockets and more often than not I found myself putting back more change than I took out. It's okay to be poor, but it's a terrible thing to be hungry. I wasn't that special – believe me, the crash had turned the whole country into bums, and like everybody else I was hanging on by my fingernails, hoping that the next town would be better than the last.

By Christmas of '29 there were more companies going bankrupt, more suicides and four million working stiffs who were stiff, but not working – standing on soup lines with shattered spirits, their souls rubbed raw by ruin and shame.

So, like a bad penny, I turned up in San Francisco again. As I got off the train at Third and Townsend, the platform was crowded with people going in the opposite direction – the waifs and strays, the flotsam and jetsam of a failed society. Most of them couldn't even speak English as they struggled to board a train or a bus to another exotic-sounding place: Chicago, Philadelphia, Milwaukee, Dallas, Minneapolis or St Louis. They didn't know it, but they were all headed toward just another

Depression city. Truth is, America was all the same in those days: it didn't matter where you set your compass, the needle always pointed to zero. From where I stood, there didn't seem to be any sign of the country crawling out of the Depression pit. Everyone kept closing their eyes and hoping they'd wake up in some long-promised American dream, but it wasn't going to happen – not while that fat pig Hoover was still sitting behind the desk in the White House.

A week earlier I'd been pinched in Santa Cruz, hooking a wallet from a guy at a dive called Skoozie Allen's Dance House. It was one of the strangest things that ever happened to me in my days as a cannon. I had just walked off the street into this joint hoping to find a backdoor bar, which, with a nose like mine, I duly found. Maybe it was dark in there, or maybe it was the homemade booze they called Jake, but I must have got a little careless. I had promised myself only two glasses, three at most. I had been trying to drink less because it had left me with the shaky clanks. Also, they made this jake-juice stuff from Jamaican ginger, and the Anti-Saloon League people used to hand out these leaflets saying it caused blindness and paralysis, but everyone said you needed a whole barrelful inside you before that could happen. And anyway, if we were all so blind, how could we read the leaflets?

I was standing at the end of the bar, fanning the back pocket of this skinny, clean-shaven guy with a bald head so shiny you could shave by it. Curiously, I sensed that he could feel me touching him. Either he was extra sensitive in the buttock area, or the liquor had made me a little clumsy, but he definitely knew I had my hand in his pocket. Now normally, in circumstances such as this, the mark would scream blue murder and I would be out of there fast before the door monkeys nabbed me, but this guy just turned to me and smiled. He had puffed-up red cheeks like he was sucking golf balls and one of those sweaty top lips with a wide gap between his teeth, so I might have known he couldn't be trusted. Anyway, before I knew it, he had his hand squeezed tight around my genitals. I thought he must have been one of those dickey licker, boy-jockeys you hear so much about, so this time it was me who did the screaming. He kept smiling and squeezing my flapdoodle so hard that my eyes began to water and I felt kind of woozy. I stuffed his wallet in his mouth, which made him let go of my bat and balls, but didn't seem to stop the booze-gob from smiling.

His sweaty grin was the last thing I remember, because the next thing I knew I was coming to in the back of a meat wagon, cuffed to a Santa Cruz sheriff.

When I told my story to the judge, he laughed and gave me seven days for loitering. I think he felt sorry for me.

And so once more I was back in Frisco, which, as it turned out, was providence itself, because it was there that I met up again with Effie.

26

The distance between a baseball pitcher and a batter is about sixty feet. If the pitcher throws a knuckleball at eighty miles an hour, the batter has about a fifteen-thousandth of a second to make up his mind. A knuckleball isn't even thrown that fast, or even with knuckles, but with the fingertips, and is consequently unpredictable.

Moral No. 1: Some things come at you so fast, it's probably wiser to let them go past you.

Moral No. 2: Sometimes no one knows where the heck the ball is headed. Including the pitcher.

We bumped into one another kind of by accident. Well, to be more accurate, it was *in* an accident. I was skipping off a Washington Street cable car after fanning a couple of pokes when I saw this beautiful girl. As usual, I took a quick picture of her with the Kodak inside my head. She was wearing a slightly out of fashion, long woolen coat: single-breasted with patch pockets and piped seams. I liked her sling-back pumps, even though it was a while since I'd seen those in the catalogs. Her coat must have been missing a button or two because it kept flapping open and I could see her ivory voile skirt and a pretty sateen blouse with *lace de venise* collar and cuffs. She swung a burlap bag as she kind of slid along the sunny sidewalk like she was wearing invisible roller skates – one of those swaying walks that whispered sex but shouted trouble.

At first, I thought she was a model from the toothpaste billboards because she looked kind of familiar. Suddenly it hit me, I *did* know her – it was Effie. And just as suddenly, something hit her. It was a swanky, tomato-red Studebaker convertible, to be precise, which had turned the corner as Effie stepped off the curb and she seemed to sleepwalk straight into it. Smack! Cars skidded all around and people were screaming at the driver – a fat, tub-of-guts guy with a pitcherful of illegal happy juice inside him. I dashed across the street and knelt down at Effie's side as the curious and the lecherous gathered around.

'Don't touch her, fella.'

'Lot of blood.'

'She's hurt real bad.'

'Cute legs.'

'Can someone cover her crotch?'

'Has anyone called a cop?'

'Jeez, look at the blood.'

'An ambulance?'

'What did she break? That sure is a lot of blood.'

At first glance she seemed to be really badly hurt. Her ivory skirt and linen panties with the *broderie anglais* were stained red. I pulled her skirt down over her knees and with my other hand, almost as a reflex action, reached inside the burlap bag and felt broken glass. I peered inside to see three smashed wine bottles. At that moment Effie came to, fluttering her eyelids. A woman from a nearby shoe shop held Effie's head as she sipped at a cup of water. Another woman, with a face like a watermelon, wiped the blood from Effie's cheeks.

'You okay, honey? You're sure bleeding a lot. Don't move now, I think you could be hemorrhaging. We need a doctor here, folks, can someone start hollering?'

'Are you pregnant, honey?'

'No, no, I'm not. It's . . .' Ignoring the woman, Effie pulled herself up on her knees. 'It's not blood,' Effie offered, handing back the cup.

'It's not?' said the Watermelon Woman. 'Then what the heck is it?'

'It's wine,' I answered.

It was then that she turned her head and saw me. Boy, did she have a cockeyed look in her eyes, like she had died and gone to hell. At any rate, she blacked out.

Effie sat on a broken-backed chair in the corner of a seedy joint called Izzy's Café. In the corner were a small sink and a mirror and I dabbed a wet towel on her forehead. The storefront said it was a café, but behind the dirty velvet curtain at the back I could see a metal door leading to what was obviously a root-and-toot speakeasy. The waitress handed Effie a coffee, into which she upended a shot glass of liquor. I was right; this was no coffee shop.

'She okay?' I turned to see a cop sitting in the dark,

hidden by a half-curtain. Every speak had an on-duty cop in the corner just like this one, eating his free corned beef, cabbage and beans, washing it down with a mug of beer – all on the house.

'Yeah, she's fine, thanks. Just a little bruised and shaken up,' I answered.

The cop got up, finished his beer, walked out the door and continued on his beat as though we, and the joint we were in, didn't exist.

As Effie slightly parted her legs, I noticed she had a run in her stockings forming a long ladder, which climbed up into the darkness of her underwear. Considering that the Studebaker had hit her harder than Dempsey had hit that powder-puff Frenchman Carpentier back in '21, she was in surprisingly good shape. I was itching to know how she was. She sipped from her cup.

'Tommy, is it really you?'

'It is.'

'Wow, it's been a long time.'

I shrugged in agreement. It's hard to make excuses for being ten years late for a date.

'I waited,' she said softly.

'At the gas station?'

'By the red bench.'

'I'm sorry.'

'I waited for three hours the first day. Two hours the second day. And an hour the next.'

I shook my head. How many times can you say you're sorry? Boy, did I feel like a shit-heel. Her lip had stopped bleeding.

'I went back to the gas station every week for a month. You know what I kept telling myself?' She smiled at the distant memory.

I shook my head, no.

'I kept telling myself that it takes six months to build a Pierce-Arrow. Do you remember saying that?' I smiled and nodded at my dumb-ass remark about an automobile, which had taken on such significance for her.

'But six months turned into eighteen months and there were no Pierce-Arrows on the horizon.' She laughed at her own joke. To me it was all kind of sad.

Effie looked me straight in the eye and stroked my cheek. 'Where the hell were you, Tommy?'

I shrugged, 'Name a place.'

She shook her head, trying to think of somewhere unlikely. 'Tuscaloosa.'

'Alabama. Yep, know it well.'

'You were in Alabama?'

'And Mississippi, Iowa, Wyoming, Ohio, Arizona.' I could have gone on, but just shook my head. 'Just about everywhere. And you?'

'Me?'

'So, are you married?'

'Uh-uh. No.' She dipped her head and smiled and after a pause she added, 'And you?'

'Nope,' I smiled, feeling kind of, well, optimistic. All I could see was the ladder in her stocking creeping up the inside of her thigh and I was already climbing to heaven when she cut me dead.

'But I do have a daughter.' She kept her head down

as she said it, pulling her stocking tight on her foot as she slipped it into her shoe. I thought this was to avoid seeing my reaction, or maybe, more realistically, to pretend she wasn't interested in one.

'And the father?' I asked the question as if I was inquiring how the weather had been lately, but in truth the bases were loaded and she had just pitched me a hand grenade that I was expected to bat out of the park. Effie said nothing. She leaned forward into the white sink and splashed water on to her face.

'He didn't stick around.' She looked at me in the mirror, still feigning disinterest as she cocked her head to one side and tugged at her waterlogged ear.

'He skedaddled?' I asked.

'Huh?'

'Jumped the flying pig at midnight?'

She smiled. 'Something like that.'

'He's not around anymore?'

'No, he isn't.'

'How old is she, your daughter?'

She looked at me and made the connection with what I was thinking. She smiled and shook her head, no. 'She's seven. Don't worry, she was born a *long* time after you left.'

'I'm sorry.'

'Don't be. She's a beautiful girl.'

I was obviously getting nowhere, so I dropped the subject. 'And your mom and dad?'

'My mother died. TB. But Dad's still going strong, except it's been kind of tough since Prohibition. The winery's not the same . . . we had to scale down . . . kind of disheartening, but we keep going. We had to let most of the workers go. The vines that the bugs didn't kill we keep alive with a few prayers and a lot of work. But we manage. How about you? Where did you settle?'

'Oh, no place, no place at all. Itchy feet. Just kept moving. One step ahead . . . it's my job.' Once again I shrugged my shoulders matter-of-factly, unable to describe my dubious existence.

Effie looked puzzled. 'So what line of work are you in?'

'I'm a thief.'

She turned from the mirror and looked me directly in the eye. 'A thief?'

'A thief.'

'What kind of thief?'

'The kind that steals things?'

'Oh, Tommy, you never changed.'

I thought I had. When we first met long ago in the vineyard I had told her I was a magician. Maybe she had figured otherwise even then. Or maybe neither of us was innocent anymore.

'No, I never did,' I answered. I stroked the side of her head and drew my hand slowly and gently across her cheek. She took my hand and kissed it.

'I really did wait, you know?'

'I'm truly sorry. It wasn't my fault . . . well, not *all* my fault.'

She looked at me suspiciously. 'It wasn't?'

'I went to my mom's funeral and the police came.'

'Why?'

'Looking for me. Nothing important. Just another screw-up in a lot of years of facing jail.'

'You went to jail?'

I nodded, 'Yes.'

'You should have written.'

'I should have.' I bowed my head. 'I thought about you a lot,' I offered weakly.

'And me you,' she replied, and kissed me on the forehead.

For a long time I'd had the feeling that whoever was responsible for pulling my strings up there, whoever was looking out for me, had taken a break and forgotten to come back after lunch. But things were looking up – maybe Hoagie had put in a good word for me.

We walked across Washington Square, not far from where my mother, sisters and I used to live before the quake. I hardly recognized the place because all the buildings were new. After 1906, a lot of people in San Francisco made piles of dough in the construction business, only to lose it when Wall Street took the dive into the cement. Everywhere you looked there were unfinished buildings, boarded up with bankruptcy signs slapped on the walls.

There was even a brand new Saints Peter and Paul Church, which was much grander than the patched-up shanty I remembered. It had not just one, but two, lofty spires. I tried to read the Latin inscription on the front of the church, 'La gloria di colui che tutto muove . . .'

Effie helped me out by translating, 'The Glory of Him who moves all things . . .'

'Including the church,' I answered.

'Huh?'

'It used to be at the end of the block.'

There was a fancy little dress store on Columbus and I dragged Effie inside. An attentive assistant fussed over her and she finally chose a ruby-red, silk *messaline* skirt and a blouse with an *organdie* collar with a row of ebony buttons dribbling down the front. She must have tried on every dress in the store, and I swear she looked great in every one of them. I pulled down a felt hat from a peg and Effie stuffed her long brown hair inside it, cocking her head back and forth as she looked at herself in the mirror. I guessed that the assistant hadn't made a sale in weeks, and consequently she was unusually helpful, just stopping short of licking our shoes. As I counted out the bills to pay, she passed remark on my wallet.

'Oh, what a beautiful wallet. Is it crocodile? Where did you get it? It looks French.'

'No, right here, good old San Francisco, USA.'

'Oh, where exactly?'

'Er . . . the Washington Street cable car.'

'Oh, you're teasing me.'

Effie pulled back the dressing cubicle curtain, gestured me to shut the heck up, and stuffed her wine-stained frock into her burlap bag. I left fifty cents on the counter. 'Thank you for your kindness. My wife and I much appreciate it.'

I opened the etched glass door and on cue from the bell that rang above it, Effie, dressed in ruby red, glided onto the sidewalk on her invisible roller skates.

27

When I was growing up, after the grape harvest in September and October, the sidewalks all down Kearny Street were cluttered with homemade winepresses and grape boxes. It seemed as though every Italian guy in San Francisco made his own wine. I loved the Italians – they were always laughing, whereas us Irish were always crying in our beer. It seemed like all the Italian songs were happy and romantic and ours were just plain sad – the best times we Irish ever seemed to have was at funerals. I never could quite figure that out. Waxy Doyle, the barkeep at the Red Rooster on Montgomery, had a theory that it was all due to the journey to America. When the big wave of Italians started coming to America on the steamers from Naples, Genoa and Palermo, it took just ten days to cross the Atlantic. Fifty years before that, when the Irish came over during the potato famine, it took forty days if you were lucky – and that's the essential difference between us. When the Italians got off the boat they immediately unpacked their sausages and bottles of red wine and started celebrating King Umberto's birthday. The Irish, on the other hand, were still puking up from the long voyage from Cork and, it seems to me, they have been ever since.

If you were Italian, or even if you weren't, the center of San Francisco was Abruzzinni's Grocery on Columbus in North Beach. It was jammed full of chickens, fish, sacks of macaroni, jugs of olive oil, giant cheeses and thirty kinds of bread. It was also, quite possibly, the noisiest place in town. The perpetual Italian cacophony bounced around the haunches of smoked hams and chubs of salami, some as big as ferry buoys, that hung from the ceilings.

Mrs Abruzzinni was Effie's aunt, and Effie's cousins – Patrizia and Rosa – were her best friends. Effie had been on her way to the store when the brandy-brain in the red Studebaker smacked into her. I found myself invited to dinner.

The upstairs rooms of the store were no saner than the madness that went on every day below. There were hundred-pound bags of *fagioli* beans stacked on the staircase and crates marked *provola affumicata* and *ricotta tutta crema* covered in ice and piled six-feet high in the living room. It was impossible to tell where the Abruzzinnis' store finished and their home began.

For just one family, they must have had five adopted grandmothers and many more assorted elderly uncles. There was also a separate table where a dozen noisy Italian-American kids scoffed down the plates of food that arrived every couple of minutes.

Bottles of wine were lined up in the center of the long table, no labels, their shoulders glistening like the armor of a defiant Roman army – old man Abruzzinni was obviously well connected. He poured each glass generously, although possibly with a little more restraint than he would have done before Prohibition.

I sat squeezed between Effie and an elderly aunt who kept asking me to do my trick with the quarter – flipping it in and out of my fingers and stuff. It wasn't much, just what us pit workers do to keep our eyes sharp, our fingers nimble and Uncle Arthritis at bay. I made the mistake of showing the old lady this trick, coupled with another one where the quarter disappeared and reappeared in her salami, and she went crazy. It was like showing a magic trick for the first time to a five-year-old. The consequence of this octogenarian adulation was that for long periods of time I neglected Effie. She was occupied in a close huddle with Rosa's husband, Guido Brunazzi, who, although on the runty side, was one of those pinch-ass ladies' men who was frankly getting a tad too close to her for my perfect comfort. She was even showing him her huge bruise from the car crash, necessitating her dress being hoisted a little too high for mixed company, I thought. Although I must say, it did remind me of what beautiful legs she had, even if they were closer to Guido Brunazzi's shifty eyes than my own.

Effie had introduced him to me and with a limp, dead man's handshake he cocked his carrot-shaped nose and unpleasantly sniffed at me as though he could smell failure. He was hard to like and Effie whispered to me that I should be careful as he was a gangster from New York sent here to work with the San Francisco bootlegger Frankie Stutz. I noticed that he was carrying a gun under his belted flannel jacket.

Effie must have sensed my feeling a little separated from her and gently squeezed the back of my hand, praising me for being her Sir Galahad and coming to her rescue on the street. I shrugged off the applause that followed with false modesty and took the opportunity to hold her hand. I felt her stroke the tips of my fingers with her thumb while she continued to speak to people around the table. Touch. Oh, boy, everything is touch.

Effie leaned across and whispered, 'You're doing great.'

She made it sound like I was some nut who had been allowed out for the day from an asylum – a home for the lonely, the misfits and the socially inadequate. I smiled and thanked her for these moments of freedom, 'That's good.'

They say the only thing you can't take away from someone is that which is inside of them. I guess that's mostly true. In my profession I could steal almost anything from almost anywhere from almost anyone. But Effie went one better and tore the rule into little pieces, turning the tables that night – she dug down and hooked something way deep inside of me. We clinked our glasses and remained looking at one another just long enough for it to matter to the two of us, though not for so long that it would be noticed by anyone else.

Now, I have to say right up front, that as I got older the charm of Italian music had worn thin. Well, put it this way – why do Italians always play the same old three or four organ-grinder tunes when they've got so many other ones you never hear? By good musicians, too. And

I'm not just talking show tunes; I'm talking big shots like Verdi and Rossini. Old man Abruzzinni was an exception. He must have had the biggest record collection this side of Milan: he was a complete music nut, and very knowledgeable, considering he spent most of his day slicing prosciutto. Old Abruzzinni had even closed his store when Caruso died back in '21.

There was a photo on the mantel showing the store draped with black crêpe in big semicircles across the front and great fat salamis dangling from each corner. For the old man, it was the greatest way to pay his respects.

He kept cranking up his Victrola and slapping on record after record. I think he grew to like me for trying to name each tune as he polished the disks with his sleeve and gently put down the gramophone needle.

'Okay, here you go, Tommy,' he said.

'*Button Up Your Overcoat!*' I would shout and, '*Hush-a-Bye My Baby.*'

'Easy. Okay, here's a hard one.'

'Er . . . er . . . *Mi chiamano Mimi.*' It wasn't hard at all. I'd spent too many nights waiting to score from the pockets of silk-scarved opera audiences during the intervals. I'd passed the time memorizing a program or two.

'Yes, but by who?' yelled the old man.

'Puccini?' I offered, hoping he wasn't going to ask me for the name of the soprano, which of course he did.

'Of course it's Puccini,' he said. 'But who's singing?'

'Nellie Melba?' I guessed. The old man grimaced like he'd swallowed a jar of pickles and so he moved on to 'Mammy', which of course was a whole lot easier. Effie's extended family applauded whatever I said. I'm telling you, old Abruzzinni could have started his own record store, he had so many. From Luisa Tetrazzini to the Rhythm Boys, from *Carmen* to 'K-K-K Katy'. He had them all. They said that when things started to get rough after the '29 crash his customers used to barter a dozen records at a time, in exchange for a half-pound of scamorza cheese.

As always, Effie was surrounded by admirers and I had to wait my turn to dance with her. Reluctantly, I volunteered to take to the floor with the elderly aunts and, curiously, some uncles, with whom my complete lack of rhythm went unnoticed.

Effie stood on a chair and loudly revealed what she politely described as my 'magician's tricks', whereby I had the embarrassing task of returning the watches and wallets I had been collecting all evening. Of course, I would have anyway.

Everyone seemed overwhelmingly impressed by my party tricks and no one suspected for a moment the more practical application of my dubious talent in the wider world. Except perhaps Guido Brunazzi, who looked at me down his carrot-nose with more than a hint of suspicion. I didn't like the look of him either, come to that, and it wasn't just because he had his eye on Effie. Rosa nuzzled up to Guido and he was eventually distracted from Effie by two very fat children climbing all over him. Patrizia and Rosa's younger brother Joey dragged me up to dance and pushed Effie in my direction. I liked little Joey.

Effie and Patrizia vainly tried to teach me the rudiments of some kind of dance.

'Begin on the balls of your feet, bend your knees, push out the hips, don't slouch the shoulders, stick out your backside!' yelled Effie.

'Rock-step, step back, shift forward,' yelled Patrizia.

'Rock-step, kick, step, double kick,' I tamely repeated. Little Joey was convulsed with laughter at my clumsy efforts, because it was clear that I was no Fred Astaire. Boy, was I useless – too much of a late starter – but Effie tenderly persevered until we were the last ones left dancing.

Effie walked me along the alley at the rear of Abruzzinni's store. She had arranged to stay the night with Patrizia, and Mrs Abruzzinni had made up a bed for her. As we said goodnight, I fluffed my lines, shuffled my shoe and stared at the wine stain on my cuff. Effie leaned in and floated across a kiss in my direction. It was deliberately fleeting – two, three seconds, no more. As she turned to walk away, I still had hold of her purse and, although a little ring-rusty in the love department, I pulled her back towards me, kissing her once again – this time with a good deal more purpose. As my left hand stroked the hollow of her back I could feel that there was no corset. With the same butterfly twist of the fingers that normally vanished away old men's cufflinks, I flicked open two of the ebony studs on Effie's blouse. The opening was just wide enough for me to slip my hand in, and I softly stroked the *crêpe de Chine* bandeau covering her breasts. I could feel her breathing more deeply as she suddenly realized how far I had intruded into her under-wear and she audibly sighed as my fingers crept inside her inner garments and cupped her breast, squeezing her nipple between my fingers.

As our tongues touched, my right hand reefed her skirt upwards and following the line of her silk stocking and the smooth flesh inside her thigh, I slipped my hand ever upwards into the no-man's-land of her sateen panties. Effie briefly opened her eyes when she realized the enemy was at the gate and then fluttered her eyes closed, which I took as a signal for us to proceed. I pulled down the loose panties and she opened her thighs, hooked her left leg around me and then I was inside her, our bodies rocking back and forth. 'Up on your heels, down on your toes.' I didn't feel like an outcast anymore. I pressed her up against the wooden shutters and she dug her nails deep into my shoulder. It didn't last much longer than the '06 tremor, or the long count that Gene Tunney took when Jack D smacked him to the canvas back in '27. But for me it seemed to last so long that when I opened my eyes I could have sworn that we were out of the Depression.

Effie walked back to the Abruzzinnis and I watched her each and every step. She stopped. 'Oh, I forgot.' She walked back and reached into her bag. 'Do you believe in miracles?' she asked.

'No, I rely on them.'

'Close your eyes.'

I obeyed and could hear her walking away. I didn't need to look at what was in my hand. I could feel it.

My thumb rubbed the surface. It was a silver dollar. Year 1919. It was the same silver dollar that I had given to her, while lying in the yellow poppies, all those years ago.

28

With a certain lightness of step I walked on and found myself whistling the Charleston tune, 'Up on your heels, down on your toes'. Boy, did I feel good, maybe I could get the hang of this.

I fumbled for matches in my pocket, lit up a Lucky cigarette and walked a couple of blocks. Across the street on Kearny I noticed Farruggio's, or more accurately, as the green and yellow sign said, 'The Farruggio's Sausage and Table Meat Company', which must have supplied the whole of Northern California. Their salami was famous, made the traditional way from the best shoulder of pork, packed and cured in pork-gut casings and mold-ripened for months. Some say it was even better than salami from Italy, where they had been known to throw in the odd donkey.

The meat was delivered to Farruggio's in great wooden barrels from the abattoir out at Hunter's Point, where I remembered Sammy Liu and I working one summer for fifty cents a day. Sammy used to bag up the discarded animal guts – the pigs' intestines, the cows' stomachs and the horses' dangles – and sell them in Chinatown. If you ever asked Sammy why they ate that stuff, he would always answer, 'It gives you a hard-on.' With a sales pitch like that, how could you fail? If you could sell a horse's dick, you could sell anything.

I smiled at the thought of my old buddy Sammy when a Plymouth Sedan screeched past me in a hurry, splashing dirty rain water on my legs. I brushed my pants dry and noticed the old Rex movie theater in the alley at the side of Angelotti's shoe store. The front was no wider than the box office where the very large Mrs Peggano used to sit. It was such a tight fit, it looked like they had built the box right around her while she sat there. When we were kids, we used to wait for her to doze off and then we'd duck underneath her window and sneak in. I often thought that she wasn't dozing at all, just doing a couple of poor kids a favor. Once you were down the alley, it opened up out back to a giant barn of a place. In that passion pit you'd always find some guy too busy trying to get his hand up his girl's skirt to worry about his wallet, but Sammy was always more interested in the movies. I remember watching *Alkali Ike's Auto* and *The Musketeers of Pig Alley* – we loved those Gish girls. Sammy preferred Lillian, but in my bed in the depths of the night I had the secret hots for Dorothy.

Next to the Rex, an iron sliding door clanked open and a couple emerged. From the crooked route they took to the curb it was obvious that they'd both had a snootful. The woman had bobbed hair, short skirt, rolled-down hose, powdered knees and looked like a hooker, so I guessed that there must have been a bucketshop speakeasy hidden back there. I stopped to straighten my tie in the window of Folino's Barber Shop and ponder the notion that when the whole country was in Depression, sex, liquor, drugs and gambling all thrived, while everything else went bust. I nodded at my observation when suddenly there was a huge explosion that smacked me straight into Folino's wooden shutters. I picked myself up, my ears ringing like ten fire trucks. Or maybe they were real fire trucks. I looked down the street towards where the front of Farruggio's sausage factory used to be. The entire front of the building had been dynamited away and the street was covered in chunks of sausage. It looked like it had been raining salami. People gathered to look at the damage and I mingled among them. Under my feet the sausage meat squelched and crackled. Crackled? I looked down. Broken bottles. Wine bottles. I picked up a snapped-off bottle neck and sniffed at the cork inside. I'm no expert, but it seemed like it would have been a very good wine. All around me there must have been a few thousand bottles of it smashed into little pieces amongst a million sausages. The crowd outside Farruggio's had got bigger as the speakeasy customers emptied into the street since the view of the damage was preferable to the cheesy cabaret. I hooked two pretty good pocket watches, three wallets, a nice leather cigar case, a cheap powder-puff vanity compact and headed down Broadway.

At the corner of Columbus I stopped at a diner for a coffee. I still had a ringing sound in my head and felt kind of woozy. Whether this was because of the effect of Effie or the dynamite at Farruggio's, it was hard to tell. The guy behind the counter was real friendly and gave me a Bromo for my headache.

'Don't I know you?' he asked.

'Nah, don't think so.'

'Didn't you go to the Salesian School at Saints Peter and Paul on Filbert?'

'Yeah, long time ago.'

'I recognized you. It's the droopy eye.'

'Yeah, it's quite a handicap.'

'You can't see out of it?'

'No. Being recognized.'

'I'm sorry, I didn't mean to be rude . . . it being an affliction and all.'

'Oh, it's not an affliction . . . d'you know that Beethoven was deaf, Milton was blind and Sarah Bernhardt had only one leg?'

'Sarah Bernhardt had only one leg?' Apparently she was the one he had heard of.

'She did.'

'I didn't know that,' he said, wishing he'd never mentioned my eye in the first place.

'Didn't bother her a bit. She used to hop on stage like Long John Silver.'

He laughed and changed the subject. 'Did you hear the explosion?'

'Yeah, what was that?' Considering the contents of my pockets I sure wasn't going to tell this hash-slinger that I was standing right outside the place when it happened. Two fire trucks screamed past the window, which caused the guy behind the counter to let out a long whistle.

'They say they blew up the sausage factory,' he said, topping up my coffee.

'Who?'

'Those crazy Italians. It started in New York. They're all trying to kill one another.'

'Yeah, I read that in the paper.'

'You see, it's this Marzipano guy who's muscling in on this other guy, Mass . . . er . . . Mass-something.'

'Masseria,' I helped him out.

'You know about this stuff?'

'Just what I read in the papers.'

I wasn't about to contribute further to the conversation because I couldn't stop thinking about Effie and my head was ringing louder than the fire alarms – and a cop car had just pulled up outside the diner. If I had been in a more talkative mood, I could have told the diner guy that marzipan is sweet stuff that you coat a cake with and that Salvatore Maranzano was not so sweet and more likely to coat you in cement. He had been sent from the big capo in Sicily to take over Joe 'The Boss' Masseria's rackets and for a year and a half the Italians had been slaughtering one another from New York to Chicago.

'Fifty murders so far, they say,' chirped the hash-slinger.

'Here's my tip,' I replied. 'Avoid Italian restaurants and barbershops.'

He laughed, 'Ain't that the truth.'

'Thanks for the Bromo.'

I left him a nickel tip and held the door open for the cop. Good manners go a long way with cops.

29

It's true that I had avoided a permanent situation with the opposite sex – or maybe, more truthfully, they hadn't been interested in *me*. Throughout my life, whenever 'hello' had developed into, 'Why don't you stick around a while?' I usually hit the wind faster than a shovelful of Oklahoma topsoil. I had always imagined love as a rope thrown to a drowning man: a rope that would form a noose around your neck and garrote you the moment you said, 'I love you.' This time, I told myself, it was going to be different.

When I got to Abruzzinni's the next day, the daily madness of the store was in full flight. I tried to get Patrizia's or Rosa's attention over the heads of some particularly feisty ladies who could have killed me with one swipe of their shopping bags.

'She's left,' Patrizia had to shout at the top of her lungs while tossing hams to her Uncle Nando, ten feet away.

'I thought she was staying till tomorrow?'

'Something came up,' said Rosa.

I felt sick. How could I have missed her? I even took my hand off the purse of the lady who was in front of me on line. Anyway, what kind of shit-heel had I become, stealing purses with a dollar-fifty in them – from old ladies at Abruzzinni's Grocery? What a jerk. I waved to Rosa and Patrizia and turned to leave.

'Thanks.'

'Say, Tommy, where are you going?' asked Patrizia.

'Are you going to see her?' shouted Rosa.

'Should I? You think so?'

'Sure, I think so. She's expecting you.'

'She . . . ?'

'Get your butt down to the ferry, Tommy . . . she likes you!'

'She does?'

'Oh, yeah, are you crazy?' I was enjoying the good news when Rosa's face suddenly turned nasty and she screamed even louder at her younger brother.

'Joey! Where've you been? We need some more mortadella from the yard.' She turned back to me. 'Go see her, Tommy, she's gonna be real mad if you don't. She's probably cooking dinner already. D'you know where to go?'

'No. It's been a long time.'

Rosa scribbled onto a paper bag and a dozen hands passed it back to me.

An old lady in a cornet bonnet, who had elbowed her way across the sawdust floor and barged in front of me, had grown less interested in getting her bag of macaroni and more interested in my conversation with Rosa. She turned around and whispered, 'I think you should go see her.'

'You're right,' I nodded and held her arm with a familiarity that probably wasn't appropriate, as though she were a long-lost aunt who I'd spoken to twice a week for twenty years rather than a total stranger. I gave back her watch. It was a nice one, too – old gold from Palermo most probably – and she strapped it back on her wrist.

'My Lord, did I drop that? Well, thank you so much, hon. You're an honest person.' She patted the side of my face. 'Now, you go see your girl.'

I climbed the stairs of my flophouse to pick up my things. The Vallejo Ferry left at noon – enough time for a haircut, shave and a shoeshine. In a matter of hours, I could be with Effie. As I searched in my pocket for the key, I noticed that its function in life had been made redundant because the door to my room had been kicked clean out of the lock. I pushed the door open and saw a fancy pair of shiny leather lace-up boots, which were the walking end of a very large gentleman lying on my bed. He looked like a relative of Big Mike Abrahams, the guy who beheaded the Chinese comic at the Dwyer Theater when I was a kid. If he'd had just a little more body hair he could also have been quite an attraction at the San Francisco Zoo. He had already gone through my stash that I kept in an old shoebox. It takes a thief to know a thief, and he'd easily found the loose floorboard under the linoleum. He was flipping through one of the wallets as I walked in. The guy had curiously rouged cheeks and a squashed nose that looked like it'd once had a serious confrontation with a baseball bat. Puffing up his cheeks, he looked up at me and smiled. It was one of those smiles that never seem over-friendly and because of his past encounter with the baseball bat his speech was predictably adenoidal, like someone had stuffed a pair of oven mitts up his nostrils.

'Nice wallet.'

'Yep.'

'Crocodile?'

'I think snakeskin.'

'Oh, yeah. You're right . . . snakeskin. Nice.' Pocketing the wallet, he eased himself off the bed and walked to the dressing table. He tipped the shoebox upside down and the contents tumbled everywhere. Snatching at a gold fob watch, he shook it violently until the delicate innards satisfied him with a tick. His nose being blocked, he breathed by sucking in air noisily through his teeth. He held up the timepiece and swung it from the gold albert chain.

'You know whose watch this is?'

I shook my head, 'No.' I racked my brains to think of just whose pocket I'd been stupid enough to pick.

'Well, it's not yours, is it?' What a dumb question. I had never owned a solitary thing that didn't start out life as someone else's, but I wasn't about to argue. And anyway, I don't think he would have been terribly interested in debating the concept of possession being nine-tenths of the law. So I shook my head again.

'No.'

'This watch belongs to Oakie Doolan. You know Oakie, right?'

Again, I shook my head, no. I lied a little, as I knew *of* Oakie, but didn't actually *know* him. Who would want to? He was a crazy, lowlife killer from Russian Hill and a bagman for the bootlegger Frankie Stutz. Slowly I was beginning to get the message.

'Oh, you *should* know Oakie.'

'Should I?'

'He's my boss. He's a big shot, a real big shot.'

In actual fact, Frankie Stutz was the big shot in San Francisco, and Oakie just stood in his shadow – and Frankie stood in the bloody shadows of whichever Italian called the tune in New York, but right then I wasn't in a position to correct my visitor – an enormous sonofabitch who now blocked any exit that I might have attempted. I consequently kept my answers on the humble side.

'Look, I'm just a nobody doormat thief. Don't know no big shots.' I could see that he was unimpressed by my candor.

'Oakie's real mad at you. This watch used to belong to his pa. Says it was all his old man had to his name when he walked off the boat in Hoboken.'

If he thought this would make me cry, he'd get more tears from an onion. Oakie's old man had probably strong-armed it off of some other poor sucker from Lithuania or someplace when he was coming over on the boat, because anyone who owned a gold watch sure didn't need to leave Ireland, where they didn't even have potatoes.

Once again he shook the timepiece violently and held it to his ear. 'It's not too good a timekeeper, but it's a sentimental thing, you understand. Someone recognized you outside Farruggio's. You're the droopy-eyed pocket dip.'

Yes, I was. My droopy eye was the bane of my life, my Coca-Cola sign, my mark of Cain.

They say the easiest person to stiff is another thief. For me it wasn't the first time, and probably wouldn't be the last. But this time it hurt more than most because Mr Gorilla suddenly punched me very hard in the pit of my stomach. In the fight game, I think this would have been termed a low blow because, frankly, any lower and he would have crushed my nuts. Suffice to say, it really hurt, and I had trouble catching my breath, like someone had tossed a shovelful of sand down my throat. It only took one punch, but he was a big guy and, in my experience, punches seem to hurt a whole lot more when you stop one in real life than they seem to do in the movies. I thought I couldn't hurt any worse but I was wrong. I fell to my knees and with a woozy head watched as his calfskin lace-up with Yale toe, heavy sole and Goodyear welt, stamped down hard on my hand. I screamed as I heard the bones crack, and even louder when he did it the second time. He picked up my crushed mitt and it flopped in front of his face like a wet glove while he examined his handiwork. He sniffed at my talcum-powdered fingers. 'You smell nice. Kind of girlie-fied,' smiled the gorilla. He tossed back my hand, puffed up his rouged cheeks once more and laughed as I yelled in pain.

'I guess that'll keep you from poking around inside other people's jackets.' He was still laughing as he waddled down the flophouse stairs.

I looked down at my mangled, useless hand. I couldn't touch it and I couldn't stop it trembling. My solar plexus burned like a bucketful of hot coals, but worst of all, my right hand had gone completely numb, hanging from the end of my arm like a slab of dead flesh. I staggered along the corridor and down the stairs, clinging to the banister like a back alley drunk.

Out in the street, the light blinded me. Everything seemed drained of color. I squeezed my eyes together to clear my head and felt for my sunglasses with my good left hand. 'I still have one good hand,' I repeated over and over. 'I still have one good hand. I still have one good hand.' With my record and parole violations, I couldn't risk waltzing into a regular hospital, otherwise I'd be doing another six months in the slammer. But my hand needed the best attention – or it would heal like a drunken lobster. I decided to make my way over to Siskin's Pawn Shop on Powell and see a fence I knew. Maybe he would have a tube of Zam-Buk ointment he could sell me. Harry Houdini advertised Zam-Buk on the billboards and that was all I could think of at that moment. Harry Houdini who, buckled into a straitjacket, was padlocked in a mailbag upside down and submerged twenty feet into the Hudson River always came out okay, didn't he? Except that one time Houdini got a surprise punch in the stomach – that killed him.

'I still have one good hand. I still have one good hand,' I repeated to myself as I struggled down the length of Grant, leaning against every lamppost to catch my breath and stop the buildings from swaying. At the corner of Clay I stumbled through the doors of a small Chinese store and bought a soda. My left hand started to shake as much as my right. The Chinese lady behind the counter offered me a bottle opener on a string. She saw me struggle with one hand and kindly held the bottle while I flipped the cap. My damaged right hand was beginning to throb again, and I felt the bottle slip out of my hand as the Chinese lady suddenly grew to seven feet tall and rising fast as I slipped to the floor and blacked out.

All my life I had been obsessed with my own hands and everyone else's as I had watched them slip away their wallet, fasten a button or close a purse. Now they reached into my head from all directions. There were veined, calloused, wrinkled, grimy, chafed, arthritic, bloodstained hands and sunburned, sinewy, warty, stubby, blistered, diseased and greasy hands. Hands that could pitch a fly ball, spin a coin, sign a death warrant, soothe a brow, flip a card, take a vote, form a fist, cup a breast or wipe away a tear. My dad's hands, red and raw; my mom's hands, cold and dead. My own hand, once pampered and powdered, was now a chunk of crushed meat.

30

In Chinatown there used to be a guy called Dan Heu, which meant 'Big Ox'. He did this routine where he had a live chicken on a pole and he'd toss two fat short swords high into the air, catch them by the blades in the palms of his hands, spin them up to the handle and slice the throat of the chicken with the razor-sharp blade. He'd then rub his hands in an ointment he called 'tiedayanjiu' and show everyone that he didn't even have the slightest cut. People would then line up to buy a jar. He did pretty good business, too.

Moral: It pays to advertise. Unless you're a chicken.

The voice said, 'Drink up!' My eyelids parted and I could see an elderly Chinese man with a billy-goat beard. It seemed as though he was looking at me from the other side of a goldfish bowl, but then his face straightened out as my eyes shifted in their sockets and found their focus. My head hurt, my stomach hurt, but my hand felt okay. I obediently drank the liquid. It tasted good. Medicinal, but with a kick that made me want to go back to sleep. But the voice kept me awake. The voice was disembodied – it wasn't the old man speaking, unless he was a ventriloquist. 'Hi, Tommy. Trouble still following you around, I see.'

The voice was familiar. Almost *too* familiar. Like my own voice. Like a brother's or a father's voice. Except I had neither. I tried to move my head towards where the voice was coming from.

'Long time, no see.' My head became a little clearer. It was a fancy room with the latest modern furniture and a steel fan that buzzed away on top of a Victrola. Behind the big desk sat the owner of the voice. He stood up and a shaft of light crept up his face dramatically, like a vaudeville act at Dwyer's Theater. It was Sammy. The same Sammy Liu who, aged ten, smoked eight-inch cigars, which he claimed had been rolled on the thighs of Chinese virgins deep in the heart of Chinatown – where white guys didn't dare to tread. The same Sammy Liu who earned a nickel a hit by scraping out the pipe bowls in his uncle's hoodoo opium joints; the same Sammy Liu who helped me save the whole of San Francisco from dying of the Black Death by catching rats as big as tomcats. It was the same Sammy Liu, my best and only childhood friend.

He spoke Chinese to the old physician, who snapped closed his leather bag and made for the door. Sammy peeled a few bills from a sizable wad and stuffed them in the old man's top pocket. Billy Goat kissed Sammy's hand and performed a deep, reverential bow, like Sammy was royalty or something. I looked down at my neatly bandaged hand. A wooden splint held it straight and it looked like one of those flat spoons they use to dig out noodles at Chinese restaurants.

'You should be okay, as long as you don't move it for a while. The old man is the best doctor in San Francisco, but he's kind of exclusive. Not many people know him.'

'Chinese patients only?'

'And one dumb Irishman,' Sammy said as he hugged me.

'How did you find me?'

'One of my guys recognized you when they were dumping you in the back alley behind the store where you passed out. Gave me a call. I talk about you a lot with my guys. You know, from when we were kids and stuff. It makes them laugh. You're famous. They know you pretty good from my stories.'

I looked around the room and noticed the paintings, wall silks and expensive lacquered bowls filled with shiny red Chinese apples. Sammy was always unusually tall for a Chinaman and had grown beyond six foot. He had a long, slender body and soft, elegant hands. His narrow face now sported a natty toothbrush moustache and the suit was expensive silk and wool weave, double-breasted and beautifully hand-stitched. 'So, you're doing well, it seems,' I said.

'Can't complain, Thomas. How about you? Still swiping quarters from pay phones?'

'Oh, yeah, and still stealing purses from old ladies who can't run after me.' Sammy laughed, and I smiled like it wasn't actually true, but he knew that it probably was. You can fool a lot of people in life, but never your oldest friend. I continued, 'What kind of business are you in anyway, Sammy?'

'Family business. Company business.' He poured two fingers of Scotch and handed a glass to me.

'You work for your Uncle Joe?' I sipped at the Scotch. It was very good – the real thing, all the way from Scotland – it must have cost a fortune.

'No, Chin Ju Bing is dead.' He used the reverential name for his crazy Uncle Joe. 'So I ended up . . . boss of the store.'

'I'm sorry about your uncle.'

'It happens.'

'He had a good life.'

'You know why my uncle came to this country in the first place?'

'Not really, in search of the Golden Mountains, I guess?'

'No. Not Chin Ju Bing, he never wanted to leave China. He loved China. It was his family before him who came here to mine for gold. But one day a relative of our family was attacked by white miners in Yuba County. It happened a lot. Except this time, deep in the mine shaft, they cut off his legs with a rail cart and he screamed in pain for two days before he finally bled to death.'

'I'm sorry,' I apologized, as if I too were responsible for the unfathomable cruelty of all white guys. I sucked down another mouthful of Sammy's whisky down my throat – not backyard Kentucky horse sweat this – but real, magical Scotch.

'The Chinese miners decided that enough was enough and shipped Chin Ju Bing over here – he already had something of a reputation over there in Kwantung – and within a week he had sliced the throats of all five miners responsible, tied their bodies to railroad sleepers and dumped them in the Sacramento River. They were never found, of course.'

'Of course.'

'The white retribution would have been too great, you understand.'

I understood.

'So the bodies stayed at the bottom of the river and my uncle rose to the top.'

'So he died of old age?'

'Oh no. Lead poisoning.'

'Lead poisoning?'

'Fifteen bullets in the head.'

'I'm sorry,' I stuttered again.

'Don't be sorry. They buried twenty-three members of the *Si Yi* a week after my uncle was assassinated.' I shook my head as Sammy continued, 'A tooth for a tooth. Like in your bible.'

'Twenty-three teeth for one tooth.' I corrected his math.

'The Chinese bible is different,' Sammy answered with a mischievous smile. 'And you understand, my uncle was no noodle cook.'

I blinked in order to take it all in. Young Sammy had taken over from the biggest, meanest Chinese gangster San Francisco had ever known. And I'm telling you, these guys were meaner than any Mob guy – Italian or Irish. I'd heard there had been a bloodbath while I was on the road. I seemed to recollect that a whole bunch of killers were brought in from mainland China to sort out the uppity local tongs. I never dreamed that Sammy would be in the middle of it, let alone end up on top of the heap. What kind of mean sonofabitch had he become? You don't get to be boss of this outfit by being Mister Nice Guy.

I remembered that as a kid, he was so gentle – well, most of the time. He was no good at the pickpocketing game. The Chinese are never very good at it. They don't like the bodily contact. It's a cultural thing. If you ever bump into a Chinese person, just watch him jump three feet in the air. Sammy said it was a superstition from the *fan tan* tables – if someone touched you it was considered bad luck.

But that's not to say that young Sammy Liu didn't have other attributes. I remember a Chinese heavy called Rice Boy who worked for Sammy's Uncle Joe had caught young Sammy in one of the booths at the Mansion brothel – he humiliated him in front of everybody, first chance he got. I don't know what he said about young Sammy's private parts, because he was jabbering away in Chinese and wiggling his little finger. It made Sammy mad. Real mad. The next time we saw this guy Rice Boy, he was dipping fried octopus flakes into green tea at some back-street dive when Sammy pulled out a giant pistol that he'd found in a trunk under his grandma's bed. The gun was so old, it must have been made in Peking the week after they invented gunpowder. He fired just once at the guy and the kick on the old gun knocked Sammy back against the wall, dislocating his shoulder. Rice Boy didn't come off so well. Sammy had put a hole in the guy that you could drive a Cadillac through. I think Rice Boy lived, but Uncle Joe smacked Sammy around quite badly, as I remember – not because of the shooting but because he did it in front of so many witnesses. These were the same witnesses that Uncle Joe soon spirited away on a slow boat back to China. For weeks, Rice Boy's demise was the talk of Chinatown and Sammy was not Little Sammy anymore – just Sammy.

I stared at my beautifully wrapped hand. Whoever that doctor was, he was an artist. Sammy noticed me looking at it. 'So how did you hurt your hand?' He sipped at his whisky, flipped a Chesterfield into his mouth, and offered one to me.

'In the comfort of my hotel room. Courtesy of one of Frankie Stutz's guys – some gorilla who works for Oakie Doolan.' With my good hand I pressed my nose against my face to demonstrate Mr Gorilla's palooka profile. Sammy seemed to know him.

'Mook the Homo? Big guy?'

'Very.' I ignored the homo part. Sure, he had rouged cheeks, now I came to think about it, but he sure didn't act like no sissy pink-pants.

'That would be Mook Mosso.' Sammy looked at me oddly, probably wondering what the hell a two-hundred-and-fifty-pound butt-dancer was doing in my room. After all, it had been a few years since he knew me, and my life's journey could have taken all kinds of exotic turns. 'So, what was his beef?'

'I hooked his boss's gold watch. It had belonged to Doolan's old man.'

Sammy nodded. 'You want me to deal with him?'

I loved the sound of that. Now, don't get me wrong, I'm not big on retribution. I always thought revenge, however much you dress it up with phony morality, was kind of a waste of time and effort. Also, I never had the luxury, frankly. I was always the little guy – I had wits in the places where other people had muscles, and whenever it was possible I always avoided the rough stuff – not that it always avoided me.

But my hand still throbbed, and I didn't know if I could ever pick my own nose again, let alone a pocket. I had powdered my fingers and polished and filed my nails so often that I had become fond of my hands. I *needed* my hands. I *loved* my hands. My hands were all that stood between me and a Salvation Army soup line. Frankly, I was mad at the gorilla in the shiny tie-up, fancy boots with the Goodyear welts. So Sammy's guys would just rough Mook up a little. So what? Didn't the gorilla deserve it? I found myself nodding, like a kid asking a favor of his big brother to sort out the class bully in the schoolyard. Yeah, screw my theories on the pointlessness of revenge. I cleared my throat and heard myself say, 'Sure. Do you mind?'

Sammy's pen scratched away as he made a note on his desk pad.

31

Funny how you don't see certain people for ages and then the moment you meet up again you're gabbing away right where you left off twenty-odd years before. We walked all over Chinatown and everywhere we went it was obvious that Sammy was the cat's pajamas. From every store people would rush out, bow low and old ladies would kiss his hand. The two guys who walked behind us kept an eye on anyone who lingered too long or got too close. Sammy waved for his car and a glistening, midnight blue Pierce-Arrow Straight 8 pulled up. Sammy and I climbed in back and the two bodyguards squeezed in front next to the chauffeur, Willi Chu. I relaxed back into the embroidered seats and admired the maple wood with silver trim. It's true what they say – these Pierce-Arrows are pretty great cars – however long it takes them to make one.

'Nice car,' I said. 'Is it new?'

Sammy's face lit up with pride. 'Just a week old. Pierce-Arrow model B, Sport Phaeton. Just four people in the whole world own this model. Babe Ruth, J.D. Rockefeller . . . and who else, Willi?'

'The King of Belgium, Mr Sammy,' answered Willi Chu.

'The King of Belgium, and me.' Sammy shook his

head, as if even he couldn't believe it. I let out a short whistle to show that I was impressed. Effie would have been too.

'Babe Ruth? Are you kidding?'

'Nope. He has the very same car, only he paid full price.' Sammy and Willi Chu laughed out loud, sharing some secret that it would be better not to inquire into further. My old pal had certainly come a long way since we played all those games of stickball in Piss Alley.

Sammy had inherited the entire family business – from restaurants to fish and pork shops to laundries. Also, there was the 'less legitimate' side of the business, to say the least. The two heavies who sat in the front weren't real-estate agents or waiters after all, and the machete that the guy by the door clutched between his knees was not meant for the filleting of fish.

When the Chinese were banned from becoming American citizens, they just went ahead and evolved their own system, including their own police, if you could call it that. The Chinese Consolidated Benevolent Association, or 'the Six Companies', controlled every aspect of Chinese life in San Francisco.

Chinatown was a predominantly male society and so naturally vice and gambling were the biggest business, and Sammy's 'company' being the one with the most muscle, he pretty well controlled things. Apart from the other Chinese tongs, their only competition was Frankie Stutz and the ragbag of Irish loblollies like Oakie Doolan who were never smart enough, or sober long enough, to ever be a threat.

By 1 a.m. Sammy and I were alone in the back corner of one of his joints on Stockton. Earlier in the evening his friends had joined in with laughter as the two of us went through our old stories. But as the yarns got bloodier and bloodier, they had gradually drifted away as we recounted Ah Soon's throat-slitting and Police Chief Biggy's dick in his pocket. The more Sammy and I yammered away, gripping our sides with laughter, the more Sammy's friends had excused themselves from the table and the evening. Out front in the crowded *fan tan* room, a serious game was still in progress as one guy pushed the porcelain buttons around with a black stick and another, perched high on a stool, raked in the gamblers' money.

Sammy was a little drunk, as was I, from his endless supply of excellent Scotch whisky. My head was still clear, but the whisky helped to numb the pain in my bad hand. Sammy and I were laughing about the times we sneaked past Mrs Peggano at the Rex Theater, and I mentioned that I had rolled Oakie Doolan outside Farruggio's Sausage Factory. Suddenly, Sammy sobered up.

'He was there? Immediately after the explosion? At Farruggio's?'

'Sure. Must have been him, unless he'd loaned his watch and wallet to someone else. And the Farruggios weren't just storing sausages.'

I placed on the table the neck of the broken bottle I had slipped into my pocket outside Farruggio's. Sammy took it and twisted it in his fingers. He drained his whisky and looked at the empty glass. He was thoughtful, with one of those faint smiles that certain people have when they know more than you do. I've often noticed this smile on others in my life. He placed his napkin over the broken bottle neck, picked up the bottle of Scotch and smashed it on the table. Gently unwrapping the napkin, he fished out the cork from the shards of dark green glass and inspected it closely. Sammy, like a lot of Chinese it seems to me, was a little deficient in the eye-ball department. Someone once told me it was because they eat too much rice and not enough hamburgers. Have you noticed that? Sammy held the cork six inches from his face, rolled it between his fingers and gave it a long, knowing sniff.

'I tell you, Tommy, the whole goddamn country has turned into alkies. They can't get enough of the stuff. Prohibition has got the cash registers ringing like sleigh bells,' he said quietly.

'Ain't that a fact,' I agreed and raised my glass. Seems like Sammy and I had the same politics even though, due to his obvious fiscal success, he was probably a little more enamored with the principle of capitalism than my cynical and pathetic self. I picked up the cork and looked at it more closely. Burned into the bottom of it was a curly letter 'C'. I copied Sammy and gave it a sniff. 'And you? Are you in on this?'

'Not really. Frankie Stutz and the Catholics have shut the door on the booze racket, so it's not a business that interests me. It's one-way traffic from here to New York. Sure, I take a little for Chinese needs, fortified wine,

Chinese brandy. Just a few barrels for local use. You know how the Six Companies work, Tommy. We look after everyone's needs.'

'Cradle to the grave.'

'Whatever your pleasure, we can provide it.'

'Yeah, from the crotch upward.'

Sammy started to sing a tune from the old days. He had a truly terrible voice. '*There's three ways to make a bucky, make a bucky . . .*'

'*Feeling lucky, sucky-fucky and Old Kentucky,*' I finished the verse for him.

'Gambling, sex and booze.'

'The three pillars of society.'

'And speaking of sucky-fucky, how would you like to sample the Chinese version of the Mansion?'

I admit I once had a soft spot for Chinese girls, but I waved my bandages. 'Oh, no, Sammy Liu, I think I have to put my hand to bed.'

32

The next morning my head hurt so much, I'd forgotten I had a bagful of crushed bones for a hand. Sammy's bodyguards must have put me to bed with a shovel. At any rate, I hoped so. I lay there naked and, through one eye, I could see my clothes perfectly stacked on the chair. I *never* folded my own clothes, except under the mattress, so I assumed another person had intervened. The night before sort of came back to me, but maybe I was too embarrassed to admit *who* it was that put me to bed. And in any case, it was Sammy Liu's fault. He had always led me astray, putting all sorts of ideas in my head since I was nine years of age, and he was *still* doing it. I think her name was Su Fu or something. I forget. Maybe I was hallucinating – who knows what the guy with the billy-goat beard had slipped in my Scotch? I stared at the crazy man in the bathroom mirror. I had eyes like broken windowpanes and a yellow tongue that would attract a small crowd at Coney Island.

I packed my clothes in the cardboard suitcase that I called luggage and checked out of that flophouse not a moment too soon. The old guy downstairs who gave me my bill was one of those 'I finished school' bluffers, as he obviously couldn't write. The bill just said, 'maintenance' – an all-purpose word he could write and had obviously practiced endlessly instead of learning any others. 'Maintenance,' he had scrawled on the yellowed square of paper, and the number six – that being what I owed. He had deftly squiggled the dollar sign preceding it, of course. Let's face it, in America – even if you're a dumb-ass illiterate – you sure as shit know the sign of the snake with the two lines through the middle.

The big clock on the Ferry Building tower said 11.50. I had ten minutes before the ferry left. I paid for my ticket and hauled myself along the crowded waterfront in the direction of the Vallejo Ferry slip. Dragging my bag with my good left hand, I stopped to buy smokes at the newsstand and as I paid and jerked a Lucky to my mouth I nearly had a heart attack. There on the front page of the *Examiner* was a large photo and a headline that said, 'Double Mob Killing'. I snatched a copy from the rack for a closer look. There in the photograph, slumped at the end of some anonymous back alley, were two dead bodies. Gangsters. Each of them had two crisp bullet holes perfectly placed in their foreheads – what the Mob called a simple case of two deuces. The photo was extra gruesome because the cops were holding up the dead guys by their collars so that the photographer could get a better shot. It seemed that these days everyone was in show business, even the cops and a couple of corpses. I gulped hard. All that I ever imagined Sammy's guys doing was roughing up Mook Mosso. Perhaps they'd just push him around a little or split his lip, maybe. Surely not kill him *and* his boss, Oakie Doolan. I mean, it was me who stole the guy's watch in the first place. The dead men stared out from the photograph like a couple of those creepy wooden statues of Jesus I was telling you about. They were dead, but they were staring straight at *me*. I looked down at my hand – the cause of this carnage. Blood was seeping through the bandage from the wound within like an iron nail had been driven into my palm. I had stolen a dumb watch from a guy, and now the very same guy was sitting in a puddle of his own blood and piss with two bullet holes ventilating his brain? Jeez – my friend Sammy was even crazier than his Uncle Joe.

'You gonna pay for that, fella?' I turned with a start, expecting to see a cop at the very least. The skinny youth behind the newsstand waited patiently as I scrambled for change with my good hand. I was sweating and I looked at the newsstand guy like *I* was guilty – as if I *personally* had put those slugs in the skulls of Doolan and Mosso. 'You want me to deal with him?' That's all Sammy had said. I could hear it real loud, with an echo, bouncing around inside my head, as if it was coming over the Ferry Building loudspeakers. I could clearly hear him scratching down their names on his desk pad. I didn't realize it was a death warrant.

I found myself saying to this stranger behind the news counter, 'I thought he'd just rough them up. Just rough them up. That's all, honest.'

'Huh? What'd'ya say, fella? Someone rough you up?'

'No, nothing! Nothing!'

I stuffed the newspaper under my arm, grabbed my

bag and made for the ferry. As I ran along the pier, a large woman – her line of sight impeded by the dead fox curled high around her neck – bumped into me. I screamed as the clumsy lard-ball barreled into my bad hand, causing me to drop my suitcase.

'Shi . . . Jesus, Mary!' The woman's even larger husband put a friendly hand on my shoulder as I went down on one knee.

'You okay, buddy?'

'I'm fine, really,' I stammered. 'I have a bad hand. It's not your fault.' The woman stared at me, convinced that I was crazy and I guess she wasn't completely wrong.

'It's *really* not your goddam fault,' I shouted, like they were hard of hearing. I was terrified that Sammy's guys would be watching and that this completely innocent couple would be punished for merely bumping into me.

'My fault entirely,' I said.

With Sammy's ruthless efficiency, I was fearful that before I even reached the boat this poor woman would be hanging by her fox stole from the highest wharf-lamp.

The ferry spewed out bilge water, chains clanked and the hull creaked as the engines throbbed into motion. We pulled away from the slip to the sound of the showy boat-horn, which was always more Louis Armstrong than maritime necessity.

I bought a coffee on the first-floor deck, got a shoeshine from the bootblack and found an empty seat. There was a busy card school in progress among the regular ferry passengers as they expertly balanced squares of wood on their knees, acting as makeshift tables. I stowed my bag and stuffed the newspaper under the seat so that I wouldn't be reminded of it anymore. I was off to see Effie. Whether she would welcome me, I couldn't be completely sure. After all, I was already a day late.

Out of the window I could see that the skyline of the city had changed once again and I tried to pick out the new buildings that had grown ever taller. In the distance were half-built scrapers stuck up in the air all over the city like the skeletons of decaying fish. As these behemoths reached for the sky, the people had hit rock bottom – except for the ones who fed off of society's missteps. Guys like Frankie Stutz. What the hell would he be thinking right now, with two of his guys tagged and stiff in the morgue? Would he be taking my flophouse room apart right now, ripping up the floor plank by plank? No, he didn't know me from Adam. But I sure knew all about him, the vicious sonofabitch.

When Frank was younger he wanted to play the violin or rather, it was his mom and dad's ambition for him. Old man Stuzzi, an Italian immigrant and dry goods importer, dreamed of hearing his son play at La Scala and the Vienna Opera. The only snag was that Frankie took after his sizable Austrian mom and consequently had massive finger pads more suited to swatting flies in a cow barn than nailing an F-sharp on a Stradivarius. By all accounts, he was a terrible violinist.

In his teens, Frankie persevered in any orchestra that would have him, which was when he met the future Mayor Schmitz, who was a conductor. Some people said that Schmitz was no conductor – except maybe on a cable car between the Hyde Street turntable and Union Square. Eugene E. Schmitz got to be the head of the San Francisco Musicians' Union and young Frankie Stutz, as he called himself, tagged along as his backdoor string puller and head breaker – a job for which he showed a far greater talent than for the violin. With the help of the unions and political boss Abe Ruef, Schmitz was elected Mayor under the banner of the Union Labor Party and young Frankie's non-musical career prospered. Not a hammer was lifted, pipe fitted, brick laid, wall plastered, painted or papered, without the unions' say-so. However, by the time 1906 came around it was evident to most people that Schmitz was as phony as Barnum's South Seas' Mermaid. People joked that he was taking so many backhanders that he had to have a special suit made with the sleeves facing the back.

And so, once the quake and the fire were out of the way, Mayor Schmitz was indicted on twenty-seven counts of graft and bribery. Soon after that, Ruef and eleven out of the eighteen of the Board of Supervisors were also put away for oiling the skids of corruption. These guys were in the pay of everyone from Pacific Telephone and United Railroads to the French whorehouse restaurants above Market Street.

The only one they couldn't nail was little Frankie Stutz, and he'd been filling the rotten vacuum, free as a bird, ever since – and now, with Masseria's New York Mob's approval, he was the biggest bootlegger west of Chicago.

I looked down at my hand once more and tried to cup it, but it hurt too much. At least I could move it, which is more than can be said for Frankie's boys being displayed in the *Examiner* photograph with four bullet holes in their foreheads.

33

The ferry pulled up to the wharf and I took the bus into Napa Valley. The old electric railroad had gone bankrupt, though the rails still snaked into the valley and I curled up on the back seat as the bus drove along the road at the side of the tracks.

I opened my eyes, not knowing how long I had slept. Through the bus window the red evening sun dropped fast, bleeding into the pale green haze of the horizon. This was wine country.

They'd come from all over to settle here – hoping to find the soil and climate that roughly mirrored the land they'd left behind in Europe. The land their families had worked for centuries, which would never belong to them. But here in California, they could own their own land, as well as their own vines, and benefit from their own labor. Well, *that* was the theory, at any rate. If you were Chinese you weren't allowed to own a bucket of gravel, and since they passed that dumb Exclusion Act in 1892 they weren't even welcome in America.

First came the Spaniards, and then the dutiful Chinese. These quiet, docile workers were replaced by the hysterical Italians, the cagey Swiss, the stoical Mexicans, the snobby French, the crazy Germans, the friendly Greeks and the unfathomable Armenians. Some came as refugees with their fortunes in their trunks, but most came pulling their cartloads of belongings into these hills and valleys, grasping at the vines to graft a little of their forgetful past onto a hopeful future. Above them, gentle and pre-dictable skies; to the west of them, cooling fogs billowing in from the ocean and beneath them the forgiving red earth – the magical mix of mud, silt, sand and gravel that nurtured the temperamental plantings. With enough hard labor, and good luck, they could produce the pre-cious grapes from which they could squeeze small for-tunes for themselves and their families.

But, as for many hard-working Americans in those dif-ficult times, in the harsh light of the waking day the American dream didn't always deliver. Before then, the root louse phylloxera had been the disease dreaded most by any vineyard, until the man-made disease called Prohibition crept into their lives and declared a death sentence on most of their livelihoods. In the name of 'morality', decency, temperance and a dry society, a handful of zealots had imposed their will on an entire nation with disastrous effect. Little did the people in the wine country think that the new law would actually affect *them*. It was wine, for heaven's sake, *aqua vitae*: the water of life – not the crude, rotgut liquor of ten-cent saloons. Wine is sacred, isn't it? St Paul said it was 'the good creature of God' – it wasn't the piss-bucket hooch in some elbow-bender's mug. Two hundred years before, the Franciscans had planted their vine cuttings and harvested the grapes. They thought that wine would reveal to them the mysteries of

God. Hadn't wine been the chosen drink of man for six thousand years? Didn't the Bible say, 'Wine that maketh glad the heart of man.' 'No,' the drys countered: the Bible clearly said, 'It biteth like the serpent and stingeth like an adder. The wine may be from God, but the Drunkard is from the Devil.' Surely a few elderly ladies misquoting the Bible couldn't alter history? But they did.

I got off the bus at Yountville, crossed the road to the gas station and made straight for the pay phone. After a short telephone chase around Chinatown, I finally reached Sammy Liu.

'Sammy, did you kill them?'

'Did I kill who?'

'Oakie Doolan and Mook.'

He laughed. 'No, too neat. Not messy enough for Chinese. They still had their heads on.' He laughed again, even louder.

'Don't mess with me, Sammy, I know you.'

'You flatter me, Tommy.'

'Who knows what Stutz will do now?'

'Yes, who knows? These kind of things are very irritating.'

'Irritating? Those guys were suffering from bullet holes in the head, not fucking shoe blisters.'

'Calm down, Tommy. It wasn't me.'

'How do I know it wasn't you?'

'Because I'm not that dumb.'

He was right, he wasn't, and it seemed the most likely reason to believe him.

'Then who did it?'

'Probably out of town people that the Farruggios pulled in. Maybe they were mad about their store being blown all over Kearny Street. Wouldn't you be?'

'I would.'

'Maybe they blamed Doolan, he was there that night. You stole his watch, remember?'

'I remember, I've still got a broken hand to remind me.'

'You want to see my doctor?'

'Yeah, next time I'm in town, maybe.'

We said our goodbyes. I hung up the phone, went inside and bought a soda from the lady behind the counter. It was a long walk to Effie's place and after maybe a mile or so I stopped for a breather and lit up a Lucky. I sat on my suitcase and looked at the fields on the valley floor. The last time I was here, the rows of vines were full of workers and the air was thick with the music of many languages: Chinese, Italian, Greek and a few curious ones that sounded like diseases of the throat. Back then, the vines were immaculate, proud and healthy in their soldierly rows, their leafy boughs bending from the weight of the ripe grapes. But now, in the tenth winter of Prohibition, everything looked a little sadder. Some growers had ripped out their vines and replanted with apricots, figs, pears and plum. Others had replaced the precious wine grapes with eating grapes. But much of the land was empty, with rows of untended, decaying vines: mildewed, crippled and dying from gray-rot and neglect.

'From 12.01 a.m., July 16th, 1920, no person shall manufacture, sell, barter, transport, import, export, deliver,
furnish or possess intoxicating liquor.' That's what the
Eighteenth Amendment had said, and it shouted the
death knell across this once beautiful valley. Though not
for everyone, it seemed.

As I turned the corner, surprisingly there were row
upon row of immaculately kept vines, neatly trimmed
and winter pruned, and between the vine rows, a carpet
of mustard weed covered the floor. Someone, it seemed,
had managed to be unaffected by Prohibition.

Another mile on, I checked the map that Rosa had
scribbled for me and turned into the steep curved road
leading up to Effie's. The dirt road was pockmarked with
deep holes and the once-tended grass banks which in
spring would be spattered with wildflowers were now
dreary and choking with weeds.

The painted sign on the post simply said, 'Eichelberger-
Monticule', and on either side of the road were two
hillocks planted not with vines but with cabbage. In fact,
it looked more like a run-down cabbage farm than a vineyard. An early Fordson tractor lay abandoned in the ditch
and was home to animal refugees from the fields, comfortable in its rotten, rusty carcass.

I kept walking and, once over the hill, all was revealed
to me. Through the low-hanging curtain of fog, was the
small but immaculate hidden valley where Effie's father,
old man Kazarian, had planted his vines in steep terraces. The vines followed the contours of the hill and
the lines of some subterranean soil map inside his head.

There was only a fraction of the acreage that was once all vines, but what was left was a gem. On the horizon were silhouettes of sycamore and California oak and in front of the house a line of olive trees and a small orchard. I realized what Effie's old man was up to – the whole place was an illusion. Nothing discouraged the Prohibition agents more than a steep hill and a pot-holed road. Even if they got as far as the gate, they would see only a sad cabbage farm, a rusty Fordson, a steep hill, and then turn right around.

Behind the house, the vines had been plowed up and replaced with a large planting of vegetables. At the top of the drive was the old house, made from pinkish volcanic lava rock at its base and faded rust-red painted clapboard to the roof. It had kept its dignity and looked very imposing – if a little less than spick-and-span – clad with the spindly, leafless winter branches of the Virginia creeper that curled around the shutters.

I nervously straightened the knot in my tie and approached the front door, trying hard not to tread on one of the dozens of chickens running freely in the yard. I rapped on the door with my good hand and brushed chicken feathers from my pants.

Mr Kazarian opened the door. I smiled and introduced myself, but either he disliked me on sight, or he had an extraordinary distrust of strangers. Both of which were understandable.

'Hi, I'm Tommy.'

'Tommy?' He stared at me like I was from the Feds. This was a man unused to visitors climbing the hill and knocking at his door. For a few seconds, which dragged into minutes, he just stood there, looking me up and down.

'Tommy Moran . . . I'm a friend of Effie's. Is she there?' I offered.

His hair had gone completely white since I last saw him, but he was still an imposing man with a strong, erect back and a no-nonsense, baggy-eyed stare. His piercing brown eyes were hooded by his intimidating bushy eyebrows, which made me instinctively drop my head and look at my shoes. He had a red face and a head like a coconut on a telegraph pole – small as it was, set atop a sturdy, crinkled, leathery neck. I guessed that the last ten years had put twenty years onto most of us, but the old Armenian, like his vines, had aged well.

He led me into the house, which I took as a sign that he was expecting me. I felt kind of sissy as I offered my good left hand in friendship. His rough working hands made me feel like I was holding a pound of walnuts and boy, was he strong. He gripped my left hand so hard that for a minute I thought he was trying to emulate what Mook Mosso's boot had achieved with my right.

Opening the door wider, he vaguely shook his head in the direction of what could have been Minneapolis. I followed him inside and in the large main room he nodded, indicating that I should wait.

He continued on through the tall French doors out to the backyard, leaving me to twiddle my thumbs in the center of the room, which was warm from a large wood-burning stove in the corner. The room led into a large kitchen where a picture of the Sacred Heart and a small painting of Pope Pius XI hung on the wall. On top of the polished walnut radio a pig-iron statue of a German shepherd dog shared the space with a child's plasticine version. On closer inspection, the iron statue had a plate that read, 'Rin Tin Tin'.

I waited there for five minutes, maybe ten, admiring the embroidery on the chairs and nosing through the framed photos on the mantel. There were photos of Effie as a kid, standing next to her mother and father in happier times. Another photo showed Mrs Abruzzinni and Effie's mom as smiling teenagers. My browsing was interrupted by a child's voice.

'Hi.'

I turned to see a little girl who, to be honest, didn't look much like Effie at all, except that she was also beautiful, with dark chestnut hair, and I assumed that this must be Effie's daughter.

'Hi, how you doing? I'm Tommy.' Once again I awkwardly held out my left hand, which she found kind of strange, so she took it with her own left hand.

'I'm Mara. Mom says to come down to the winery.'

The old joke was that you could tell if someone worked in the wine-making game because they always had purple feet. Well, Effie's feet weren't purple, but her legs and hands were. She was on top of a ladder resting against a giant redwood cask, holding a small hand pump and a long hose, which sucked up the wine from the bottom of the cask and splashed it over the surface of the vat.

Effie jumped down to kiss me and I hugged her with my good arm, watched very closely by an inquisitive Mara. Effie held her wet arms in the air as we embraced, and she noticed me protectively cupping my bad hand.

'We were expecting you yesterday . . . what happened to your hand?'

'Er . . . silly accident . . . you know those tire jacks, can't trust 'em.' Who was I kidding? I didn't even own a car.

'It's just a few broken bones. Nothing too serious.' I waved my hand, caught Mara smiling, and realized how dumb the bandaged, Chinese wooden paddle must have looked.

'I could play Ping Pong without a bat. It should heal soon. How about you? How's the Studebaker bruise?'

Effie hoisted up her skirt to reveal her handsome legs. I was kind of embarrassed with Mara standing there, but I looked anyway.

'It's fading fast, although I think I twisted my knee from the dancing. So, you two have met?'

Mara and I nodded. I winked at her in a friendly way and she winked back. Well, kind of – I don't think she'd quite got the hang of winking yet – she opened and closed both eyes rapidly, without much success. Maybe she was trying to imitate my droopy eye. We both giggled. I thought she liked me.

34

Effie showed me up to a room in the loft above the winery. There were bunks for twenty workers tucked up in the rafters, but I was to be the sole occupant. Effie pushed open the stiff windows facing out on to the healthy side of the vineyard.

'I'll hang these out a while,' she said, pulling a face while sniffing at the pile of blankets sitting at the bottom of the mattress. I nodded my approval at my new quarters.

'Nice place, nice view.'

'Nice folks. And all you can eat,' she added. Little Mara was standing at the door, her stare unwavering as she continued to look me up and down, not quite sure if I was friend or foe.

'There's a washroom at the end of the corridor – plumbing's not great, but I think you can get a half-decent shower. Dinner's at seven-thirty.'

'Sounds good to me.' I smiled and winked at Mara, who tried once again to wink back but again with little success.

I took a shower, put on my clean white shirt, rolled up the sleeves to hide the frayed cuffs and went for a stroll. I could see Effie cooking on the barbecue and her old man still digging away in his vegetable patch. Boy, were these hard-working people. I walked around the outside of the house and barns and a scruffy yet friendly mutt tagged along. I made my way along the dirt path through the untended side of the vineyard. In a small paddock were a chestnut Belgian mare, a goat and two pigs coexisting quite peacefully. I held out a branch with a few leaves for the goat to gnaw on but instead it licked my bandaged hand, the smell of the Chinese ointment apparently being more desirable. I heard giggling and looked up to see three Mexican children laughing at me on the far side of the paddock. Behind them was a small clapboard shack that I hadn't noticed before. I went over to introduce myself and to my surprise they seemed to know who I was and why I was there. Their father, Isaias, and his pregnant wife, Calida, had worked for Kazarian for five years. Calida brought out a plate of empanadas and insisted I try one. I bit into it, and though it burned the roof of my mouth, I smiled, complimented her on her cooking and headed further up the hill.

At the top, I looked down into the valley. It was a hard life out there, there's no doubt, but it did have its compensations, and this magnificent view was one of them. Mount Helena loomed in the distance and I sat there trying to pick out Napa and Yountville while stroking the head of my new friend, the mutt. I'd spent my whole life in the stench of the city, where damp armpits and stale makeup were always inches from my nose as I plied my trade. They say the nose gets exhausted easily, but sometimes I would scrub my hands for ten minutes at a time to rid myself of the sweat from other people's bodies. Up on the hill, I opened my mouth and gulped in fresh air. It felt good and I wanted more. The fox sparrows and dippers chirped away and as the breeze hit me in the face, and for the first time in my life I thought there was the possibility of a little contentment. Maybe, Hoagie, a crab *can* learn to walk straight?

The table was all set for dinner. I sat down and tried to engage Mr Kazarian in some lighthearted conversation, but he sure was tough going. Frankly, I've had livelier conversations with wooden cigar-store Indians. I told him I had traveled the country doing many jobs, but avoided the full confessional at that point. I guess he was suspicious enough already without me telling him right off the bat that he had a ten-cent, sticky-fingered thief, with a past as crooked as the Kickapoo River, sitting at his dinner table. Not that I was embarrassed about who I was, or what I did. Treading water as I had in the dung and scum of life, I had seen that there was horseshit everywhere in the world, however much you dressed it up in fancy feathers. But old Kazarian was different. He was a *good* man of uncomplicated dignity, and you kind of felt clean sitting at the same table with him, like it was a privilege or something. I instantly liked him, although I couldn't say the feeling was mutual.

After dinner, Effie put Mara to bed. Kazarian had mellowed somewhat from the two bottles of wine consumed at dinner and was now offering me a glass of his precious cognac, which he kept locked in a giant oak armoire in the kitchen.

'Thank you, Mr Kazarian,' I said as I took the glass.

'Kaz,' he said, 'Everyone calls me Kaz.'

'Thanks, Kaz.' I sensed I was making progress with the old man.

I sipped the cognac slowly and felt its warmth as it drizzled downwards. To tell you the truth, I hated cognac – it always played havoc with my digestive tubes – but it was the first sign of him being nice to me, so I sure wasn't going to say no. The old man stared out at his precious vines. His dark eyes appeared more angry than sad.

'How long have you been here?' I asked.

'Come All Saints' Day, twenty-three years since November, 1907.' His previously perfect English was now muddied by his Armenian accent, which seemed to grow thicker as the evening drew on and he sucked down more cognac. 'And maybe this will be the last.'

'Things that bad?' Funny how you say dumb things when you're trying to be sympathetic to someone's problems. Have you noticed that? You'd have to be blind to not see that the old Armenian, like most people in the valley, was up shit creek without a paddle. He shrugged, then let out a sigh and his tobacco-stained bronchial tubes added a layer of harmony. His eyes looked into the distance, full of the confusion and pain of a strong, proud man resigned to inevitable defeat. He'd put in too many hours, days and years of his life to see the triumph of his labors crumble through his fingers like a handful of the red dirt on the hillside.

'Worse than bad. If the bank don't take it, the bugs will.' His glass clinked against his teeth as he searched for his mouth to finish his drink. 'Never thought it would come to this, but . . .' The old man shrugged his shoulders and stood, waving his arms to indicate that he had nothing more to discuss.

He didn't like talking about it, and who could blame him? The cognac would help him through the night and the hangover the next morning would give him a good reason to work his old Armenian butt off until he dropped once more from exhaustion. 'Good night.'

He waddled to the back of the house, kicking at the mutt tangled up in his feet as he stumbled to bed. He cursed at the dog quietly in what was, I assume, Armenian. Whatever language it was, the animal seemed to understand, and ran for cover. The old man closed his bedroom door at the side of the stairs. I could still hear him cursing quietly and farting loudly.

Effie returned from the kitchen carrying another bottle of wine. We finished our coffee and she took her coat from a hook and handed me a less than elegant, worn tweed jacket, which by the smell of it might have belonged to the dog. We climbed the hill, bottle and glasses in hand, sat and looked down at the valley.

Above us in the night sky the stars were brightly strutting their stuff as though they were showing off just for the two of us.

'It's very peaceful up here,' I said. 'I know a guy who's

up there someplace, someone I met on the road, it looks like he's opened up his own Coney Island in heaven.'

Effie laughed and poured wine in my glass.

'What was his name?'

'Hoagie . . . well, depending on what day of the week it was. Sometimes he was Illyich. He said he was from Russia, but I think he was from Philly.'

'He was your friend?'

'He was. He taught me a lot . . . he got killed under a train somewhere between Kansas and Missouri.'

'He taught you how to steal?'

'Kind of.' I shrugged and looked up at the sky as I repeated from Hoagie's book:

'When he shall die,
Take him and cut him out in little stars,
And he will make the face of heaven so fine
That all the world will be in love with night . . .'

'That's pretty.'

'Yeah, good old Hoagie, he also taught me to read.'

'Did you really live by stealing from people, Tommy? I can't believe that's all you did.'

She asked in a kindly way and with an understanding smile that was a lot more generous than I deserved.

'That's all I did . . . because that's all I knew, and I figured that everyone was taking your wallet from you some way or other . . . a back-to-front way of looking at the world, I know . . . but it seemed to get me by. I'd sometimes lie there late at night in some two-horse town and wonder why I let it all go. Loneliness can make you so numb, you stop seeing the world like a normal person . . . I was a blind man peeping through a fence.'

Effie smiled sweetly, but I didn't want her to feel sorry for me. She listened patiently as I rambled through my questionable yet eventful life: how I was crushed at Valentino's wake, saw Niagara Falls, the Kentucky Derby, Dempsey box, the Glasgow caves, Laurello's revolving head at Coney Island. Boy, I even saw them hang an elephant in Tennessee. I missed out the Mackintosh twins and the contribution of Soapy Marx's Romola elixir to the benefit of genital improvement. I know that sometimes not telling the truth can be an even bigger lie, but one day I would tell her everything. Effie must have read my thoughts because she came right back with: 'Did you ever fall in love while you were away?'

'No. I never did . . . I always thought that love was kind of . . . not really for me . . . too fragile . . . like a glass of whiskey that could be so easily knocked over on a bar top.'

Effie raised her eyebrows and sipped her wine.

'How about you?' I asked.

'No,' she shook her head emphatically. 'Too busy with the vineyard . . . looking after my dad . . .' She stopped herself and stared down into the valley. The long shadows that sneaked out from the pruned vines grew ever larger, like giant witches' hands, as they crept up the hillside towards us. After a long silence I had to ask, 'How about Mara? I guess she has a father?'

'I guess she does.'

'Was he from around here?'

'Yes, and no.'

'Where did he go . . . why did he leave?'

'Philadelphia or someplace, I'm not sure.'

'You didn't love him?'

'It was a mistake . . . it's something I can't talk about. I'm sorry.'

'That's okay . . .' She had stopped smiling and I kissed away the secrets of her tears.

'So many lost years, Tommy.'

'I know,' I whispered. 'I thought of you often, waiting on that red bench. I wondered what kind of life you had . . . I always meant to come back, Effie, but . . . I was caught by a railroad cop who busted my jaw with his shotgun butt.' I told her of Mose and Dex and his wife with the pignut eyes. And how I had blacked out and woke up in Fresno when the boxcar door slid open and a dozen railroad cops were standing there, waving their lanterns and cocking their shotguns.

'Mose must have jumped off the train when it had slowed at Madera. They'd found a bull with a broken neck at the side of the tracks and a migrant worker with his belly hanging out, but it didn't answer all their questions. Dex's wife started screaming hysterically when the horror of it all finally got through to her. They gave me sixty days for vagrancy and more time for some cocka-mamie legal stuff that helped them explain away my broken jaw and the two dead bodies. I did a year in Fresno County Jail. I guess big Mose got to Kern County to pull his potatoes.'

Effie leaned across with a forgiving kiss. 'Yeah, your chin is kind of crooked.'

Effie apologized again about the musty smell of the blankets in my loft room. She unhooked her *toile* dress and it fluttered to the ground. She stepped out of her sateen chemise and panties, then slipped under the blankets of the iron cot.

By the time the rooster announced the new day, she was gone.

35

On my second evening there, the old man had lined up ten dusty wine bottles on the table. Out in the yard I could see him sniffing the air and mouthing a silent prayer as he watched the fog roll up the hillside and settle at just the right height to cool, but not harm, the vines. Mara and Effie sat at the table plucking feathers from a chicken.

'Are you expecting guests?' I asked.

'No, he wants you to taste his wines.'

'Ten bottles?'

'You won't taste them all. Well, I hope not.'

At dinner, old Kaz opened each bottle in turn. Wine was his life and he had made it Effie's too – she was equally expert at helping me through the rituals – and boy, was it wonderful wine.

'Hold the glass at the bottom, by the foot. Look at the color against the light. What do you see?'

'Red?'

'Not red,' said Kaz. 'Ruby. Garnet . . .'

'Deepest cherry,' said Effie. 'Never red. Red is for fire engines and nosebleeds.'

'Now, swirl it around in your glass.'

I obeyed, as Effie and old Kaz stared into the bowls of their glasses.

'Do you see the streaks on the glass – the tears? Some say the more tears, the greater the magic.'

'The more tears, the greater the magic . . .' I repeated, staring into the uncharted territory inside my glass.

'And more alcohol. Now, sniff.' The old man's nose was practically dipping into the surface of the wine as he sniffed in the bouquet like some hophead in one of Sammy Liu's opium joints. Effie pressed onwards with my education.

'Now, taste it.' I took a nervous sip and gulped it down.

'No, don't swallow,' she said. 'Take another sip and kind of swish it around your mouth.' I obeyed.

'Inside your cheeks. First there. What do you taste?' I dutifully sucked in my cheeks. I sucked so hard that I went cross-eyed. Effie and Mara laughed, as did the old man, who then farted loudly and uncontrollably, pushing Mara over the edge and into hysterics.

'The tannins. You should taste the tannins in your cheeks. They should pucker the mouth.' Whatever a tannin was, I could taste it. I nodded.

'Okay, swallow. What else can you taste?'

'Fruit.'

'Yes, what kind of fruit?'

'Plums?'

'And?'

'Cherries?'

'Which one?'

'Both?' I hedged my bets.

'Good. And . . .'

'Maybe . . . maybe a little tartness at the back of the throat . . . kind of a . . . bite?'

'That's the alcohol,' said Kaz.

'And the taste is still there?' said Effie.

'Yes,' I frowned.

'No, that's good. It's meant to be.'

'So, do you like it?' asked the old man.

'I do. I do,' I stammered. I put down my glass, exhausted from losing my virginity, from swimming the whirlpool rapids, from flying the Atlantic solo, from scoring sixty home runs in a season at Rec Park. I took a deep breath and Effie leaned across to kiss me on the lips in front of the old man, in front of Mara and in front of the picture of the Sacred Heart. I started to feel quite at home.

On the third day, the old man showed me his treasure. Built against the hill was what looked like an old, broken-down, slatboard lean-to. Inside, he slid back a tall oak door, revealing long, dark tunnels that had been dug into the hillside fifty years before. On wooden racks he proudly showed me the barrels and puncheons of his aging wine. My nose was confused by the smells – dank and musty, but not vinegary. It was the smell of the earth, of plums and of cedar – like the inside of a cigar box. On each oak cask he had chalked his markings: *Cab* and *Pin* with numbers and Armenian scribbles that only he could decipher. And piled high were hundreds of bottles, thick with dust and cobwebs. He waved away a flapping bat as he knocked free the wooden bung from one of the casks with a mallet. Taking an instrument with a rubber bulb on the end, he sucked up a mouthful into a cup, sniffed it to his satisfaction and handed it to me. The old man had hoarded this wine since before Prohibition and it sat there aging away, just getting better and better as his own life got worse and worse. Each year he, Effie, Isaias and Calida had tended to the vines with a little extra hired help for the fall harvest. The old man would make his wine and put a little away, blending the old with the newer casks. They couldn't sell their wines legally but they had hung on, spending every last penny they had and praying for an end to Prohibition.

'So how can you survive?' I asked.

'To tell you the truth, after they declared Prohibition, we did okay. More than okay, as a matter of fact. The price of grapes went from ten dollars a ton to a hundred. We could harvest and sell off our surplus grapes, and if the Prohibition agents left us alone, we could put a little wine down to age. I thought Prohibition was such a dumb idea that it couldn't possibly last more than five years, but here we are at the end of ten and we've ended up the dumb asses.'

'But the price of grapes skyrocketed?'

'For a while. When they shipped the grapes east, most of the fruit rotted and so people started grafting Alicante and Petite Sirah – shit quality but thicker skins, so they traveled better.'

'You didn't do that?'

'No.'

Kaz knocked out the bung from another barrel and sucked up the wine.

'Why?'

'Because I'm a winemaker, not a fucking fruit farmer. Anyway, if it's cheap grapes you want, they grow them aplenty over in San Joaquin.'

You had to admire the obstinate old Armenian, even though his stubbornness had made them go broke. Kaz held out the nozzle with the bulb on the end and I held out my glass for a refill.

'Anyway, greed got the better of them and in '26 the grape market collapsed and . . .' He shrugged and buried his nose in the glass.

'That's tough,' I said lamely.

The old man swished the wine around his mouth and swallowed.

'We get by. The Abruzzinnis take a few puncheons. We also make some money on the olive oil and Effie's hens.'

'I passed a big vineyard on the way here that seemed to be doing okay.'

'Sacramental wine – for the Eucharist. The Cana-Carpentier vineyard has a monopoly.'

'Can't you sell them your wine?'

He shook his head most emphatically. 'No. I hate those bastards.' He gulped another mouthful, pursed his lips, slurped in the air and spat it out. He gestured for us to leave. Something had given him a bad taste in his mouth.

36

During Prohibition, each household was allowed to make two hundred gallons of fruit juice a year. They used to sell these dried grapes in solid bricks with names like 'Vine-Glo' and 'Forbidden Fruit'. All you had to do was add water and you had legal fruit juice. Except they also included a yeast pellet so that with a little coaxing it became wine. They had these strict instructions saying, 'WARNING: You absolutely must <u>not</u> add the yeast pellet to the grape juice because of the extreme danger of it fermenting and becoming alcohol, which is illegal.'

Moral No. 1: No one is ever that dumb, whatever the law says.

Moral No. 2: If you don't want people to break the law, why not leave out the yeast pellet?

Who ever thought that I'd end up working for a living? Old man Kazarian told me what to do, and I did it. It wasn't easy for me because I'd never had a boss in my life – well, not since the Hunter's Point abattoir when I was a kid.

'Do this! Do that, you dumb shit! Are you stupid? Have you got rocks in your head?' And I'm not even mentioning the Armenian stuff that mostly spewed out of the guy's mouth, which I'm sure was worse. Mara would giggle as he scolded me – I guess she realized how useless I was, and maybe even knew an Armenian word or two.

The old man busted my conk all day, every day, and you know what? I loved every minute of it. I just lapped it up, every single goddam insult, because I worshipped that guy. Maybe he was the old man I never had. Who knows? I never went along with all that, 'Your family can screw you up for the rest of your life,' shit. Hoagie used to say that bread always falls on the buttered side, but right then, my life seemed sunny-side up. I'm telling you, just sitting on the back of that crooked cart as the old man whupped the horse up the hill made me feel proud to be part of the human race.

Getting up with the sun, working those vines, weeding and cutting brush and walking up and down old Papa Kazarian's hills kind of brought me closer to my Maker or something. Now, I wouldn't want you to think that I was having some dumb epiphany or religious experience or anything. Let's face it, my soul had probably jumped a freight car to damnation the day I rolled my first sucker – there was nothing that I could do about that – and I have to say it never worried me for a second because guilt can drown you quicker than a barrelful of brine. That's not to say that I didn't talk to God and Hoagie about it – and you know, I think they understood. My point is simply this: I had never met a man like the Armenian before. Sure, I'd met some halfway decent people – not a whole lot, but some. But before then I had never met a totally honest one because, sadly, it's hard getting through life without telling a lie, and in the world I had lived in, most people couldn't tell the difference between truth and lies anyway.

Those months were tough, but my broken hand healed and I flipped that quarter back and forth, in and out of my knuckles a thousand times a day to get the feeling back.

Little Mara and I used to ride down the hill in old Kaz's bucket-of-bolts Ford 'T' pickup to Swann's general store and barter a puncheon of wine, some olive oil and Effie's eggs for the things she needed in the kitchen. A sign behind the counter said: *If we don't have it, you don't need it,* which was just as well because our needs were small.

When we drove back over the hill, Mara and I would dig into a bag of Chuckles candies and sing at the top of our lungs, 'Me and My Old Kentucky Darling' and 'Why Don't the Sun Ever Shine in Albuquerque' as she practiced flipping the quarter in and out of her fingers. No one could hear us singing out there in the fields, which was probably a godsend, as neither of us had a voice worth writing home about. But she was getting quite good at the quarter flipping, I must say, she was a natural. If I'd had her with me as my bag-hand working the street, she could have been quite an advantage.

The old Ford T, with a mind of its own, refused to go any faster than a lazy putter over those steep hills, which frankly didn't bother us one bit since we were in no hurry and had a lot of songs to sing and things to talk about.

'Did you really go to the Statue of Liberty, Tommy?'

'Yep. Right to the top, all three-hundred-and-fifty-four steps.'

'And Coney Island?'

'Sure did, a couple of times.'

'Do they really have a full-size racetrack with mechanical horses that even kids can ride?'

'They do. It's called Steeplechase Park.'

'Is it dangerous?'

'Oh, no, it's exciting. It's like riding in the Kentucky Derby.'

'Tell me about the House of Fun.'

'It's this big glass building, as big as St Helena, where you can fire real bullets at the shooting gallery, there's Skee-Ball bowling, penny arcades, oh, and the freak shows.'

'What's a freak show?'

I wasn't going to tell her about the premature babies in their incubators, which for some curious reason always had the longest lines.

'All sorts of freak people.'

'What kind of people?'

'There's Professor Graf, the man with tattoos all over his body, there's Laurello, the man with a revolving head.'

'Eeow!' she grimaced. 'A revolving head?'

'And Alice from Dallas, the world's fattest girl.'

'How fat?'

'As big as three cows.'

'Three cows?'

'Maybe your dad can take you there some day.' Why did I suddenly say that? What kind of a bozo would say something so thoughtless to a kid? Fortunately Mara took it in her stride.

'I don't have a dad.'

'Everyone has a dad.'

'Not me.'

'Where is he, then?' I knew I shouldn't be pushing her in this way, but I couldn't stop myself.

'Don't know. Mom won't talk about him. I think it's a secret. He left before I was born. Maybe he's dead. Did that guy really have a revolving head? Did it turn all the way around? Did you see it?'

She sure wasn't going to talk about her father and I felt like a jerk for asking. Anyway, Laurello's head never revolved. It was a trick, an illusion. All of life is an illusion, Hoagie said. And I guess that included women like Effie who gave birth to a beautiful daughter without the help of a father.

When we got home, Mara jumped out of the Ford and ran shouting to Effie.

'Mom, Mom, watch me!' She flipped the quarter through her fingers and spun it in the air.

'That's great,' said Effie unconvincingly.

'Give me your hands,' said Mara.

'I'm busy, I have a pot boiling.' She reluctantly held out her hands and Mara grabbed them.

'Close your eyes and say, "abracadabra".'

'Abracadabra,' Effie repeated.

'Da-daaaaa!' Mara opened her hands and revealed the bracelet that she had unfastened from her mother's wrist.

'Tommy showed me how. Tommy, tell her about the man with the revolving head . . . no, tell her about fat Alice from Dallas.'

Effie was not at all impressed by Mara's new skills or by my notions of parenthood. She scowled at me and stormed into the house. She was right. What kind of father could I ever be? That was the last time I ever showed a trick to Mara.

Apart from such minor mishaps, Effie and her old man seemed genuinely happy that I was there. Or maybe I was kidding myself. I did all I could, at the old man's instruction, to help keep the vineyard on an even keel. Isaias and I would walk up and down those terraces a hundred times a day trying to do the work of fifty hands. At times, quite honestly, it felt like we were bobbing around in the middle of some vast ocean in a small boat that was leaking badly, and scooping out the water with a thimble. It was obvious that however hard all of us worked we could never save everything, so we concentrated on what we *could* look after.

Effie had read in the paper that kids had become taller since Prohibition because of all the vegetables they were eating. So we started to plant all kinds of vegetables, including some I had never even heard of – from Japan or someplace.

Sometimes I thought that I was in need of a new back as I hoed and watered the rows of baby plantings. But it was the grapes that were Kaz's and Effie's first love.

Every day Kaz taught me something new. He said the best vines were those that grew on his red gravelly hillside: the finest varieties of Cabernet Sauvignon and Pinot Noir. As the fog blew in from the San Pablo Bay, dodging between the mountains it would be sucked north up the valley and settle just a few feet from Kaz's vines. Thirty miles up the coast in Calistoga, the grapes would be heating up – the fog and the ocean breeze wouldn't roll that far, thereby over-ripening the fruit, so they could only grow Zinfandel and red Rhône up there. Old Kaz said his Cabernet was better than that grown by Cana-Carpentier on the valley floor. He said that we were fifteen hundred feet up in the hanging valley and so bud-break came a little later. The soil was volcanic and not as fertile as on the valley floor so it was better for the vines because it stressed them. There was less fruit and his grapes were smaller so the wine was more intense.

I must say, if you've ever worked or lived anywhere near a vineyard, it's like contracting some strange disease – and I don't mean the louse bug variety, either. No, it's a crazy, inexplicable, all-consuming obsession, because if you lost just one vine you'd been nursing it was like a death in the family. It sure put everything into perspective to think of the deep pain the old man must have suffered when he saw at least half of the precious vines that he had planted and cared for over twenty hard years crumble and die before his eyes.

* * *

After listening to 'Amos 'n' Andy' on the radio, the old man slept heavily most nights due to the plentiful supply of wine and his dwindling stock of precious cognac locked in the armoire. Most nights Effie would tiptoe out of the house and join me up in the bunkhouse, high in the winery rafters. Each morning I awoke to find she had already slipped back into her own bed next-door to Mara.

Mara, this magical child with a beautiful mother, but no mentionable father. The more tears, the greater the magic, Effie had said. Dear, sweet Effie, who carried her heart on her sleeve but kept one deep secret inside it. I would look at her over and over and ask the silent question in my head: Who was he, Effie?

This same question ricocheted in my mind every day and through every task; every hen I chased, every vine I tied, every barrel I rolled, every bottle I washed, every log I split, every yard of the red hillside dirt I climbed.

But why the heck did I have any right to ask anyway? I was an outsider creeping into their lives with no claims or expectations, except that I genuinely loved these gentle people.

I used to walk to the top of the hill at the side of the house and, alone amongst the wild lupine and foxglove, I would light up a Lucky and actually begin thinking *good* thoughts about my fellow humans. That was a first for me, I'm telling you. Well, at least about the ones I was currently privileged to spend this part of my life with. I have to admit that these kinds of thoughts unnerved me and made me think it might be better for me to move on. That's what I usually did, after all. At such times I would have conversations with whoever up there was passing as my God, hiding beyond the clouds. But more often than not I found myself talking to Hoagie.

'So, what do you figure, Hoagie?' I'd ask him. 'Should I get out of here before I become a sap, before I become normal?' I'd look up at the sky, expecting a sign. A revelation. A clue? There wasn't a peep out of Hoagie – nor his Boss: nothing. Not that I was expecting heavenly music or anything – just a hint, that's all I needed. But I didn't hear any harps, not even a goddam banjo. Hoagie hated the banjo. He said that if you listened to it for long enough it could put you in the bughouse. Whatever was happening, I guessed I was going to have to figure it out for myself. I turned back down the hill, rather disappointed with the lack of response from my old pal up in the blue stuff, when I clumsily stepped into a mushy wad of very recent cow shit. I looked up at the clouds that some call heaven. Boy, if that was an omen, it was one that I could have done without.

'Is this your answer, Hoagie?'

I could have sworn I heard him laughing.

37

Every Sunday I would drive Effie and Mara to the nearby small church at St Ursula's College, which was an agricultural school run by the Catholic Brethren. The Church of the Sacred Heart was a mission-style church originally built for the novitiate who attended the college. But sometimes there were some pretty fancy church big shots up there glad-handing it in the court-yard after the celebration of the Mass.

One Sunday, I was waiting by the old T truck, leaning on the window and watching a hawk hover over the field, when the oak doors of Sacred Heart opened and the yard filled with color and voices. The church guys stood there in a gaggle, like some fancy dress ball, in their silk vest-ments and pointed hats. They were a grand group and I thought they looked a little out of place for a tiny church in the middle of nowhere. Effie seemed to know a lot of the churchmen and was busy introducing them to little Mara, who looked bored at having her cheeks pinched.

Effie saw me waiting and beckoned me to join them. I stamped out my Lucky and was introduced to Monsignor-this and His Excellency-that. I kind of lost count of how many bishops were there. I'm sure she said the bishop of New Orleans. What the heck was he doing there? It was a long way from Decatur Street. Did he get lost on the streetcar? The bishops chatted away with their sing-song voices and superior smiles and I felt very uneasy. The only 'friendly bishop' I had previously encountered was on a chessboard fronted by trapped pawns.

Effie also introduced me to Jean-Baptiste Carpentier, who owned the next-door Cana-Carpentier vineyard. Carpentier oozed snake oil charm and had a sunburned face of deep peach, with the smooth, tight skin of a much younger man. His neck, however, was red and scrawny and his hair flared up in a wild, uncontrollable gray-red crest. He had a sharp Julius Caesar nose and a pencil-thin moustache that followed the contour of his thin upper lip. Smelling of *Fleurs de Paris*, he held his head back on a pivot somewhere in his neck, which gave him the appearance of a strutting rooster. As his coat opened slightly, I also noticed that he had a knife sheathed at his hip. I took an instant dislike to him. Perhaps I had known too many guys like him on my travels and even a bucket of *Fleurs de Paris* couldn't hide the bad smell I got from him.

Carpentier was kissing those church rings with the eagerness of someone trying to tap-dance his way out of purgatory. He was also a tad too friendly with Effie for my complete comfort. He gave her a kiss on both cheeks like the French do and the second smacker came a little too close to her lips. Was he the guy who had lit her torch? Is that why I instantly hated him so?

'So, how come you know him?' I casually remarked, as I drove them home.

'Who?'

'The John the Baptist guy.'

'You mean J.B.?'

'Yeah, J.B.,' I said.

'Oh, we go a long way back. I used to go to agricultural school at St Ursula's and he was always around.'

'He was?'

'I know his daughters, Irène and Edith, don't you remember them?' I did. They were the crazy sisters who tried to kill me in their Ford coupe back in 1919 when I first visited the valley.

'I didn't see them today.'

'They live in Paris. They hate California.' It took a while for things to sink in.

'You went to school at St Ursula's?'

'Sure did.'

'I thought it was for men only?'

'Officially, but we got special dispensation.'

'We?'

'Irène, Edith, Rosa and me.'

'Rosa Abruzzinni? She went there too?'

'Sure. Where else are you gonna learn about wine?' she said cheerfully.

We passed by the entrance of Cana-Carpentier: a giant basalt arch that straddled the entry road to the vineyard. Above the arch perched the letter *C* in cast iron. I looked over to see if Effie's eyes moved towards the gate. I wanted to see if she registered, with the faintest of giveaway smiles, the word 'Carpentier' on the green painted sign at the side of the workers' bunkhouses. Did she look across at the great stone house in the distance? Did she look sad? Was her head full of secret thoughts that she was anxious to share with me? I tried to read her face but nothing seemed to be hidden there. She unraveled the braid in Mara's hair and gently smoothed it into a barrette.

I steered Kaz's jalopy up the hill towards Eichelberger and slowed to avoid the potholes and the old sycamore that the wind had blown over. My mind was still flooding with suspicion and mistrust. Hadn't Effie just said 'J.B.'? Not 'Jean-Baptiste'. Not 'Mr Carpentier'. But 'J.B.' I shuddered as I remembered the familiarity. Hadn't he kissed her a little too close to the lips? Didn't he hold her hand a little too tightly?

Little Mara was licking stamps depicting biblical scenes and sticking them into the inside cover of her prayer book. She started singing 'Why Don't the Sun Ever Shine in Albuquerque', and I joined in. Just to take my mind off things.

Every third Saturday Effie would take Mara into San Francisco to stay with the Abruzzinnis overnight and attend Sunday Mass at the cathedral on Van Ness. I would drop them at the Yountville crossroads, where the bus took them to the Vallejo ferry. On my way back home I would pick up kerosene for the smudge pots – the burners that the old man and Isaias used to stop the cold air settling on the vines. One Saturday, after the green mustard seed had blossomed and crept alongside the vines, flopping over the hills like yellow dusters, I was driving past the Cana-Carpentier property when I noticed rows of workers lining up in their old, beat-up jalopies waiting for the chance of work. I had known these dirt-poor migrant workers so well from my days accompanying them as they followed the harvests all over California – picking cotton in Corcoran, or doing back-breaking stoop work for ten cents an hour in the pea fields of Nipomo. But here we were, months from harvest and obviously word was out that there was plenty of work at Cana-Carpentier.

Back at Eichelberger, the old man ordered me up into the winery rafters above the huge, open-topped redwood fermenting casks. It was my job to punch down the cap – the thick crust of the grape skins that collected on top of the wine. I carefully edged along the beams, carrying a ten-foot wooden punch. As I pierced the crust it released an intoxicating gas, which I swear was the equivalent of drinking a fifth of Old Kentucky.

Old Kaz laughed as I nervously tiptoed along, which for someone with my shabby history of courage was akin to being pushed over Niagara in a barrel. I tried to catch him off guard.

'So, do you get Effie to do this?'

'Sure. She has good balance, but she's not so strong with the punch.'

'Kaz, how come Carpentier is doing so well?'

'I told you. Church wine. For the Sacrament.'

'They have a lot of workers.'

'They make a lot of wine.'

'Can't we get in on that?'

I hated saying *we* – I was a guest here – but it was the only way to make the old man think about it. Once again, he answered emphatically, 'No.'

'You don't like Carpentier?'

'I don't like the Church.'

'You don't believe in God?'

'I used to.'

'Effie seems to get on okay with Carpentier.'

'That's how she is.'

'All the priests over there seem to know her quite well.'

He looked up at me, held my stare for a second and then shrugged his shoulders. 'She likes the Church.' With that, he turned away through the winery doors and into the sunlight. What had his god done to him, I wondered? Sammy Liu always said the Chinese never rely on just one god for the whole bag of bananas. He reasoned that if some other guy's god got pissed, then you could get the rap for it. He always said that the 1906 earthquake was a case in point, and I never could disagree with him. It was clear that old Kaz had some big beef with whichever god was looking out for Carpentier.

Carpentier? I knew that name. I punched into the crust on top of the casks. *Whack.* Left hook. I punched again. *Smack.* Right cross to the jaw. I was thinking of the fight between Jack Dempsey and Georges Carpentier, this guy's namesake, in Jersey City, July 1921.

38

They called the French boxer the Orchid Kid because he was kind of handsome for a fighter and had great legs that made the ladies swoon. Jack Dempsey wasn't quite so enamored and consequently broke Georges Carpentier's pretty nose with his first punch, but he carried him for four more rounds for the sake of the newsreels. Finally Dempsey put his opponent down for the count with a vicious punch. It took five minutes for the Frenchman to recover.

Moral: A right shovel-hook to the heart gets you every time.

I tightened my grip on the wheel of the old Ford. I didn't want to be there, but Effie had been sent the invitation and insisted that we go. Apart from being Archbishop Meehan's birthday, it was a special party for San Francisco Mayor 'Sunny Jim' Rolph, who was running for Governor of California in the fall.

Effie straightened my tie as I drove under the Carpentier arch. The road was straight and elegantly lined with Greek walnut trees and flowering camellias. On either side stretched the immaculately tended rows of Cabernet, now sprouting leafage on the spurs of the vines a little earlier than ours. The fog had started to creep in and shake hands with the dusk just as Effie and I had watched many times from our perch up on the hill.

In the west field the word *Cana* was spelled out with a hundred kerosene torches. I remembered that Jesus had turned water into wine at the miracle at Cana. When I was a kid I was always fascinated by miracles, but that one was particularly amusing to me. They ran out of booze, and Jesus pulled a smart move on the jugs of water and abracadabra – they had jugs of wine. Now that's a Bible story those Anti-Saloon League people never quoted.

The field hands stood by with fifty buckets of water in case the flames from the kerosene smudge pots accidentally leaped across to the vines. No chance of *their* buckets being turned into wine, I thought – they weren't even invited to the party.

It was a beautiful house. Well, it was hard to tell where the house ended and the winery began because the ivy-clad building seemed to stretch for a mile. I parked the old car in the lemon orchard amongst the Packards, Buicks and a fancy De Soto roadster. If the crash of '29 had bankrupt the rest of America, the people here sure hadn't noticed.

We crossed the front lawn, avoiding some aggressively territorial geese, and walked up the steps, flanked by women servants – wives of the field hands, most probably – dressed in neat uniforms and starched linen aprons. They held trays of various fruit juices as well as trays of what looked like red wine. I handed one to Effie. She sniffed it and took a sip, as did I.

'Pinot Noir?' I asked.

'Oh, yes.' She sniffed some more. 'Three, maybe four years old. Not bad. Not great, but not bad.'

I dutifully swished, sniffed and drank. It didn't taste much like the sweet sacramental wine I remembered as a kid – the kind that tasted like diluted treacle and made you gag. 'Pretty fancy wine to wash down a Body of Christ wafer?' I offered. Effie raised her eyebrows, indicating that this was not an area of conversation she was about to take further.

The Most Reverend Raymond Meehan, shepherd of his flock, his excellency the Archbishop of San Francisco and birthday boy, stood at the door in his black cassock and red sash greeting the guests alongside his host, Jean-Baptiste Carpentier. I watched like a hawk as Carpentier formally kissed Effie on both cheeks and she curtsied and kissed the archbishop's ringed hand. Both the archbishop and the vintner blanked me out and I was forced to introduce myself. I took the Catholic big shot's hand and shook it heartily. He was a devout but jovial man, jowly, slightly effeminate, and he smelled of cloves. I then bumped Carpentier as he turned from shaking another guest's hand. He looked straight through me as he shook mine, standing erect and formal, like he was being mugged. Effie said hello to another priest, and I excused myself to slip into the bathroom.

In the Spanish tiled room I went through the contents of our hosts' pockets. The archbishop had on him a pocketbook thicker than Luke – that's the gospel according to, not the baseball player. He had a bundle of hundred-dollar bills on him that no Catholic priest had a right to – and a silver box full of clove-scented snuff. Along with gin and young boys of St Ursula's Novitiate, snuff was Archbishop Meehan's favorite tipple. The flowery inscription inside the snuffbox lid read, 'Your Excellency – to God's ear. With respect, J.B.' There was a knock on the door.

'You okay in there, Sir?' asked the bathroom servant.

'Fine, just fine,' I answered. I stuffed Carpentier's wallet and a very nice tortoiseshell fountain pen into my pocket and palmed the archbishop's pieces.

In the main room I saw the archbishop patting his side, obviously in need of a pinch of snuff, so I nudged the waiter towards him. This domino effect allowed me to make slight contact with the archbishop and apologetic pleasantries were just enough, as he raised his arm to adjust his red skullcap, for me to replace the snuffbox and wallet – minus a hundred-dollar bill. Handling charges, I reasoned. From the size of his wad, he wouldn't miss it and it would pay for old man Kazarian's kerosene and make a down-payment on the new tractor Isaias and I needed. Anyway, what the heck? No God-fearing priest should be carrying around a wedge like that in the first place, especially an archbishop. I watched as he finally found his snuff, took a dip and furtively rubbed it on his teeth and gums.

I felt very uneasy around these people because I stood out like the wart on Teddy Roosevelt's nose. I joined Effie, who was talking to a tall priest and, to my surprise, Effie's cousin Rosa and her creepy husband Guido

Brunazzi were also there. The priest seemed to know both girls very well. I stood at the edge of the group and heard him introduced as Monsignor Jack Cathain. He was a good-looking guy, in an elegant black cassock with purple buttons; he had heavily greased black hair and a mouthful of white teeth. He looked more like a movie actor than a man of the cloth. Effie kept laughing at jokes that only the two of them seemed to understand.

'Jack, this is Tommy,' she finally said, and he leaned forward to shake my hand, flashing an ivory smile. I never liked people who smile too much. The guy was so smooth, he could polish apples with his tongue. Effie said Jack Cathain was their old friend from the days when he was the priest at St Ursula's.

'That's a pretty church,' I said.

'It is, but sadly I'm not there anymore. I work in the city.'

'Jack works for Archbishop Meehan at St Mary's Cathedral.'

'I've heard so much about you, Tommy,' he said.

Why had he heard so much about me? I never knew any priests personally, so it was hard to hear Effie refer to Monsignor Cathain as Jack. Jack? I'm always suspicious of priests who go by their first names. Cathain was also very friendly with Guido, who rudely pulled his arm and took him off into the corner to talk. The monsignor excused himself.

Just then the band struck up the tune, 'There Are Smiles That Make You Happy', which was Mayor 'Sunny Jim' Rolph's campaign song.

The guests looked towards the door and in sprung the dapper guest of honor to a round of applause. Ever the snappy dresser, he wore a cutaway coat, starched wing collar, silk cravat and his lapel sported a carnation the size of a small cabbage. Rolph, the seasoned politician, smiled, pumped the men's hands and hugged the women. Sunny Jim loved women. They said that in the twenty years he'd been mayor of San Francisco he'd spent at least nineteen of them in the Tenderloin bordellos between Larkin and Market streets. He was fond of saying in private, 'Nothing focuses the mind like the attentions of a blubber-breasted scuffer.' They said his wife used to have him tailed by detectives and their incriminating reports were routinely fed to his opponents, but they were never made public because no one would ever believe that someone could perform the duties of mayor so visibly and yet still get through so much fornication. No wonder he got on so well with that greaseball Carpentier.

We all sat down to dinner at a long table bedecked with blue and white flowers. After a meal of trout from the Cana stream and vegetables from the Cana fields, the mayor made a speech about his gubernatorial ambitions, which was quite impressive considering that he must have easily put away a good bottle or two of Carpentier red.

I was separated from Effie and seated next to a Swiss guy called Ulf Kriegel who, with his brother Stefan, owned the Frederic Frères vineyard. I had seen their property from the hillside and they seemed to be doing okay. He explained that they supplied bulk wine to Carpentier. I have to say that he was somewhat heavy-going in the conversation department, having learned very little English during his ten years in America. To be frank, I was surprised he didn't have maggots crawling out of his ears, because the guy had the personality of a corpse.

Across the table, Effie sat between her pal the Monsignor Jack Cathain and Stefan Kriegel, but it was the priest who got most of her attention. At least she wasn't sitting next to that flesh-louse Carpentier, who was licking his chops, talking into the ear of a very tanked-up Rosa. With her chin-length bob, heavily powdered face and scarlet lips, I thought that she looked kind of blowsy, but Effie said that was how Guido liked her. From where I was sitting I could see a lot of pain behind her painted face, and it also seemed to me – with my professional eye for other people's hands – that Carpentier's was a long way up Rosa's skirt, but I could have been mistaken.

I was anxious to know more about old Ulf and how his business worked, but he was one of those extra-nervous people you come up against occasionally so that when my hand touched his back pocket he jumped a foot in the air. I had been caught red-handed, so I promptly patted him on the backside and gave him a lustful wink. He smiled nervously at me, unsure of what to make of his pansy neighbor, turned to the woman on his other side and talked to her for the rest of the evening.

A large opera singer announced that she was going to sing the aria 'Casta Diva' from *Norma* by Bellini and that she was going to sing it in English. Most of the Italians immediately left the room, which was my cue to go outside and light up a Lucky. I went to find Effie in the lobby and saw that she was placating a crying Rosa. Guido walked up, grabbed Rosa's arm and dragged her to their car in the lemon orchard.

'Is everything okay?' I asked.

Effie shook her head. 'No. Let's walk.'

The opera singer had a nice voice and the music was quite beautiful, but it's a well-known fact that only when you hear it sung in English do you realize what a load of baloney opera is:

> On us with favor gleaming
> Free from rain clouds, please shine
> Oh! Calm thou hearts, too ardent burning.

We walked across a narrow bocce court down to the Cana creek and stopped in the middle of a wooden bridge. Despite the evening's feast, the water was still alive with fish, illuminated by kerosene flares that filled the air with black smoke.

'What's the problem with Rosa?'

'Too much to drink . ... and Guido gets jealous.' I felt, for once, that maybe creepy Guido and I had something in common. And from what I could see of Rosa she wasn't just a little noddy-headed from one glass too many, she was as tight as the bark on a tree.

'Jealous?' I said innocently, as though this were an emotion I had barely thought about, much less experienced.

'J.B.'

'Really, why?' I asked, as if I didn't know that the frock-lifter Carpentier was about as subtle as a dog in heat.

'It goes back a long time. When we were young, long before Guido, we used to come here to visit Irène and Edith a lot. J.B. always had a soft spot for Rosa – and she for him – and sometimes Rosa would spend the night with J.B. Guido found out about it recently. I don't know how. Rosa never told anyone. J.B. is very . . .'

'Affectionate?' I said, even though meathound and cocksmith were the words that first came to mind.

'And Guido is . . . rough on her.'

I felt sad for Rosa and sorry that she was married to her runty New York meatball husband. But mostly I stopped feeling sorry for myself. I had allowed jealousy to eat into my mind like the root louse eats into the vines and chokes all that is good and healthy. I leaned into Effie and kissed her. The kerosene smoke billowed and swirled all around us, but for me the air had become a lot clearer. The opera singer warbled her conclusion to Bellini's aria and I think I heard her sing, 'Peace on earth again returning.' I don't know about peace on earth, but personally I felt that someone had lifted a two-ton Cadillac V-16 off my head. This lasted about ten seconds because as we walked back along the narrow bocce court I wondered, if Carpentier wasn't the one who had lit Effie's torch while I was away, then who was?

39

A rainstorm blew in from San Pablo Bay. I walked up to my room and fired up the old potbellied stove. It had a chimney on it that snaked in four directions before hitting a hole in the outside wall. After some coaxing the kindling lit and I threw on a knuckle of Spanish pine.

I sat on the cot and took out J.B.'s fountain pen and wallet. The pen was a good one, French with a gold nib, and the tortoiseshell was real. Digging my thumbnail under the wallet's fastening stud, I flipped it open. Intuitively, I swiftly fanned the greenbacks and stuffed them in my back pocket. Once a thief, always a thief, but there were only a few singles; this wasn't a man who needed to carry money. In the back fold of the leather were torn-out advertisements for hemorrhoids and rootstock from a French newspaper and a few photographs. There was a fuzzy Kodak Brownie picture of a proud dog with a large bird in its jaws, professional photos of his youthful parents – fresh off the boat wearing their Old World clothes and frozen New World smiles. There was a formal photo of a woman with two small daughters. And then I flicked to a photo that made me smile. I've fished a lot of dirty photos in my time, usually from the more respectable wallets. I once hooked a stash of photos from a preacher in Duluth that would bring up your dinner. The picture in my hand was tame compared to some I've seen.

The blond girl was lying amongst the crumpled sheets of a bed that looked like it had seen some action. She was on her knees with her back arched right back so that her curls rested on a large bolster pillow behind her. Her thighs were wide apart and her nooky smiled right at you. Another girl, a brunette whose face was turned away from the camera, was leaning over, her face six inches from Blondie's hairy crotch, getting ready for lunch. I stared at Blondie's face. She had freshly marcelled curls and dark painted lips that turned down at the corners in perpetual disappointment. Her narrow plucked eyebrows arched across the top of lids heavy from a smoke or two of something other than tobacco. It was a pretty face, yet a face full of sorrow. I flicked on to the next photograph. The brunette had moved around so that her fat ass poked in the air, her garter belt loose around her waist and her stockings down at her ankles. Blondie, her legs now staddling the brunette, had lifted her head from the pillow and opened her eyes. It was almost as if she had sensed me watching. Her eyes sparkled and stared straight out at me and I could almost hear her saying, 'Hi, Tommy, remember me?' Sure I did. I closed the wallet and looked away. How could you forget your own sister?

40

On the day before Easter, I walked Effie and Mara down the hill to the Yountville crossroads for them to catch the bus to the Vallejo Ferry. As usual they would overnight with the Abruzzinnis and then attend Mass at St Mary's cathedral.

On either side of the road the wildflowers had sprung up everywhere. I could see irises and English daisies and cow parsnips, but Effie and Mara found flowers I'd never even heard of, with names like Indian Warriors, Monkey flowers, Milkmaids and Shooting Stars.

As I helped them onto the bus I made a joke that one of these days Effie would wear her knees out praying. Mara laughed, but Effie didn't.

'Belief is everything, Tommy,' Effie whispered in my ear as she kissed me goodbye.

As I walked back up the hill to Eichelberger, I wondered why she wanted to visit the city so often – and always without me.

If belief was everything, why didn't *I* believe? Why did I suspect every man she ever came in contact with or cast half a smile towards? Had all sense of love and trust in me been blinded by the shadows of too many city streets and dusty country roads? Hadn't I been the one who had always run away from attachments? And here I was, afraid that some other pickpocket thief, or worse, the man who had plucked her petals, would one day steal her away from me.

They say suspicion always haunts the guilty mind. Throughout my life I had looked over my shoulder ten times a minute, every hour of every day, turning my feelings into a pillar of salt. Sometimes your heart reacts a little differently than your mind. After all, hadn't she shown me only kindness? Hadn't she offered me the semblance of a life? Hadn't she given me her love? Hadn't I found some scraps of pleasure in contentment? Maybe I just wasn't ready for it.

Oh, boy, sometimes happiness can take you by surprise.

Isaias and I had bought a good Fordson tractor cheap from a pea farmer over in Petaluma. The bank had foreclosed on the poor guy and he'd gone belly-up which was bad for him but good for us because we got a 1928 model tractor for a steal. The bank auction was sad as they sold every last thing the guy owned – and I mean everything – from the bells around the cows' necks to a spare pair of dentures. At least I hoped they were spare, otherwise the poor guy would be sucking grits from a spoon for the rest of his life.

I often used to work farm auctions when I was differently employed and the sight of a crowd with all attentions on the auctioneer was, I have to admit, very tempting to me. I felt my fingers flex and, cracking my knuckles, I stuffed them into my pockets. As the lots got knocked down I noticed that there was one really tall guy who was buying everything. Isaias and I threaded our way through the crowd and stood next to him. He had a leather satchel over his shoulder and looked like a professional buyer and it was clear that there was no way I was going to beat him to the tractor. As the Fordson lot was announced, I flipped the buckle on his satchel and slipped my hand inside and felt a sizable wad. As I did so, I realized Isaias was watching me, kind of in shock. I put my finger to my lips to encourage him not to say anything. The bidding started and I pulled the money from the satchel. With one hand I fanned the notes and sprinkled them on the ground. I winked at Isaias, who was either disgusted or impressed, I couldn't tell. I nudged the tall guy.

'Hey, fella, is that your money down there?'

'Jeez,' he said, holding up his satchel like there was a hole in it. He dropped to his knees and gathered up the dollar bills. We got the tractor. I swear, Isaias laughed all the way back to Yountville.

The two of us took turns plowing the mustard weed. The mustard sends down deep roots and encourages the vines to do likewise, but now it had to be plowed in so that it didn't suck too much moisture from the vines.

The Mexican was an incredibly hard worker and I asked how he managed to do so much with so little help. Isaias explained that less than a century before, these hills were home to the Wappo Indians, until they were wiped out by European diseases like typhus and cholera, leaving only their ghosts to tread the hillside roads. Every so often, Isaias said, on bright moonlit nights you could see dozens of friendly Indians tending the vines. With a big smile and a twinkle in his eye, he told me that was how he coped.

Calida had prepared tamales and jicama and we sat at the small table in their yard. Kaz wouldn't dream of eating any meal without a glass of wine and arrived with an uncorked bottle. Calida brought out small glass tumblers and we drank and talked.

'So, how come Carpentier has such a hold over Archbishop Meehan?'

Isaias looked at Kaz and they both laughed. Kaz took a long swig before answering.

'Carpentier kisses the archbishop's ass. His yard boys kiss Meehan's dooley and J.B. Carpentier hands Monsignor Cathain a nice envelope every month to feed the poor, aid the underprivileged and bring comfort to the disturbed – including disturbed old priests.'

'And the Kriegel brothers?'

'I don't know the Kriegels. They only came here ten years ago. They bought the old Winnetz parcel. Good land and good vines. The wine could be excellent. Maybe they're smart.'

'They supply bulk wine to Carpentier.'

The old man raised his eyebrows as Effie had. 'That's not so smart. Let them.'

'You never thought about it?'

'Thought about what?' said the old man testily. Isaias

collected the dishes and went into the shack to help Calida.

'Selling your wine to Carpentier.'

'No.'

'No, why?'

'Because I know that bastard too well and the hog-fuckers he sells to.' Old Kaz loved swearing when Effie and Mara weren't around.

'Are your difficulties to do with the Church?' I said.

'No, it's personal.'

'Jean-Baptiste?'

'We worked together at L.M. Numuth.'

'You did?'

'Best vines in the valley. The 1906 Numuth is the best wine the valley ever made. Carpentier stole the rootstock. And everything else. We fell out. He's a thief and a phony. He's not even French.'

'He isn't?'

'Belgian,' said Isaias, who had rejoined us.

'When he got the sacramental wine license, I went to see him. I hated him, but I was scared we'd lose our vine-yard. So I ate shit and went to bury the hatchet.'

'How well did you know him?'

'I bunked with him for five years when we were appren-tices at Numuth's. I knew him, believe me, I knew him. The guy had too much ink in his pen. I watched him dab carbolic on his dick the first time he got crabs and watched him cry the first time he got old Joe clap. The guy was incapable of buttoning his dick in his trousers and just getting it out to piss with. He was so sick, he would get a hard-on looking at a cow's ass.' Isaias laughed and poured more wine in the tiny tumblers.

I smiled and urged the old man to continue. 'So you went to see him?'

'I did.'

'And?'

'He offered me five dollars a barrel or ten cents a ton of grapes.'

'That was bad,' said Isaias, who had heard all this before. 'We couldn't live.'

'What did you say?'

'I told him he should have taught his wife to swim.'

'To swim?'

'Yeah, they'd just dredged her out of that trout stream of his.'

'Drowned?'

Kaz nodded.

'Suicide?'

'Suicide.'

'Why?'

'She just got sick of being humiliated.'

'That was a pretty cruel thing for you to say.'

'If I could have made it crueler, I would have.'

'And the daughters?'

'They left for France the day after the funeral. They haven't spoken to him since.'

'So, I take it you didn't get his business?'

'No. But I got the smell of him on my clothes. You know that sweet and fancy French goat's piss he wears? The stink was on me and it made me want to vomit. I climbed the hill, burned my clothes in the field and walked home naked.'

Isaias and I chuckled at the thought.

I had some time before I picked up Effie and Mara, so I drove over to the library in St Helena. There were row upon row of shelves stacked high with thick ledgers stuffed with old *St Helena Star* newspapers. I must have gone through six of them before I found what I was after.

Apparently the whole US Roman Catholic Church needed about 100,000 gallons of sacramental wine before Prohibition and now, according to the paper, they were pulling down way over a million gallons. It didn't make sense. Unless the whole goddam country had converted to the Church of Rome, it had to be a scam. If there was a scam, then The Most Reverend Archbishop and his bagman Monsignor Cathain had to be in on it.

I hurried to meet Effie and Mara at Yountville. Everything raced through my head – I felt like St Paul on his way to Damascus.

I was late getting to the bus stop and they were already waiting by the gas station. Mara looked scared and Effie was sobbing into her handkerchief. I jumped out of the truck and ran across the road.

'What happened?'

'Poor Rosa. They killed Guido.'

'Who? Why?' She shook her head and looked at Mara as though it was too awful to put in words and unthinkable to repeat in front of an eight-year-old child.

She was right. Guido Brunazzi had been found hanging upside down, a rope tied around his ankles, dangling from a construction crane on 22nd Street in Protrero. His head had been split open with a five-pound monkey wrench. It must have taken hours for him to bleed to death.

41

Father Cathain conducted the funeral service at St Mary's cathedral. Rosa's older sister Patrizia propped her up on one side and Mrs Abruzzinni on the other. We sat immediately behind the family and I comforted Effie, who seemed to be more upset that she could do nothing to ease Rosa's grief than shedding tears for the unfortunate Guido.

Old man Kazarian, the unbeliever, dressed in his funeral suit, looked kind of awkward and out of place in the cathedral, amongst the clacking of rosaries. He tenderly held Mara's hand and chewed on a licorice root. He said it helped with his flatulence, which was always worse when he attended church. His wife and daughter had clung to their faith, but he had long since lost his own. A million of his fellow Armenians were slaughtered in 1916 for being Christians in a Moslem Turkey and it had turned his head away from organized religion. Kaz worshipped his precious vines and the only gods he trusted were the soil, the sun and the rain.

Across the aisle sat San Francisco's lowlifes all spiffed up in their Sunday best, smelling of roses and stinking with corruption. In the opposite pew was the short and stubby figure of Guido's bootlegger boss, Frankie Stutz.

I looked to the altar and wondered what squalid mischief had resulted in Guido lying there in that casket. The Italians had been murdering one another on a daily basis and now it was Guido's turn in the wooden box.

Frankie Stutz stared straight ahead at the altar, vacant and without a speck of grief or emotion on his face. He was about as interested in the proceedings as a whorehouse piano player.

My eyes drifted across the beautiful statuary and gold filigree of the altar and up to the tall windows with the unfathomable biblical stories in stained glass. I looked at the confession box, which I had long since visited. The last time I had been behind a velvet curtain like that was in Chicago when I stole the Mafia bible. I shuddered at the memory, considering the assembled mobsters across the aisle. Looking along the walls, I tried to recount the Stations of the Cross I had memorized in childhood. But I couldn't get past Jesus falling for the second time.

Effie seemed to be the only one who was interested in Cathain's elegant Latin, and as I stroked her arm her attentions were riveted by the handsome priest with the apple butter voice. Maybe Cathain was the epitome of worldly piety, but I knew Stutz had him in his back pocket just as Joe Masseria in New York had Stutz in his. I couldn't help thinking what a screwed-up place America had become since Prohibition. Everybody had everybody else in his or her back pocket. The hooker had the barkeep in her back pocket. The speak owners had the cops in their back pockets. The booze runners had the politicians in their back pockets. And I once had my hand in all of their back pockets. It seemed everyone was on the take and everyone had a racket. Even Mother Church.

After the service we gathered on the cathedral steps, taking it in turns to comfort Rosa, who was still bawling.

'I guess she must have really loved the guy,' I said to young Joey Abruzzinni as I lit his cigarette.

'Yeah, she did,' he sucked down the smoke. 'She always had terrible taste in men.'

The rest of the family seemed to agree with Joey that Rosa was best rid of her husband, but right then no one was sharing their opinions with the tearful widow. Effie and I kissed Mara goodbye and Kaz took her off to see the latest Rin Tin Tin movie, *Rough Waters*, which the papers said might be Rinty's last. If they caught the matinée it would give them time to make the two o'clock ferry while Effie and I stayed in town. Effie took Rosa's arm as they walked back to the Abruzzinnis' store and I excused myself as I had a few errands to run – but truth was, I hated funerals.

'I'm gonna take a walk. I'll be at my club,' I heard Stutz whisper to Cathain.

I shook Stutz's hand and said, 'Thank you so much for coming.' Stutz had a sour face and an unfortunate protrusion of a nose, so big that it prompted you to duck. He looked at me, smiled and threw up his hand as if to say, 'Who cares?' Mr Stutz didn't appear to be an overly compassionate man and clearly didn't give a two-cent cigar about Guido Brunazzi. Stutz had the personality of a septic ulcer. He had one eye that twinkled slyly and another that seemed to look you over for a good place for a bullet.

I followed Stutz up Van Ness. I kept my distance, but he was easy to spot. He was fatter than one of Kaz's wine casks, dressed in a gray Chesterfield melton overcoat with a black velvet collar and a high-crowned felt homburg. When he got to California Street, the Chrysler Imperial that had been curb crawling behind him pulled alongside and Stutz jumped in. It was obvious that his daily exercise didn't stretch to climbing Nob Hill. Fortunately, a cable car was clanking along California and I hopped aboard.

I smiled, thinking of all the rats – the four-legged variety – that were flushed out of Chinatown after the fire and ran up Nob Hill like they were chasing the Pied Piper. I fished through the scraps in my pocket and took out the letter I'd just hooked from Stutz's jacket pocket. I read it as the cable car climbed the hill.

Dear Frankie,

Why do you do this to me? Since last Friday night I've cried a lot and you didn't call on Saturday or again on Sunday. I love you, Frankie, always and forever, but you're getting a little too hard to take lately. You hurt me, Frankie. I can't take your tempers anymore. After you left I put butter on my arm where you burned me with your cigarette. You're just too rough on me, Frankie. Anyway, I don't think you'll ever leave your wife cuz she's a beautiful lady. If you don't call no more, I'll understand.

Respectfully,

Marcie xx

Through the front window of the trolley I saw the Chrysler pull up to the brownstone pile of the Flood Mansion, now home to the Pacific-Union Club.

'I have an appointment with Mr Stutz.'

'What name shall I give?' asked the bony stiff-neck in the morning coat and white gloves behind the walnut-paneled desk.

'Thomas Moran.'

The flunky vanished into the smoke-filled room behind us, leaving me to brush the dust from my hat and stare at the Italian marble and fancy woodwork. I took the lunch menu from a rack and noticed they were serving Waldorf Pudding, just like they did on the *Titanic* the night it went down.

The flunky returned. 'He says he doesn't know you.'

'Tell him I'm a friend of Guido Brunazzi.'

Once again, he returned. 'He still doesn't know you.'

'Say I'm a friend of Archbishop Meehan.'

When he came back the third time, the flunky had grown bored of me, and he had pleasure in saying with some finality, 'He suggests you try St Mary's Cathedral on Van Ness. This is the Pacific-Union Club.' He put his white-gloved hand into the small of my back and escorted me to the door. Ordinarily I didn't mind people getting close enough to touch me, but this guy had nothing in his pockets but lint.

'Do you have any more friends?' he asked with some sarcasm.

'Yeah, as a matter of fact, I do. Tell him: Marcie.'

Marcie was the open sesame and the flunky reluctantly walked me through the Moorish smoking room. Here, under the domed ceiling, was where fifty years of clever deals had helped shape America. Half a century of horse-trading rendered by avaricious stinkbugs sitting in these deep leather chairs and worshipping the almighty dollar. Here smart men prevailed over the stupid and fortunes were amassed at the expense of the dispossessed: stock market tips; cartels; freemasonry; nepotism; bribery; chicanery; corruption and graft wafted in the sour air and mingled with the sweet smoke from Havana. Once upon a time in my former life, I could have worked this club with some success, so I threaded my fingers and cracked my knuckles to avoid temptation. Looking around the room I noticed that everyone was drinking liquor. Some speakeasy this was – sure, there was carpet on the floor, Spanish flock on the walls and no piss and spit sawdust underfoot, but it was still a speak and still breaking the law – except that the Chief of Police was sitting in the corner sipping a Gilbey's.

I was ushered to a chair by the window. Opposite me sat Frankie Stutz, his considerable nose buried in *The Wall Street Journal*, a large glass and a bottle of Johnnie Walker on his side table. He knew I was there but deliberately didn't look at me as he turned the pages of his newspaper.

'You know Marcie?' he said.

'No.'

'Then what do you want?'

'We just met at Guido Brunazzi's funeral.'

'Yeah, I remember. You a friend of his?'

'No.'

'Family?'

'Kind of.'

'Guido Brunazzi can go straight to hell as far as I am concerned . . . he was scum.'

'Scum?'

'Scum.'

'He worked for you,' I said.

'He worked for himself . . .'

'And for his wife and kids,' I answered. 'And yet someone hated him so much they cracked his skull open and hung him up so he bled to death in unimaginable agony.'

'Unimaginable,' said Frankie with contemptuous indifference, so I moved on.

'I have liquor to sell – wine – and wondered if you would be in the market to buy?'

'Tsk,' he said piously, 'we have Prohibition, didn't anybody tell you?' He smugly sipped his whisky.

'I'm not talking ordinary wine, I'm talking great wine, ten years old. Probably the best you ever drank.'

'I drink whisky.'

'Tsk, don't you know we have Prohibition?'

He lowered his paper and looked at me once again as if I was already on the way to the morgue. 'How much you asking for the wine?'

'Twenty dollars a gallon.' In truth, I had no idea of prices.

'Two dollars.'

'Do you mean two dollars a bottle?'

He shook his head like I was considerably stupid. 'No, sonny, I don't.'

'Two dollars a puncheon?'

'Two dollars a barrel,' he answered.

'A barrel? Are you fucking crazy?'

'Lower your voice, sonny, this is the Pacific-Union, not some hole-in-the-wall guzzle shop.'

'We have the best wine, maybe the best in the whole valley – Cabernet Sauvignon.'

'Let me explain, Mr Moron.'

'Moran,' I corrected him. I hadn't heard that old chestnut since Catholic school.

'I don't care if you make your wine in a spittoon from cow shit and a rabbit's ding-dongs – just as long as it's fifteen percent alcohol, that's all that matters to me. You can piss blood and bottle it, for all I care. I'm not in business to win medals at the World's Fair.'

'That's not what I had in mind.'

'Well, get it in mind. Go shove salt up your ass, sonny. You don't know shit.'

'You're right, I don't.'

Stutz went back to his newspaper and waved his hand, indicating that our meeting was over, but I continued.

'What I *do* know is that you cheat on your wife, which is fine, because half of the fine gentlemen in this room do that – except they don't use their girlfriend's arm as an ashtray.' Stutz looked up and our eyes locked. I concluded my speech with some pleasure.

'Now, *that's* scum.'

He didn't react at all; he just neatly folded his paper, sunk the last of his Johnnie Walker, put down the glass on the side table and pushed himself up from the leather armchair.

'Wait here,' he said, 'I have to take a piss.'

Sure he did. In two minutes the only dick he'd be holding would be yours truly with the other hand jamming the barrel of a .38 Smith & Wesson an inch from my brain. I wasn't going to wait around long enough for him to whistle up one of his heavies to crack open my head like Guido Brunazzi, and so I slipped through the kitchen on my way to the rear door on Sacramento Street.

42

I walked past the Tin Fook Goldsmiths and Jewelry Store on Jackson. The basement store below had a sign that said, 'Freshly Killed Chickens'. The Chinese never minced their words because a live animal was always preferable to a dead one. The belief was that if you took it home kicking and squawking, at least you knew it was fresh. I looked into the jewelry store window to see if there was something I could buy for Effie.

Inside, old Mr Yu showed me an attractive ruby ring, which he insisted was real, but at fifteen dollars we both knew it wasn't. I bought it anyway. The Yu family had become famous during the gold rush because the Chinese miners wanted to smuggle their gold home and Mr Yu's grandfather made objects to sneak past the customs officials. They say he once made a solid gold frying pan, blackened with soot to make it look like the genuine article.

On Stockton I ran into the Chinese chapter of the Salvation Army banging their drums and shaking their tambourines. Those rice bowl Christians sure looked out of place amongst the abalone, seaweed and sea slugs. An elderly female Sally Army officer handed out copies of *War Cry* as the band played and she sang 'Onward Christian Soldiers' – with every other verse in Chinese.

There was a basement noodle shop on Clay where the Chinese workers ate their *juk* rice porridge and on the first floor was a more elaborate restaurant for the local merchants and tourists. Sammy's office was one floor above and his apartment was in a pagoda on the roof.

Sammy told Willi Chu to bring up a nice bottle of wine in my honor as I filled him in on the past three months. He smiled at the absurd notion of my doing hard labor and was very impressed by my once smooth, talcumed hands which were now calloused and, to the touch, felt like knotted rope.

'You must be in love,' said Sammy, concluding that there could be no other possible explanation for my involvement in manual tasks that didn't involve putting my hand in someone's pocket. 'What's her name?'

'Effie. It's short for Euphemia.'

'Pretty name. Greek?'

'Armenian. Her mother was Italian.'

'I thought you were looking very natty, Tommy.'

'I just came from a funeral.'

Sammy looked concerned. 'Whose?'

'Guido Brunazzi.'

Sammy looked less concerned. He shrugged and pulled the cork from the unlabeled bottle of wine. 'He was a friend of yours?'

'I didn't know him, but he was married to Effie's cousin.'

'That guy would steal milk from a porch, he was not to be trusted.'

'That's what Frankie Stutz just told me.'

264

'For once, Frankie Stutz is right. And anyway, what were you doing talking to a cockroach like Stutz?'

'I had wine to sell.'

'Why didn't you come to me?'

'I didn't think you were in the wine business.' Sammy appeared not to hear me as he unwound the cork from the corkscrew.

'You know it was Stutz that had Brunazzi killed?' he said, carefully pouring two glasses.

'That I figured. But why?'

'Guido Brunazzi worked for Stutz because Joe Masseria in New York said so. It was the Italian big boss's way of keeping an eye on Stutz. It was an arrangement that worked well.'

Sammy tasted his wine. I swished my glass, sniffed and took a sip. It was Pinot Noir – in the oak for at least three years, maybe. Kaz would probably have found it a little too young and grapey, but it tasted pretty good to me.

As Sammy gulped his wine, I continued the conversation, 'Carpentier made the wine legally for the Church, the Church handed it over to Stutz, and Stutz shipped it to New York. That much I've figured out for myself.'

'And you're right. Those holy guys don't even get their hands dirty. The liquor goes straight to Stutz's warehouses out in San Mateo County.'

'So what went wrong?'

'Stutz and Masseria haven't been singing from the same hymnbook for months. Stutz got nervous about who was killing who in New York and then he found out that

Masseria had instructed Guido Brunazzi to slowly move the Carpentier wine through the Farruggios.'

'Stutz didn't know Guido was betraying him?'

'Sure he did. He was always the fox guarding the henhouse from the day he arrived. It was just a matter of time.'

'So Stutz dynamited Farruggio.'

'And tit for tat, the Farruggios got some out of town guys to put the holes in Oakie Doolan's head. Stutz loses his patience, gets pissed at Brunazzi two-timing him and so he finally knocks him off. My people tell me that Frankie did the deed himself. He hit him with a monkey wrench – got blood all over his shoes. Then Frankie's guys strung him up to bleed to death.'

'Is that an Italian thing?'

'No, Tommy, it's an American thing.'

'So, *are* you in the booze business?' He seemed awfully knowledgeable if he wasn't, but he shook his head in the negative.

'No way, those Italians can all kill each other as far as I'm concerned. Anyway, the Church would never do business with me; they're all so fucking racist. It's hard for a Chinaman to get his knees under the table.'

'This is good wine, where is it from?' I sniffed the cork.

Sammy shrugged his shoulders in total innocence.

'No idea. Carpentier, probably,' he laughed. 'How about you? Did you do your business with Stutz?'

'No. He didn't like me. I think I upset him. I swiped a letter from his pocket – it was from his girlfriend. He'd been burning her arm with cigarettes. I let him know that I knew.'

'You should be careful.'

'I know.'

'And anyway, you shouldn't be selling off the old guy's pension. You should be in business.'

'Sure, if they changed the dumb law.'

'Not my dumb law, Tommy.'

'Mine either.'

'Maybe I can help you.'

'You can?'

'Let me make some calls.'

'Legally?' I asked.

'As legal as a Chinaman is allowed to be,' he shrugged.

As I put on my coat to leave, I turned and flipped onto the table the photograph of Gracie that I'd found in Carpentier's wallet. Sammy picked it up and smiled.

'You collecting dirty pictures now, Tommy?'

'It's my sister.'

'I'm sorry.'

'I found it in some guy's pocket.'

'This is little Gracie?'

I nodded. 'Not so little, apparently. Ask around for me, will you?'

I walked down the stairs of Sammy's building and the smells from the kitchen wafted up the stairwell. Out in the street, the Sally Army band was thumping away and singing:

> Crowns and thrones may perish,
> Kingdoms rise and wane,
> But the Church of Jesus
> Constant will remain.

As I turned the corner on Grant, for some reason I began to have a conversation with myself. I thought of Jesse James, who went through all those shoot-outs with the law. He must have ducked a thousand bullets robbing all those banks.

'But do you know how he died?' I asked myself. 'Shot in the back while he was hanging a picture. His best pal Bob Ford did it.'

I answered myself rather too loudly because people were staring at me like I was some lunatic from Agnew's Asylum.

'The dirty little coward who laid poor Jesse to his grave. You know what the moral to this story is, Tommy? Be careful when you hang pictures? No. Never trust anyone, even your best pal.'

I looked down at the cork from the wine bottle I had taken at Sammy's. It had the initials *FF* burned into it. Frederic Frères, the winery owned by Ulf and Stefan Kriegel. Now, I'm not suggesting that my dear friend Sammy would ever do me any harm, but I thought that sure as shit he had more than a passing interest in the wine and bootlegging business.

43

I slept the night on the Abruzzinnis' couch, kept awake by a crate of clucking chickens. Effie bunked with Rosa. The next morning in the usually noisy downstairs store there was a somber silence – just the sounds of the salami slicer swishing back and forth and of Joey chopping up a lamb's carcass.

Willi Chu picked me up on the corner of Columbus and Stockton and drove me out to the synagogue in Fillmore. Not that it was much of a synagogue, but Rabbi Weissmuller looked authentic enough. The sign above the door of what was previously a bankrupt nickelodeon said, 'The Assembly of Hebrew Orthodox Rabbis of America'. Inside, the empty synagogue looked like it could hold a congregation of thirty at most. Judging by the dust on the wooden seats, they didn't congregate very often. I sat in the back row and the rabbi, who must have been less than five feet tall and had taxi-door ears and a beard that stretched to his navel, sat in front of me. He talked over his shoulder so that if anyone were watching, they wouldn't think he was talking to me. As Rabbi Weissmuller and I were the only ones in the synagogue, this seemed rather odd to me. He had a thick accent – maybe Russian or

Hungarian – I couldn't tell, because he talked out of both sides of his mouth, dipped his head after every three words, looked over his shoulder and noisily sniffed considerable phlegm up his nasal passages.

'I think I could get you a permit for five hundred gallons.'

'That's a big congregation,' I said.

'The law says we're allowed a gallon per worshiper, and a lot of our people worship at home.'

'That's very handy,' I answered, observing the thirty dusty seats.

'This was the arrangement I had with my previous supplier.'

'What happened to him?'

'He went bankrupt.'

'That's a shame.' Shame for him and good for us, I thought.

'I'll have to check out your facilities, of course.'

I looked puzzled. Did he think we were running a bed-and-breakfast?

'Kosher-wise,' he said.

'Oh, of course.'

I asked Willi Chu to wait while I walked a block to the Haas candy store. I joined the long line and read the enameled signs on the tiled walls: *It's worth the wait because it's the best candy you ever ate. Made from all the good stuff.* I bought a giant ten-cent bag for Mara.

On the way back to North Beach I couldn't believe the rabbi was for real, but Willi Chu insisted he was. I'd once heard of the Prohibition agents nailing a thousand-member synagogue that turned out to be a deli in Russian Hill – but at least this guy had a proper building. Willi Chu also said that Rabbi Weissmuller was related to Johnny Weissmuller, the Olympic swim champ. That made me laugh – the funny little guy sure didn't look like him.

Before we caught the ferry home I took Effie for a meal at Lucca's – 'all you can eat for fifty cents' – and then to the movies to cheer her up. We saw Greta Garbo in her first talkie, *Anna Christie*. Garbo surprised us when she opened her mouth and said, 'Giff me a visky, ginger ale on the side, and don't be stingy, baby.' Boy, did we laugh. She had this funny accent that sounded just like Rabbi Weissmuller. Can you believe that? All those years in the silent movies and we thought she was speaking American.

At the Ferry Building I bought Effie a small bunch of flowers from a guy with no legs. He probably left them in someplace in France, like Chateau-Thierry or Vaux.

As we climbed the gangway, the choppy water in the bay was barely visible through the fog and rain. Effie and I snuggled up on a bench on the lower deck next to the warm wall of the engine room. We dipped into Mara's bag of candy and Effie admired her bouquet. As she sniffed at the flowers I reached into my pocket and pulled out the ruby ring I'd bought from Mr Yu at Tin Fook.

'What's that?' she said, looking over her shoulder as if we were being watched.

'Don't you like it?'

'Did you steal it?'

'No, of course not.'

For the first time, Effie was looking at me in the same way everyone else had done all my life. She was looking at me as if she was seeing only a thief.

'I bought it in Chinatown, I promise you.'

'But how can I ever know?'

'Because I'd never lie to you.'

She sighed, 'Don't you get it? If you stole it then it means nothing to me.'

I fumbled in my pocket for the brown paper with the Chinese writing on it that Mr Yu had wrapped the ring in. I could only find the letter I'd swiped from Stutz's pocket. I felt cheap and squalid. 'Effie, I swear, I never stole it.'

'You have to promise me you'll never steal again.'

Never steal again? That was like asking me never to breathe again. But I answered without hesitation.

'I promise.'

'I'm not kidding here,' she said, taking my hand and holding it above her breast. I could feel her heart beating.

'Say, "In God's name."'

'Whose God?'

'You can't treat God like another sucker, Tommy.'

'In God's name,' I dutifully repeated.

'Swear you'll never steal again.'

'In God's name, I swear I'll never steal again.'

She leaned across and kissed me, as though absolving me of a lifetime of sin. I pulled her close and stroked her hair. Boy, what had I agreed to? And all because of a fifteen-buck ruby ring that wasn't even real.

44

When marathon runner Dorando Pietri entered the stadium at the 1908 Olympics in London, way ahead of his rivals, he became disorientated, staggered and was helped up by the officials who escorted him in the direction of the finishing line and declared him the winner. Some considerable time later, the American runner entered the stadium in second place. The US team appealed vociferously, Dorando Pietri was disqualified and the US runner was then declared the winner.

Moral: It doesn't matter how far you've run in life, it's the last lap that counts.

I went to visit my mom up on the hill in Agua Caliente. Before I left, Effie and Mara had picked a small bunch of wildflowers for me to lay on the grave. Perhaps when things got better I could get her a proper headstone to replace the wooden pauper's marker. I tugged at the weeds and it was obvious that Maeve hadn't visited too often, even though she still lived less than a mile away.

I sat alone in the quiet of the graveyard wearing my suit, collar and tie. Why I'd gotten all dressed up, I didn't know, except that I knew my mom would have liked it.

I noticed I had a hole in my jacket, which she would have grabbed and easily mended in minutes. I put my finger in the hole and wiggled it in the direction of the wooden marker.

'Sorry, Mom, if you were alive, you could have fixed this for me. Do you remember old Mr Kittleman? He's dead now . . . of course you know that. Maybe he's keeping you busy making those white robes up there, wherever you've gone. I'm sorry they took away your sewing machine . . . that made me mad. It must have broken your heart. I did send you money and stuff. But Gracie said you gave it to the Church . . . I can understand that . . .'

I snatched at the weeds around her grave and promised myself I would come here more often. Maybe plant some flowers. We never had flowers in our apartment and a garden was a pleasure that I had always seen other people enjoy as I walked past their picket fences.

'Mom, I thought of you a lot when I was on the road. Every time I saw a lady in a hat and an apron, I thought of you. You know, I read in the bible that when Adam and Eve ate from that tree in Eden and sewed fig leaves together . . . you know what they made? They made an apron. That made me smile and I thought of you when I read it. I guess God wanted people working even then.'

I knelt down and with the flat of my hand smoothed the red dirt surface of her grave, tossing away the loose pebbles. I pinched at the hundreds of tiny leaves that had sprouted through the earth and then I stopped. Maybe she had planted these in heaven? I sat cross-legged and continued my conversation.

'Oh, and thanks for letting me look at Kittleman's catalogs. I remember them well, every page . . . sounds kind of dumb, huh? You know, I've always thought it kind of screwy that I was so interested in those catalogs. I mean, what sane person fills their head with garbage like double-twisted serge and embroidered voile? But what the heck . . . they were the only books in the house, so what else could I read? That's not your fault of course, Mom . . . and I've sure done a lot of catching up with my reading since. You'd be pleased with that. In a funny kind of way, I think I've bettered myself. Don't get me wrong . . . I'm nothing much in the big scheme of things, sure . . . I know . . . but even old Abraham got to be ninety before God said he was perfect . . . so I've still got sixty years to go . . . by the way, that was a joke.'

I looked down at the stands of pear trees planted along the road that snaked up the hill to the graveyard. We never shared such a view, my mom and I. If she hadn't been padlocked to her sewing machine, maybe we could have gone on a trip – a vacation they called it. But my mom was too busy, head down at her Singer, to be able to plan such an excursion to the most beautiful country, just a nickel ferry ride away across the bay. I looked back at the rough wooden cross.

'I know in your eyes I was never a son, only a thief. I was a thief, but . . . hang on, I forgot . . . I brought something to read to you.'

I reached into my pocket and pulled out my tiny

battered book. I flicked back and forth through the pages until I found what I was looking for.

'Now, don't go thinking this is more excuses, Mom, I'm just saying this is how this guy saw things, and he was a pretty important guy.' I began to read:

> 'I'll example you with thievery:
> The sun's a thief, and with his great attraction
> Robs the vast sea: the moon's an errant thief,
> And her pale fire she snatches from the sun:
> The sea's a thief, whose liquid surge resolves
> The moon into salt tears: the earth's a thief,
> That feeds and breeds by composture stolen
> From general excrement: each thing's a thief.'

I put the book back in my pocket, rearranged the wild-flowers and kicked away the weeds.

'I hope you like the flowers. They're from Effie and Mara. They're good people. Just like you. I think you would have liked them. I'll tell you about them next time I come see you. Maybe they'll come too.'

I stood back and pulled my jacket straight.

'And don't go worrying about Gracie. I'll look after her, just like I always did, I promise. She's a crazy kid, but . . . I'm her brother and I'm back now.'

I bent down and kissed the wooden marker. 'Sláine Moran' it said, spelled the Irish way. In Gaelic it meant 'good health'.

As I walked down the hill I thought what a strapping woman she had been and how, when I saw her dead, she had shriveled to nothingness. She was barely in her fifties when the Spanish flu kicked her upstairs. Spanish flu? That's a laugh, because the poor Spanish had nothing to do with it. Everyone knew it started at the army barracks at Fort Riley in Kansas. How come the Spanish guys took the rap for the flu that we started? How come it wasn't called the Kansas flu? Go figure it.

I knocked on the door of Maeve's house on Sunnyside Road. After the third attempt the door opened and Maeve greeted me with as much enthusiasm as she would a multiple murderer. My sister wore her unhappiness like a shroud that covered her from head to toe, but she still managed a slight smile. She made some tea and her big fat arms carried a tray into the room. I asked about Gracie.

'I haven't seen her in five years. Last time I spoke to her, she was working as a chocolate dipper in a candy factory in Vallejo.'

I sipped the tea and listened really carefully, like that black-eared mutt in the Victor Records advertisement.

'Then I got a postcard from the city,' she said.

I thought of the photograph of Gracie I had in my pocket, the one I had taken from Carpentier's wallet. I thought of getting it out and showing it to Maeve, but it would ruin her dinner and overcrowd her prayers that evening.

'Did she have a boyfriend?'

I had touched upon a subject that Maeve found distasteful. She still lived alone and it was obvious that no one had ever got Maeve's oyster near the plate, let alone opened it. She looked down and busied herself with topping up the cups. 'You know Gracie,' she shrugged dismissively.

'No, I don't.'

'She's your sister.'

'I saw her just once, at Mom's funeral, in seventeen years.'

Maeve put down the teapot and draped a knitted jacket over it to keep in the heat. She cleared her throat and spoke. 'She had a lot of men. A lot.'

'She did?'

'She couldn't say no. She was always feebleminded, so men took advantage of her. Once Mom died, she just went crazy.'

'Crazy?'

'She was a slut.' It would seem the photograph in my pocket would only confirm Maeve's low opinion of her sister.

'Gracie's postcard. What did it say?'

Maeve went to the sideboard and opened a drawer. She returned with a cardboard box. Sifting through a pile of old photos and letters, she found what she was looking for and handed me a postcard. It was a hand-colored photogravure of Chinatown, which by the look of it was taken from the corner of Clay down Stockton. I turned it over and read.

Dear Maeve,
    Happy Valentine's Day! Today is Tommy's birthday and it made me think of him and you.

Landed a great job in a new club. Hostess. Big bucks.
Love,
Gracie
xx

I smiled that she had mentioned me and even remembered my birthday. As kids, Gracie and I always had a closeness and love that Maeve could never share. Poor Maeve, it was our fault as much as hers. The card was postmarked February 1929.

'Last year?'

Maeve nodded and I picked up some other photographs from her box. There was my mom and dad's wedding photo and a picture of Gracie and Maeve smiling away in their first Holy Communion dresses. There was a photograph of me with five other kids smiling at the camera in our dumb Confirmation suits. I pointed at each one of them as I tried to remember their names.

'Mickey Cremona, Liam Devlin, Ugo Battelo, Teddy Dorgan and . . .' My memory failed on the last name. Maeve leaned forward for a closer look and supplied the answer.

'Renzo Gamboloto. You were caught stealing his father's watch. Don't you remember?'

I didn't, but it still made me smile. Also in the box was a baseball signed 'Tommy Moran'. I remembered catching it outside the Seals' old Rec stadium when us kids used to line up on Valencia Street in the hopes of a home-run hit out of the park. Maeve had also kept my mom's sewing glasses, a couple of garnet and diamond earrings that I had swiped, and at the bottom, my photo from Winooski. I looked across at Maeve, dressed in her prim, high-necked, powder blue, cotton dress. Her thin hair was swept back, perched upon a plain, pallid, joyless face with skin like crumpled linen. I held out my hand. She hesitated for a moment and then took it in hers and lifted it to her cheek. She had the same red hands as my dad. For a long time we sat in silence and I felt her tears dribble through my fingers.

45

Old man Kaz was glad to get spring over and done with because it's the most hazardous time for the vines. He hated the windless nights when the air could settle and the slightest frost ruin the entire crop. He smiled only when the winds blew up and the rain washed down the valley.

It sure was pouring when I picked up Rabbi Weissmuller at the bus stop in Yountville. He stood with his arms wrapped around him and his big black fedora pulled down over his ears. He was somewhat disgruntled as he had been unsuccessful in avoiding the wet squalls that blew in from every direction. I ran over with an umbrella to help him to the T.

In the truck, the rabbi's many layers of clothes smelled of damp dirt. Also, I hadn't noticed before, but his flatulence rivaled that of old man Kaz.

'Nice country,' he said, looking out across the Cana-Carpentier fields.

'It is.'

'What are they growing here?' he asked as he looked at the vines.

'Pinot Noir, Alicante,' I answered with my newly gained knowledge.

'This is a Catholic property?'

'One of them. Yes.'

'So, are you Jewish, Mr Moran?' Was he kidding? I didn't know how to answer.

'No, sir, I'm not. Irish-American Catholic.' As if he didn't know.

'Is anyone up there Jewish?' I looked up at the sky, thinking he was pointing to heaven, but realized he was pointing up the hill at the winery.

'Oh, yes, sir.' I was growing ever more fearful that this little guy was a good deal more kosher than Sammy had led me to believe.

We had scrubbed and hosed down the winery until it was shiny-clean, but the unlikely possibility of Isaias's conversion to Judaism seemed as unconvincing as the removal of the Sacred Heart and the Pope's picture from Effie's kitchen wall.

At the Jefferson Market in Fillmore I had bought a bagful of food – gefilte fish, lox, a fat kosher sausage and a challah loaf. After a brief prayer, the rabbi consumed slice after slice of the sausage as though he hadn't eaten in weeks. Mara sat at the end of the table, chin in hands, transfixed by this eccentric-looking visitor in his multi-layered clothing.

But it was Kaz who made the breakthrough. The rabbi said that in order for the wine to be kosher, it had to be made under strict observation to avoid libations to idols. This mystified the rest of us, but old Kaz kept quoting Leviticus and Deuteronomy like he was Jewish, even though we all knew he was Church of Armenia.

After lunch, Kaz led the rabbi up the hill to his tunnels. Weissmuller tiptoed into the caves, mouth open, like he was entering Tutankhamen's tomb. The two of them got pretty tanked up and it was when we heard them singing, 'My Yiddishe Momme', from deep in the hillside that we knew we'd be okay.

I dropped the wobbly-kneed rabbi off at Yountville and he grabbed me in a bear hug. He was completely blotto and kissed me on the cheek, filling my mouth with curly black side locks.

'Thank you, my son. Thank you.'

'You're welcome.'

As he jumped onto the bus he turned to me and shouted, 'Wonderful wine. Nothing but the best for the children of Israel.' And who was I to argue with him?

I noticed that the rain had stopped, leaving a rainbow arching across the valley. There was no pot of gold at the end of it, but now, at least, Kaz could harvest and survive. I drove back up the hill in the T, skidding through the puddles like a motorboat and singing 'My Yiddishe Momme' at the top of my voice.

46

I pushed through the crowd waiting outside the Long-shoremen's hiring hall on Clay Street. Most of them didn't have a prayer of being picked, but they all hung around – probably more for the conversation than the likelihood of a job. I noticed they had formed a line heading in the opposite direction to the union hiring hall. There was this one guy who had laid out a table full of bottles and a sign behind it said in giant letters, 'H. ZALLERBACH: WORKING MAN'S HAIR SPECIALIST Alopecia, Ringworm, Scurf and Dandruff'. The suckers were lined up for half a block.

I stood and watched as this guy, Zallerbach, with a bald head resembling the dome of the new City Hall, did great business. His customers sat down on a chair in the middle of the sidewalk and he dragged a foot-long metal comb through their hair. I was reminded of the considerable wisdom of my old pal Soapy Marx, who always said, 'Never buy hair restorer from a balding man.' What puzzled me was how come so many deadbeats with their asses hanging out of their pants, who couldn't afford a cup of coffee, were suddenly worried about dandruff? I realized what the 'Working Man's Hair Specialist' was selling in the funny oblong bottles labeled 'Zallerbach's

Hair Tonic' – pure alcohol. I'm telling you, everyone had a racket. I walked along the line of suckers and felt my palms itching. I threaded my fingers, cracked my knuckles and took a deep breath, as I usually did when tempted. It was getting easier to forget a lifetime of easy pickings. Once, I wouldn't have thought twice about relieving these moochers of their liquor money. But I had promised Effie.

Rabbi Weissmuller and I met at a coffee shop next to Ziegler's Five & Dime on Van Ness. I was sitting at the counter when the fried egg juggler in the paper hat told me I had a visitor. I turned to see the rabbi easing himself onto the stool beside me. He pointed to the coffee-pot and then at the counter. This was not a man to waste words, certainly not the few he knew in English. He was wearing his big black fedora and under his jacket he was wrapped in layers of tassels and fringes – no wonder he was sweating like an old cheese.

'So, how've you been?' I said. Judging by his less than friendly demeanor, he apparently had little memory of once kissing me.

'Svell.' I guessed he meant *swell*.

'Do you have the permit?' I asked.

'No, there's an obstacle.' He pronounced obstacle as '*obschtakel*'.

'An obstacle?' I said. 'What kind of obstacle?'

'A paper obschtakel, a hutch.' He sniffed the steam from his piping hot cup.

'A hitch?'

'Yes, you have to complete the paperwork. The Prohib guy wants to see as a person.'

'In person?'

The rabbi nodded and gulped down the cup of scalding hot coffee. The guy must have had a steel pipe for a throat. Getting up from his stool, he gestured for us to leave and slapped down a nickel for his coffee.

I followed the rabbi across Van Ness and down Turk as the little guy swaggered with a gait that swayed a good two feet from side to side – like a pendulum in a fedora. He lengthened his stride to make sure he was always a yard in front of me – either to show me that he knew where he was going or to give the impression that he was absolutely not associated with me.

On Polk there was a large May Day demonstration on the steps of the Federal Building. A dozen cops on horse-back, nightsticks drawn, patiently watched from a distance as the crowd became increasingly agitated. Rabbi Weissmuller turned to me and whispered, 'Communists.'

I followed him up the steps and we weaved our way through the crowd of sad-faced unemployed. Just a few hundred here on the steps, but the papers said there were six million out of work in the whole country. A guard on the door smiled at the rabbi and let us through.

We got out of the elevator at a floor that said, 'United States Treasury Department'. The rabbi and I walked down the corridor and the rabbi sat on one of the hard-wood chairs outside Room 171. The sign on the dappled glass window in front of us said, 'Bureau of Prohibition', and below it a narrow mahogany counter jutted out from the wall. I looked across to the rabbi and smiled. He seemed kind of edgy and in no mood for conversation. As the wall clock ticked louder and louder, I ventured once more into the land of small talk.

'So, Rabbi, is it true that you are related to Johnny Weissmuller?'

'Cousins,' he answered, like it was a question he was very bored with answering.

'You don't look much like him.'

'Distant cousins.'

'How distant?'

'I can't even swim.'

I put my hand over my mouth to stop from laughing when a fat Prohib guy with a seriously warted face opened the counter window. The rabbi jumped up and started jabbering at the guy in a mixture of Yiddish and English, neither of which seemed to be understood by the pen-pusher, but he obviously knew who the rabbi was. Warty reappeared with a file, flipped it open and read from the buff-colored top sheet.

'Kosher wine – for religious purposes thereof: Section seven-nine-two, subsection eighty-three of the National Prohibition Act of October twenty-eighth, nineteen-nineteen.' He looked first at the rabbi, then at me. 'Rabbi Weissmuller, Assembly of Orthodox Rabbis?' Weissmuller shook his head, yes.

'Do you have your certified congregation list?'

The rabbi handed him two sheets of paper and then excused himself, leaving me alone with Warty.

'What kind of wine are you providing for the rabbi?'

'Sacramental and kosher,' I answered.

'Sure. Is it dago red?'

'Uh-huh, kind of.' I took the wop insult like a good Irishman, but he pressed on.

'So what kind of grapes are you growing? Alicante? Petite Sirah, Carignane?' It appeared Warty knew his grapes.

'Cabernet Sauvignon,' I answered, and his eyes lit up.

'Kind of fancy wine for kosher drinking.'

'It's for the children of Israel,' I said.

'Sure it is.' He'd already taken me for Italian, so he sure wasn't going to buy me as Jewish. 'I'll have to check the alcoholic content,' Warty said, and scribbled on a piece of paper. He beckoned me toward him and I leaned in so he could whisper in my ear.

'Two puncheons to this address.' He made his point by squeezing my arm, which was a mistake.

I nodded, 'Sure.' With my right hand I took the piece of paper and with my left I took his watch – the greedy bastard. Warty stamped the permit and I thanked him with excessive gratitude and left.

Outside the Federal Building, the May Day demon-stration had started to get ugly and the mounted cops were pushing the union guys back down Polk. I bumped myself up against a guy who looked like he hadn't eaten in a week and slipped the Prohib agent's watch into his pocket. I couldn't keep it for myself – after all, I had promised Effie.

47

In June of that year, Max Schmeling fought Jack Sharkey for the heavyweight title. Old man Kaz and I listened to the fight on the radio. It didn't go past the fourth round when Schmeling went down, claiming he was hit with a low blow and so the referee disqualified Sharkey. The guy on the radio said it wasn't *that* low, which I think was kind of tough. After all, if Jack Sharkey punched you viciously somewhere between the belly button and the bat and balls, you'd complain about it too. Let's face it, a low blow still hurts, even if it isn't *that* low.

The full canopy of leaves covered the fruit on the summer vines, gently filtering the light through to the purple blue clusters. I walked up the hill behind the house. There were yellow poppies everywhere, just as there had been the first time I climbed that corkscrew path in 1919.

I sat down and looked at my grimy, calloused fingers. My old hands used to be smooth and immaculate, but in fact they were full of the blood and toil of others. What a creep I had been all my life. I looked up at the sky. Hoagie, we got it all wrong. Every time you roll someone, it's not just their wallet or purse you take; you take away their dignity of making a buck for their families. You take the very meaning of their lives away from them. I had been obsessed with my old pampered hands. But those hands had never made anything. Those hands had never planted anything. They had never bandaged a broken leg, made anyone a hamburger, never bolted a chassis at the Ford plant, never chiseled a slab of coal, sawed a log, or polished anyone's shoes but my own. When you think about it, I was just as bad as all those louses on Wall Street who I despised. I rubbed my roughened hands and felt oddly better about myself. Each blister and crack was my contribution to the real world that I'd never known until then. A world I had once scavenged and stolen from. Boy, I sure had a lot of catching up to do.

Mara came running up the path screaming and waving her arms about like a red flagman on a runaway train. It seemed Calida was ready to have her baby. Effie ran to the shack and I jumped into the T with Mara to go fetch the doctor.

The christening was at the little Sacred Heart Church at St Ursula's. Effie arranged for her priest pal Jack Cathain to conduct the service and afterwards we had the best day I can remember at Eichelberger.

Joey Abruzzinni had borrowed a bus and the entire clan drove up for the celebrations. Effie sacrificed four of her chickens, there were bowls of vegetables and salads and it seemed the Abruzzinnis had brought half of their store up the hill. They even brought Rabbi Weissmuller, who immediately disappeared with Kaz into the winery.

I had seen an advertisement for a Mexican band pinned on the gas station wall and six guys turned up in sombreros like they'd just arrived off the train from Tijuana.

Old Kaz said it wasn't going to be a good vintage this year because of the overly hot summer. The heat wave had already killed seventy people in Chicago and Kaz said if it was hot enough to kill humans, what chance did the grapes have? In the distance on the valley road, you could see the dust clouds, twenty feet high, as cars kicked up the dry earth as fine as plaster of Paris. Even though the big California oak shaded the table, sweat dripped off everyone as they ate, drank, sang and danced in the sweltering afternoon. I once again bluffed my way through the dances, cutting the rug with Mara and Effie like I had won a free voucher at Arthur Murray's School of Dance. Rosa already had a new boyfriend called Gilberto and the two of them disappeared in the vineyard for most of the afternoon.

The band couldn't believe the endless supply of wine and were still playing as they drove down the hill at dusk, followed by Joey's bus and a dozen waving Abruzzinnis.

The kids had fallen asleep from dancing all day, helped along with a nip or two of wine. Isaias and I carried his sleeping children back to his shack and Effie and Father Cathain took Mara into the house.

I lit a Lucky while I patiently waited for Effie to finish her prayers with Jack Cathain. He had his own car, a shiny black Hudson, and driver from Cana-Carpentier. He was going to stay the night at the archbishop's residence, which the driver told me was on the Catholic Brethren's estate. He said there was always some church dignitary staying the weekend and he made a very nice living ferrying them back and forth from the city in the Hudson. The driver winked at me and said, 'They have to check out the godliness of the growth.' I would have liked to press him more but Cathain came out and I waved them goodbye.

Effie and I tiptoed over a snoring Kaz, who had passed out in front of the fireplace. Effie put a crocheted shawl over him and we took a bottle and two glasses and walked the narrow path up the hill. She stopped to give me a small white flower with tiny green leaves that she called 'Miner's Lettuce' and I kissed her. We didn't make it to the top of the hill.

I woke as the sun rose and dressed myself. Effie was already cooking breakfast and I could see smoke from the stove's chimney curling up into the sky.

Later we had even more visitors when Sammy Liu's Pierce-Arrow roared up the hill, scattering the hens in all directions. He arrived with an extraordinarily attractive Chinese actress called Mona Fong. Mara and Effie were fascinated by her stunning embroidered silk dress and her slicked-back oiled hair, kept in place with a mother-of-pearl comb. She had pierced ears with long gold and ruby ear danglers that made my fingers itchy. Down her back she wore a single braided plait, which indicated that she wasn't married, and woven into it were ribbons of raw silk, which indicated that she'd like to be.

She had a long ebony cigarette holder and Sammy, obviously besotted, jumped to light her cigarettes. A cloud of smoke hung around her like a perpetual veil, softening the painted face behind.

Effie threw together a great meal, which impressed Mona and Sammy. They didn't know that the Abruzzinnis had left behind enough food to last a week. Exotic as Mona Fong looked, she had a childlike fascination with seeing a live pig – a creature she had apparently only previously experienced with noodles. Effie and Mara took her off to the pigpen and Mona tripped along in her Manchu high-heeled shoes like a child on a first visit to the zoo.

Sammy took off his white silk jacket and relaxed in a chair on the porch. He appeared to have a little wine inside him already and was consequently somewhat spiky. Old Kaz said it was too hot for him and excused himself, waddling off to his hammock in the orchard.

'So, what brings you to this part of the world?' I asked Sammy.

'I had a little business to do quite nearby and it was a nice day. Too hot for the city.'

'What kind of business?'

'Real estate.'

'Around here?' I must have looked puzzled.

'Maybe. Who knows? Prohibition won't last forever, Tommy. Why do you sound so surprised?' He offered me one of his Havanas and we lit up.

'I don't know, it doesn't seem very . . . Chinese.'

'Whoa, don't go all Irish and Catholic on me, Tommy,

you're forgetting history. Remember, the Irish only got here from New York because the Chinese built the railroads. As a matter of fact, every vineyard in this entire valley was originally planted with the sweat of Chinese coolies.'

I had obviously touched a raw nerve, and he gushed onwards, 'You probably have cellars dug into the hill behind us, right?'

'We do.'

'They were carved out by hand by Chinese miners fifty years ago. Until they decided that the Chinese weren't welcome here, it was the Chinese who broke their backs harvesting the grapes. Maybe the Italians and the Germans made the wine, but they sure as shit never got their hands dusty.'

'You're right,' I said, 'I should know better.'

'That's okay. You're not alone in underestimating us. Like the local sheriff down there,' he gestured toward the valley.

'The sheriff?'

'Yes, what was his name, Willi? The sheriff?' Willi Chu was busy polishing the car and smiled.

'Sheriff Beedy?' Willi answered.

'Yes, I'm afraid that on his days off in the city he's been losing rather a lot of money at the *fan tan* tables. Money he doesn't have. I'm afraid we had to rap him on the knuckles.'

'Not with a meat cleaver, I hope.'

'Tommy, you have the wrong impression of us. We are more civilized than that.'

'That's good.'

'It was a tire iron.' Sammy and Willi Chu laughed out loud in high-pitched girlie giggles that made me laugh too. Sammy assured me he was only joking, but I knew he wasn't. They kept on chuckling, as Willi continued to jabber in Chinese.

'Nothing a good Chinese laundry couldn't fix,' Sammy replied.

'What was that?' I asked.

'Willi reminded me that the sheriff shit his pants.'

Mona, Effie and Mara came back from the pigs and Sammy said it was time to head back to the city. We loaded up his trunk with a dozen bottles of Kaz's best and hugged and kissed cheeks. Mara asked for Mona's autograph, on the off chance that she might, one day, become famous.

Sammy and I embraced and he looked down at the valley.

'Beautiful. Is that Napa?' He pointed at a speck in the distance.

'That's right,' I said. 'And St Helena over there.'

Sammy shielded his eyes and looked over to St Helena. 'Did you know that there used to be a Chinatown there?' he said, pursuing his favorite subject as he sat into the car.

'No, I didn't.'

'By Sulphur Creek. They burned it down in 1908 to get rid of the Chinamen, in case they took root like the vines.'

Sammy shut the car door and I leaned in through the window. I changed the subject.

'Any news of Gracie?'

'No, people know her, but so far we haven't pinned her down.'

'Oh, thanks.'

'Don't worry, we'll keep looking. Bye, Tommy.'

'Bye.'

Willi Chu started the engine and they powered down the hill in a cloud of smoke and flapping chickens.

Effie giggled.

'What's funny?' I said.

'So that's a Pierce-Arrow?' We walked back to the house, laughing uncontrollably. Mara looked at us like we were crazy.

48

My mom said that when she was a kid in Ireland, so many people on her street had died from tuberculosis that 15th August was known as the Consumption of Mary, rather than the Assumption. My mom wasn't big on jokes, so it kind of stuck in my head. Effie, as usual, wanted to celebrate this Saint's Day in the city at St Mary's Cathedral.

I never liked her going there, but I never complained. With my cockamamie views of the world and religion, I could never see her faith as a strength, only as weakness. But an even greater weakness would have been for me to dishonor her belief. 'Belief is everything,' she always said. But why couldn't she believe with the same passion at the church of the Sacred Heart just down the hill at St Ursula's? Didn't the same God inhabit that little church as every other – whatever the size of the altar and the roof above? And why does God always have to be in a church, anyway? Why did she always make the long trek to the city with Mara in tow? It was as if it was her lifelong penance: a pilgrimage. Effie said I couldn't pick God's pocket and so I guess I would never fully understand this part of her.

However uncomfortable Effie's visits to the city made

me feel, I always agreed to them and tried to bury my disapproval and, if I had any pride left after the life I'd led, maybe I buried that too.

Effie said it was an important Sunday for the family because Kaz thought of it as Mary's day: the name day of his wife and Effie's mom. It was also the day, Effie said, when you presented grapes at the altar for blessing. The old man said the good grapes wouldn't be ripe in California. Obviously when those guys at the Vatican were first working out a calendar, they were already hauling down the grapes from those seven hills of Rome.

Calida was worried because all of her children had caught measles and she was concerned for her one-month-old baby. Mara too was covered in red spots and so Effie traveled to San Francisco on her own. She said she would spend the night with Patrizia and Rosa, attend Sunday morning Mass and catch the ferry home after lunch with the Abruzzinnis.

We dropped Effie at the Yountville bus and Kaz and I drove to the bank in Napa.

After half an hour of waiting, Kaz was asked to go through to the manager's office. A guard with a shotgun and a cartridge belt thrown over his shoulder put his hand on my chest to hold me back. I smiled at him politely.

'It's okay, I'm with him, we have an appointment.'

'*He* has an appointment, mister. Not *we*. Not *you*.'

'It's okay, he's with me,' said Kaz.

'No, mister. Only *you* is with *you*.'

I shrugged and left Kaz on his own. I sat down on the bentwood chair and the thug with the gun hovered nearby.

I tried to make conversation with the bank manager's secretary.

'So, what's with the guard?'

''Cause this is the third manager we've had in a month.' She nodded in the direction of his office.

'What happened to the first two?'

'Last one was shot. He lived though, just a bullet in the arm. The manager before that foreclosed on someone when he was working at our Vacaville branch and the guy's wife came all the way over here and stuck a hatpin in his eye.'

I winced, 'That's nasty.'

'He lived, but has since retired.'

After not more than five minutes, Kaz came out of the inner office shaking his head. The cockroach inside had refused to lend the flat-broke Kaz any more money so that we could hire the extra labor necessary for the harvest, even though we had the rabbi's contract. The guard smiled as we left. If I'd had a hatpin I could have caused him some serious damage.

The old man and I drove home in silence. We each put our heads out the side of the T to suck in some fresh air – it seemed both of us thought that we smelled of failure. My first instincts were to drive into town and go to work to raise a little capital. How long would it take? How many wallets would I need? The only problem was, I had promised Effie that I would never steal again.

On Sunday morning, Kaz pulled the tin bath in front of the stove and began to heat up kettles of water. He said that one bath a year was all anyone needed and that if you bathed on 15th August you would have good luck for the next twelve months, and anyway, he liked to smell fresh and clean for Mary on her birthday.

I was in the yard feeding the hens when the dark blue Sports Phaeton drove up the hill. As it pulled up, Willi Chu, his fat arms sweating through his cotton summer shirt, leaned out the window.

'What's wrong?' I asked, as Willi got out of the car.

'Nothing's wrong, it's just that Mister Sammy needs to talk to you. Kind of urgent. He thought me coming here to pick you up would save some time.'

'Can I get you some lemonade?'

'That would be nice. And then I think we should get going, Mister Tommy.'

49

Jack Dempsey was the best heavyweight that ever lived. When he fought the light heavyweight Gene Tunney in 1926, in Philadelphia, no one thought Jack could possibly lose. Except that he was so good, he'd beaten all the other heavyweights around and consequently hadn't had a fight for three years. That night everyone was shocked, because Tunney didn't just beat Dempsey, he beat him really badly. For ten rounds he cut his face to ribbons and smacked him black and blue. Dempsey had never been beaten before, so his somewhat surprised wife asked, 'How come you lost, Jack?'

'I forgot to duck,' he said.

Moral: Never forget to duck.

As we dodged a cable car up the hill on Clay, Willi told me that Sammy was waiting at a restaurant, which he called by its Chinese name: *Mung Zhu.*

'What does that mean in English?' I asked.

'The swine that never sees,' he laughed.

'Sorry, I don't get it, Willi.'

He repeated the name in Chinese and translated once

again: '*Mung Zhu*. The swine that never sees.' I shook my head like a knucklehead.

'*Mung Zhu*. Blind pig. Get it? Like a blind pig speakeasy?' He let out a loud, high-pitched giggle at his lame joke.

Sammy sat at the corner table with his back to the wall, reading the *Chung Sai Yat Po* newspaper. He was jacketless in a crisply ironed linen shirt and fanned himself from the hothouse heat. We embraced as usual and sat down. The waiter, who wore an old-fashioned plaited Manchu *queue* pigtail down his back, poured green tea.

'How was the drive?' asked Sammy.

'Very comfortable.'

'Good.' He slurped his tea.

'Is there a problem?'

'No, no problem. Just a little business.' A large duck was placed in the center of the table, followed by many other platters.

'First, let's eat.' He beckoned to Willi Chu. 'Willi?'

Willi Chu came over, picked up some chopsticks and tasted the food before Sammy would eat. I remembered his Uncle Joe, during periods of unrest, used to do the same, fearful as he was of being poisoned. Willi didn't drop dead, so we filled our plates.

They brought many more dishes until we both sat there stuffed as fat as Buddha's belly. Sammy shook out a Chesterfield and offered it to me. I gestured that I had my own and lit up a Lucky.

'Tommy, I have business partners. Business partners have meetings. Business partners who think it's time that

Sammy Liu got into the liquor business big-time.'

'They do?'

'Big-time. So I need your help.'

'Me?'

'I need to stamp on Frankie Stutz's toes.'

'I don't have much pull there. The guy wouldn't scrape me from the bottom of his shoe.'

'I want you to ask your monsignor pal to arrange a meeting with the archbishop.'

'To do what?'

'To offer an alternative to Stutz and that piss-bucket Carpentier.' The very mention of his name made me nod.

'What makes you think you can muzzle in on their business? Didn't you say they had the whole racket sewn up?'

'And so they do, for now. The Catholic Church has always claimed the moral high ground. They see themselves as the real Church of God. They despise the Lutherans and the Jews and as for my people, they think we are damned: idolaters worshiping far-off pagodas. But the simple truth is that these Papists haven't held the high ground since Calvary. They abuse their right to the Sacrament and the bootleggers pass the liquor on to the juice-heads in Manhattan. We have been very patient. Now it's our turn.'

'To claim the high ground?'

'For us, it's business. It's about the booze-gobs or anyone else ready to part with a dollar for a glass of liquor. At least we don't confuse business with religion.'

'And you think you can make this work?'

'Yes. But to do so, first I need a special favor from you.'

'From me?'

'I need your expertise.' I knew what was coming, because I had only one expertise.

'I want you to steal something for me.'

I shook my head. 'That I can't do.'

'Why not?'

'Because I promised Effie that I'd never steal again.'

'But this is just a very small thing. Only you and I would ever know.'

'No.'

'Well, think about it,' said Sammy, who seemed to me rather too confident that he would eventually change my mind.

'I also need a favor,' I said as I blew out the smoke and picked some strands of tobacco from the tip of my tongue.

'Go ahead,' Sammy waved his hand.

'Yesterday I went to the bank with Effie's old man. He's flat broke and the bank refused him another loan. We'll need to hire extra labor, maybe twenty guys, to help with the harvest and the crush. The guy's ass is hanging out of his trousers; he's at rock bottom.'

'How much?'

'Five thousand.'

'That's not a problem.'

'We'll be able to pay you back as soon as we deliver to the rabbi.'

Sammy shrugged as though it didn't matter whether I paid him back or not, which is more than can be said for our local Sheriff Beedy, whose knuckles Sammy had rapped with a tire iron.

50

We stopped at Sammy's office where he counted out five thousand dollars from a thick stash in his safe. As I walked up Clay I felt the envelope inside my jacket. A sign on a telephone pole said, *Beware of Pickpockets,* which made me smile.

On the sidewalk, I walked around the wire cages filled with live ducks, geese and chickens. It reminded me of when we were kids and of the man who sold live chickens out of a basket on a pole. He thought nothing of snapping their wings to stop them flapping away, which made me wince now, but at the time it didn't seem at all cruel.

I thought how busy everything was and remembered when it was a smoking ruin in 1906. The buildings and memories spiraled around me and I could still smell the damp smoke in the air. I remembered the National Guard foraging in the ashes for melted jewelry. When the authorities finally allowed the Chinese back into the city there was an old merchant called Chong who tried to reclaim his steel safe, which had survived the inferno. When he got to where his store used to be on Sacramento the blackened safe was already sitting on the back of an army truck and he screamed at them in Chinese as he tried to retrieve it. A soldier smacked him with the butt of his rifle, pushing him into the road. Old Chong suddenly pulled out a revolver, but before he could pull the trigger the three guardsmen covering him opened fire and shot him dead.

When the dust had settled after the quake, they blamed the looting on a Colonel Peltz, who was commanding officer of the guardsmen in the Chinatown area. People said he even had Chinese pieces decorating his bungalow at Fort Ross. Many years later, after he retired, he was found dead in his bath with his throat cut. The Chinese didn't get the blame, they said it was a disgruntled soldier. What the papers didn't mention was that rumor had it that he also had his ears cut off and stuffed in his mouth, which everyone in Chinatown knew was the specialty of a gangster called 'Little Boy' Chong – old Chong's grandson.

I jumped off the cable car at Green Street and walked the three blocks to Abruzzinni's Grocery. Effie would be really surprised that I was in the city and that she would finally get to ride in a Pierce-Arrow, all the way home to Eichelberger.

Abruzzinni's store was closed on Sundays, so I walked to the back alley and rang the bell to the apartment above. Joey answered the door; he was lathering up for a shave so I hugged him with some care.

'Tommy, what you doing here?'

'I've come to pick up Effie.'

'She's not here, Tommy, you wanna come in? I'll wash off and make you some coffee. You want me to fix you a sandwich or something? I'm on my own here.' I followed him up the stairs.

'On your own?'

'Yeah, everyone's gone to visit my mom's sister in Eureka. She's sick.'

My mind was racing and fogging up with ugly doubt. Why wasn't Effie here? She never said Rosa and Patrizia were away in Eureka. She said she was staying with them and going to Mass. Didn't she?

'You haven't seen Effie?'

Joey propped up the mirror and started to shave expertly with an open razor. 'Oh, yeah, she was here. But she's mostly been at the church. Mary's Day, or something. I don't keep up with that stuff, myself. Six days a week here in the store, I sure ain't gonna waste my day off talking to statues.'

'Is she there now?'

'At the church?'

'Yeah.'

He shrugged, 'I guess so.'

'Okay. See you later, Joey.'

I took the streetcar down Broadway and jumped off at Van Ness. I found myself quickening my stride until I had broken into a trot. At O'Farrell I ran up the wide stone steps of the giant red-brick cathedral and pushed open the tall doors into the vestibule. There was a marble statue of an angel holding a giant shell containing the holy water. Her head was shyly bowed as if she didn't want to engage in conversation. I dipped my right hand in the water, crossed myself and stood at the back of the church. The air was thick with incense but the service was over and apart from an old lady in the front pew, the church was empty. She was saying Hail Marys very loudly to make sure God heard her. I'm sure He did. They could probably hear her in Oakland.

I looked up at the statue of Christ crucified on the cross with His painted bloody hands. He was looking at me again, just like He always did. His lank hair dangled over His shoulders like petrified rope and His face – the face that stared at me – was eternal pain carved in a block of wood.

It was then I heard Effie laughing. Not loudly, but softly and pleasurably as I had heard her do a thousand times before with Mara. I walked down the wide corridor flanked by statues towards the side of the church and the inner sanctum of the priests' rooms and offices.

The tall screen was a checkerboard of amber, hand-blown and cathedral-blue stained glass. The light from the giant Assumption Day candles inside the room flickered through the hanging fog of incense and silhouetted the two figures, their shadows creeping through the glass and bleeding across the marble floor.

I slowly moved closer to look through the open door. 'Belief is everything,' she always said. 'You can't pick God's pocket,' she always said. And now I saw that her words had been veiling a far more painful truth.

Father Cathain, this man of the cloth, this urban disciple, this handsome man with slicked-back, pomaded hair and a soutane of the finest silk with scarlet buttons – this man of God was touching her knee and cupping his hand high on her stockinged thigh. Her knee? His hand? So high? Touch? I knew touch. Touch was my life's blood. Touching was my art. I knew the way that fingers stroked a wool coat, a satin dress, a watch, a wallet, a cluster of precious letters, or a gun. I knew touch because touch was *my* religion. This priest in silk had an ungodly touch. This servant of Rome touched her like a man.

I stumbled away from the glass screen, bruising my hip against a pew before I turned and ran down the aisle of the cathedral. I had spent my whole life running and the sound of my feet on the marble flagstones drowned out the thoughts that were bursting in my head. There must have been fifty stone steps from the cathedral down to the street and I jumped them six at a time. A streetcar was clanking along O'Farrell and I snatched at the rail and hopped on board.

I slumped on the brown varnished bench and had difficulty with my breathing. I couldn't breathe, but I didn't want to breathe. Breath had no use for me now. Clutching at my chest in real pain, I felt as if someone had surely stabbed a pitchfork through my heart.

I watched as the streets clanked by: Polk, Larkin, Hyde, Jones, Larkin, Polk, Hyde, east, west, north, south. Where was I going? I was on a streetcar to nowhere. I brushed past a woman discreetly suckling her baby and jumped off the moving trolley. It was going so fast, I couldn't keep my footing and was tossed onto the cobbles, rolling over and over in the street like I had made a touchdown at Kezar Stadium. A crowd of people gathered to help me. They must have thought I was mad. I had grazed the side of my face and a woman from a hardware store handed me a floor-cloth to dab at the bleeding. I was running around in circles like I had a turkey on my back.

'Thank you. Thank you. Breathe. Breathe. Thank you.'

I walked up the hill to Sammy's office on Clay and, staggering across the street, I nearly lost my legs to the cable car. As I picked myself up, a car horn was hooting behind me. It was a Pierce-Arrow.

'You want me to take you back now?' shouted Willi Chu.

'No.'

'When then?'

'I mean, yes. Now.' I climbed into the back of the car.

'Effie's not coming?'

'No. No, I missed her, she took the early ferry.' I put my head down and dribbled blood on to the embroidered seats.

'I'm sorry, Willi, I'm sick.'

Willi expertly maneuvered the busy evening horse traffic on Grant. 'You want to go to Sammy's doctor?'

'No, no, I'll be fine. Maybe something for my face.'

Willi stopped the car at the corner of Sacramento. People came from all over town to get their ailments cured at the Hahng Cheun Yuhn drugstore, and Willi reappeared a moment later with a muslin pad smeared with ointment.

'Put that on the face, and you just rest. I'll get you home in no time.'

His voice was very soothing and I closed my eyes to sleep courtesy of the Chinese ointment. Everything was flooding through my head at once like screams in an empty barn. I heard the ringing of the cable car bells, the drone of the old lady's Hail Marys, Willi's faint, distant voice saying, 'Are you sure you're okay?' I saw the shy, marble statue with the bowed head that had dished out holy water for a hundred years and the flapping chickens, their necks awaiting a straight-edged razor. But louder than everything combined, I heard Effie's laugh. And more clearly than anything, I saw Cathain's hand cupped high upon Effie's thigh.

Boy, did I forget to duck.

'What happened to you?' asked Effie when I picked her up at the Yountville crossroads that evening.

'I fell off the tractor.'

'How?'

'On the steep part of the west ridge.'

She hugged me. 'I can smell camphor,' she said. I nuzzled into her hair.

I could smell only incense.

51

My old pal Soapy Marx told me that a very good cure for chronic arthritis was to bury yourself up to your neck in horse manure. It always amazed me, the extraordinary lengths that people will go to ease their pain. Even if they end up smelling like shit.

I ate dinner in silence and excused myself from the table. I climbed the stairs to my room and started packing. I took out the envelope containing the five thousand dollars Sammy had given me and with Carpentier's tortoiseshell fountain pen I wrote *Kaz* on it and put it on the windowsill. I opened my cardboard suitcase on the bed, neatly folded my only good pair of pants, took my shirts out of the drawer and looked down at my life – a suitcase full of nothing.

Back in the house Effie was busy with the dishes and I peeped into Mara's room where her red-spotted face was asleep on the pillow. I blew her a kiss and walked out into the yard to find Kaz.

He wasn't in the winery and through the crush-room window I saw him climbing the hill with Isaias.

'Is there something the matter?' Effie was standing at the winery door.

I opened my mouth to speak but couldn't. My tongue was numb, my brain was leaping a boxcar to another life and the words fell from my mouth like drunken spittle. 'Yes, there is. I think it's time for me to move on.'

'Move on? Why?'

'I can't pick God's pocket.'

'I don't understand.'

'I didn't fall off the tractor.'

'You didn't? Then how did you . . . ?'

'I fell off a streetcar.'

'Today? You were in the city?'

'I was. Sammy Liu wanted to talk to me. Willi Chu came up and drove me in. I looked for you at the Abruzzinnis'. Didn't you say you were having lunch there?'

Effie dropped her head.

'But you knew they were in Eureka,' I said.

'I know.'

'You lied to me, Effie . . . so I went to the cathedral to find you. I figured it must have been the longest early morning Mass in history . . . and then I saw you. I saw you and Cathain. I saw him touch you . . . Effie, I saw . . . I know.'

She closed her eyes, leaned against the oak cask, ran her hands through her hair and turned to answer me.

'It's not what you think.'

'What do I think?'

'Jack, Jack Cathain.'

I walked to the stone trough in the corner, turned on the hose and sucked in water as it splashed over my head.

I coughed as I spat out the words, 'I should never have stayed.'

'But Mara . . .'

'Leave Mara out of this.'

'I can't.'

She drew in a deep breath, looked up at the rafters and slowly lowered her head, locking her eyes with mine. 'He's her father.'

It's funny how someone who you loved so much, someone who gave you so much happiness, someone who had made you feel like a decent human being, could in the blink of an eye cause you so much pain. 'He's her father. Her father. Her father.' As I heard her words something snapped inside my head, sense drained from my brain and the heart I thought I had rediscovered took flight to be lost again on some dusty road. I realized that every time she had made love to me, I had been sharing her body with Cathain. I felt the knife blade of deceit twist in my gut, and spinning around I smacked her across the face. I, who had never struck another human being in my life, hit the only woman who had ever meant anything to me. She let out a cry and I stepped back, looking at my hand as if it belonged to someone else. I stood frozen, like those blocks of wood from which they carve the petrified corpses of Jesus.

'I'm sorry . . . I'm really sorry,' I murmured, leaning forward to stroke the side of her cheek as though her tears and the angry red marks of my hand would vanish away, but it was too late. Effie pulled back and crouched between the giant wine vats, sobbing in the shadows.

I picked my way through the chickens in the yard. They scooted in all directions, but to me they could have been as dead and bloody as those I'd seen at the old Kroeger farm back in Kentucky. Boy, the crazy, cruel things people do for the dumbest reasons.

In my room in the winery loft, I opened Hoagie's book. 'Doubt truth to be a liar. But never doubt love,' it said. Sure, never doubt that love can disembowel you like a Navajo knife. Never doubt that love had bit me like a rabid dog and the jealous poison had made me incapable of thinking straight.

I looked at the unmade bed and could see only Effie and Cathain lying there. How could I have been so stupid? I should have known that the man who had fathered her child would keep coming back for more.

I tossed the book into the suitcase, snapped the locks shut, put on my jacket, blew my nose, straightened my hat and left.

As I walked away from Eichelberger I didn't look back. I dared not look back. If I had, I would have seen Effie sobbing uncontrollably as old man Kaz and Isaias ran down the hill. I would have seen Mara in tears, delirious with fever, knowing more than we ever gave her credit for. What kind of father could a jerk like me ever have been to her anyway? I would have seen Calida standing at the shack door holding her baby. I was too stupid and too stubborn to look back. Butterfingers Moran, I was letting the only decent thing in my life slip through my fingers. I kept walking over the hillock surrounded by songless birds, past the field of mildewed cabbages, past the rusty old Fordson tractor, until I was no longer in their line of sight.

I tell you, jealousy is the coffin of love.

At the gas station I made a call to Sammy Liu, then started to walk. I had got as far as First Street in Napa town when Willi picked me up at the side of the road. On the way to the city in the car, I kept going through the Ten Commandments in my head.

> *No. 5: Thou shalt not kill.*
> *No. 6: Thou shalt not commit adultery.*
> *No. 7: Thou shalt not steal.*

Have you ever noticed that? Even back then, they figured that screwing around was worse than being a thief.

Willi managed to get me a small room above a pork shop on Joice Street – no mean feat in Chinatown, where it was so overcrowded that most beds were slept in with two shifts. Usually when one guy got up to go to work, another climbed in. Willi carried my suitcase up the narrow stairs and gave me a gift from Sammy: a bottle of Johnnie Walker Scotch. I finished a good half of it before falling asleep.

52

The next morning, Willi Chu pulled the car in front of the archbishop's residence on Alamo Square. To the side of the large oak door was a white porcelain bell-pull the size of an apple. Sammy casually yanked at it and bells clanged somewhere up in the attic. As we stood there waiting, Sammy looked over at me.

'Be humble,' he said to me, but I think he was talking to himself.

'Jesus was a carpenter,' I said, for no particular reason except that we were exploring the notion of humility.

'So he was,' Sammy answered. 'He made some shelves for me once.' He smiled, but it was an unfamiliar smile of a Sammy I didn't know.

A young peach-cheeked novitiate priest, who seemed to be expecting us, answered the door. We followed him up the elegant, curving mahogany staircase and Sammy ran his fingers along the shiny shellacked handrail.

'He does good work, your carpenter.'

The walls were filled with gilt-framed oil paintings – giant, grandiose images of Christ's considerable suffering, though none depicting his carpentry.

In the large upstairs room the Most Reverend Archbishop Meehan sat slumped at his desk, dressed in his black Italian silk, his red-capped head bowed in prayer. Monsignor Jack Cathain sat in front of him opposite two carefully placed straight-backed chairs. Cathain stood and shook my hand. He whispered so as not to disturb the archbishop's prayers.

'Good to see you, Tommy.'

'Jack, this is Sammy Liu.'

'Pleased to meet you, Mr Liu.'

'Pleasure,' said Sammy, and Cathain waved us toward the two chairs. We sat awkwardly waiting for the archbishop to conclude his lofty conversation. After a few minutes he looked up, fluttered his eyelids and smiled at us sheepishly like an epileptic coming out of a fit. I noticed that he had a brown snuff stain on his upper lip, which gave the appearance that his nose was leaking like a rusty pipe. By the look of it, his nostrils were in worse shape than my liver.

'Gentlemen.'

'Archbishop, my name is Samuel Liu. This here is my associate, Thomas Moran.' I nodded like I was in court, which was the only other time anyone ever called me Thomas.

Sammy continued, 'I represent certain interests in the Chinese community here in San Francisco.'

'What is your business, Mr Liu?' asked the archbishop, cutting Sammy short. He was no stranger to small talk himself, but he had little tolerance for it in others.

'Your Church requires a large quantity of wine for the celebration of the Eucharist. I would like to supply this wine to you.'

'We already have a supplier, Mr Liu,' said Cathain. Sammy ignored him and continued to address the archbishop.

'I would like you to terminate your present arrangements after the fall harvest.'

The archbishop threw a nervous glance at Cathain as he realized this was no community meeting and that Sammy was attempting to shake him down.

'Mr Liu, I don't think you understand. We have a long term . . . we have a long history of wine in this state.' He pointed to an oil painting on the wall behind us. 'That portrait there is of Junipero Serra, the Franciscan monk who was the first to plant vines in California.'

'And for sixty years the Chinese replanted, tended and picked the grapes.'

'Mr Liu, sixty years is as of nothing. We are talking about the Sacrament. The Holy Communion. The wine represents the precious blood of Jesus, as it has done for nearly two thousand years.'

'Let me remind you, Archbishop. When the Romans hanged Jesus on the cross, my people had already been civilized and worshiping their gods for thirty centuries before they hammered the first nail into your guy's hand.'

The archbishop smiled, self-consciously rubbed his own palm and fingered the large pectoral cross dangling from his neck.

'Mr Liu, thank you for your interest in providing the sacramental wine for Mother Church, but we are quite happy with our present arrangements. However, if we are ever in need of a bowl of noodles, we will call you.'

Cathain suppressed a smile after his boss's bad joke.

'You don't have an arrangement, *Mee Han*, you have a racket.' Sammy pronounced Meehan's name as if he hailed from Shanghai, not Galway. 'Only one quarter of the wine you take is religious, the rest is sacrilegious.'

'Mr Liu, the Volstead Act is an evil that we all have to live with.' He waved an Italian newspaper, the *L'Osserratore Romano*, in front of him. 'Even the Holy Father in Rome has spoken out against its ineffectiveness.' Sammy stood up. He'd had enough of small talk.

'Listen carefully, Archbishop. Stutz and Carpentier are out. If you don't hand your business over to me, you will have Stutz and the Farruggios killing one another until Prohibition is repealed. I am offering you a sensible alternative to what could result in considerable bloodshed. I have spoken to New York and they understand.'

It was there that Sammy lost me. Who was he talking about? Did he mean Joe Masseria or Sal Maranzano and the serious Mob guys? Who had he spoken to in New York?

Cathain picked up the conversation. 'How would you provide the necessary quantities we require? Close to . . .' The monsignor couldn't finish his sentence before Sammy provided the answer.

'A million gallons. We will provide. Good day, Archbishop.' Sammy walked to the door and I edged towards Meehan. Once Sammy had left the room I grabbed the archbishop's hand and squeezed it between mine. I bowed my head and jabbered away like a religious lunatic.

'Your Excellency, please accept my apologies for Mr

Liu . . . they are heathen men planted on Christian soil.'
I pressed my thumb into the veins in his wrist, loosening
his bony fingers.

'Are you a Catholic?'

'I am, Your Excellency. The Reverend Father Ramm,
who saved St Mary's in the great fire, was a family friend.'

'You knew Father Ramm?'

'I did, Your Excellency. He was a great influence in
my life.' Meehan pulled his hand free and made the sign
of the cross above my bowed head. I could smell the
cloves of his snuff.

'Go in peace, my son. God be with you.' I backed out
of the room and Cathain led the way down the curved
mahogany staircase.

I felt the gun in my pocket as I walked behind Jack
Cathain. Sammy had given me the Colt .45 automatic in
the car. For all my squalid life I had never once owned a
gun. At the time, I had said, 'No, not for me.' Sammy
said it wasn't an option as it was his own neck he was worried about, not mine. I could put the .45 to the monsignor's head and kill him there and then in front of the
giant painting of John the Baptist in the Wilderness. He
was a hypocritical sack of shit priest who had betrayed his
vows and taken Effie from me. They say you hate what
you fear. And maybe that was why I hated him so much.
I feared Effie's love for him and, deep inside, I feared the
truth that she had always loved this holy man more than
me, if only they had not been secretly imprisoned by their
faith. 'Thou shalt not steal,' went through my head. 'Thou
shalt not commit adultery.' 'Thou shalt not kill.'

Sammy said his goodbyes and, lighting up a cigar, walked out to the car. Cathain took my hand, held it longer than necessary, and locked his eyes with mine.

'Tommy, if we lose our honor, we lose ourselves.'

'I know. Antony to Octavia, *Antony and Cleopatra*, Act three, Scene four.'

'You know Shakespeare, Tommy?'

'No, never met him.'

I looked around the grand mansion. 'What do you do with it all?'

Cathain looked puzzled, 'Do with what?'

'The money you're pulling down from the booze racket?'

'It isn't for us, Tommy. It's for God's work, the work of the Church. It's not for personal gain.'

'Oh, that's right . . . a priest's holy vows. Poverty before God.'

'That's correct.'

'And celibacy?' Cathain stared at me. He knew that I knew he had not 'put his flesh to death', as his holy vows had demanded.

'I guess you stumbled along the Holy Road,' I said.

'Perhaps I did.'

I felt the gun in my pocket. I could take it out right now and place the barrel at his temple, an inch beneath his slicked-back hair, squeeze the trigger, split his skull and splatter his brains across the pale blue silk damask that lined the walls.

'When He comes to judge me, I will place my life at God's mercy,' he said.

But right then God wasn't doing the judging, *I* was,

and I felt little mercy. I moved my finger to the trigger of the Colt. In just a splinter of a second the gun would be out of my pocket and pressed against the black silk of his cassock, aimed directly at his heart. I would kill him, and to make sure there were no witnesses I would put a second bullet through the brain of the peach-cheeked novitiate who stood holding the door. I would then run to the Pierce-Arrow and Willi would floor the accelerator and we would make our escape. But I didn't. I couldn't. I walked to the door.

'God loves you, Tommy,' said Cathain, as he made the sign of the cross.

'He does? That's good. I was beginning to wonder.'

53

I asked Sammy to drop me at the corner of Stockton and Washington so I could walk for a block or two and think. I tried breathing deeply to clear my head and the air smelled of cuttlefish and salted cabbage.

I walked along Fish Alley by the Chong Tsui Fish Store and had difficulty keeping my footing because the slippery cobbles were slimy with salt water and smelled of sprats. At the end of the alley, kids were playing shuttlecock and it reminded me of the hundreds of games of stickball that Sammy and I had played in Piss Alley.

In the basement at the Yoot Hong I ate a big bowl of soup with dumplings and as I scooped them up I thought of the winery and the vines. It was just a month or so away from harvest and crush, when all the extra hands would be needed. Hopefully Kaz would have the five thousand dollars I'd left him and would be able to hire in the extra labor. I had looked forward to being around when the grapes were picked, but now I wouldn't be there. I looked at the calendar on the wall, which said that it was the Chinese year of the horse. So was that why I had run? Had some crazed, foamy-mouthed stallion galloped through my head and dragged my reason through the stable-shit behind it? Is this why I had run

away from the only scraps of true happiness that had
been so freely given to me – without my having to steal
it? Had I expected too much? Pride can eat at you like
a bucket of maggots and as I began to see how much I
had let slip through my fingers, my feelings revealed a
diseased soul born of too many years of self-preservation
– because I still could not forgive her.

It had started to rain heavily so I pulled up my collar
and ducked into a smokes store to buy a copy of *The
Examiner* and some Luckys. I walked back to my room
to drown my miseries in what was left of Sammy's bottle
of Johnnie Walker. I climbed the stairs and at the last
flight but one I stopped in my tracks.

'Hi,' said Effie, who was sitting on the bottom step.
She was wearing her old coat, no makeup and her hair
was soaked from the downpour.

'Hi.'

'Some rain.'

'Some rain,' I repeated.

'I'm so sorry,' she said.

I nodded stupidly. What could I say? I'm sorry I hit
you? I'm sorry you confirmed a lifetime's self-observa-
tion that I was a pathetic, hapless shit-heel?

'Tommy, if you leave, you'll break my heart.'

'That'll make two of us.'

'Three. You'll break Mara's heart too.'

I sat down next to her, tossed aside my paper and lit
up a Lucky. The last time I hurt like this I had a burning
ember in my eye.

Effie pulled back her wet hair, drew in a deep breath, and cupped her hands around her face.

'When I left high school, we went to St Ursula's to learn how to make wine. There were J.B.'s daughters – Irène and Edith – Rosa and me, amongst twenty boy novitiates. There was an old nun who looked after us at first, Sister Bronagh, Mistress of Postulants and Novices, but sadly she died and they never got around to replacing her. Jack Cathain was the principal of the school. We were all very religious. We prayed together and made wine together. J.B. was there all the time and got quite attached to Rosa. Father Cathain was instructing me because my mom had this crazy idea that I should maybe go into the Church. Jack and I spent a lot of time together as we tried the wine and . . . we made love. It was just once. It was a terrible mistake and I got pregnant with Mara.'

After a minute, or maybe longer, I spoke. 'So, why did he never help you and Kaz?'

'He was sent away to Philadelphia before Mara was born. Archbishop Meehan asked him to come back to San Francisco only last year. My father forbade any connection or favor, but he knew Mara should see her father.'

'Does Mara know?'

'No. That's what we were talking about yesterday. Jack would like you to bring her up, as her father. He was also saying goodbye because he's being sent to Rome. Tommy, please don't leave us.'

I shook my head. 'I think I need a drink.' I felt like I'd just gone fifteen rounds with Jack Dempsey.

'I'm so sorry. I should have told you from the start.'

'I can't rush this,' I said.

'I know, it . . .'

'. . . takes six months to build a Pierce-Arrow,' we said in unison. She smiled and kissed me on the cheek.

'Come home, Tommy.'

I nodded and stamped out my Lucky.

'I'll be staying at Rosa's,' she said and stood up, kissed me on the top of my head and disappeared down the stairs. I sat there and listened to every echoing step as she walked to the street. I went up to my room and poured three fingers of Scotch.

54

In the year 897, they dug up Pope Formosus, nine months after he'd been buried in Rome. They then dressed his rotting corpse in the pontifical vestments and placed him on the throne to stand trial before a religious court. They found him guilty and chopped off his blessing fingers.

Moral No. 1: Sometimes, being dead is not enough for some people.

Moral No. 2: Catholics are a weird bunch.

'The sheriff said the young man had been found running naked along the valley road in front of the St Ursula's vineyard. It was dusk and the Chinese cabbage farmer's truck had nearly run him over. The kid seemed very distraught and so the farmer took him straight to the sheriff. The boy claimed that someone had tried to strangle and bugger him at St Ursula's. He had two red lipstick crosses on his buttocks and a red silk sash around his neck.'

I sat silently listening to Sammy Liu, who poured me a Johnnie Walker. He continued, 'The sheriff said it looked like an archbishop's sash – there again, anyone could make one of those – but it was the ring the kid had on his finger that really concerned him, because it was authentic and no one could fake that. It was a genuine archbishop's ring and this led to some very disturbing questions.'

Sammy sipped his whisky as he recounted with pleasure his shakedown of Archbishop Meehan. I just listened, but it gave me no pleasure whatsoever.

'So, Sheriff Beedy and I went directly to the archbishop and explained what had happened. The archbishop denied everything, of course, but when the sheriff asked to see his ring, he said he'd mislaid it. Sheriff Beedy inquired whether the ring, which he then produced from his pocket, belonged to the archbishop, and Meehan nodded, yes.'

'The same Sheriff Beedy who lost all that money at your *fan tan* tables?' I asked.

'Indeed, the same Jim Beedy who said he would be happy to hush the whole thing up and avoid a messy investigation if the archbishop would listen to my business proposition. Archbishop Meehan and I later spoke alone, and I'm pleased to say we came to a satisfactory conclusion.'

'But the whole thing was a lie.'

Sammy shrugged, 'Apparently there's no smoke without fire.'

He put the ring down on his desk. The same ring that I had taken from the third finger of the archbishop's right hand. I should have stayed true to my superstition. Never roll a priest, it's unlucky.

'Can you explain something to me?' I asked.

'Go ahead.'

'Frankie Stutz is now out of business?'

'Correct.'

'Okay,' I reasoned, 'that's not a problem, because I already knew that Joe Masseria in New York was moving away from Stutz to the Farruggios for distribution. So, isn't Masseria going to be mad that you've changed the arrangement with his favored new supplier? Don't you think you should square that away before they spill a little blood on Clay Street?'

'I have squared it away.'

'You have? How?'

'I'm not dealing with Masseria. I'm dealing with Sal Maranzano . . . for the time being, anyway. You know there's a war going on, Tommy, and Masseria is going to lose. So . . .' Sammy shrugged. He really had it all figured out. While the Italians butchered one another on the east coast, he would supply his liquor to whoever was left standing.

'And by the way, where are you going to get a million gallons of wine?'

'Frederic Frères. I'm in business with Ulf and Stefan Kriegel. When we break Carpentier he'll have to sell, and we could be sitting on the most acres of the best vines in America. Prohibition can't last more than another five years, maybe less. After they repeal it, we'll be sitting pretty.'

I smiled, 'I guess you got it all figured, Sammy.'

'I guess I have,' he said, without a trace of false modesty. 'It's only business.'

I took out the Colt .45 automatic and put it down on the table. 'You can have your gun back.'

'No, you'd better keep it, just in case. At least until this whole thing blows over. Now, go see your girl . . .'

That sounded good. It reminded me of the old lady in the Abruzzinni's store when I first went up to see Effie at Eichelberger.

I ran down the stairs of Sammy's building and from the restaurant kitchen I could smell dinner. Sammy appeared over the banister rail.

'Hey, Tommy! I almost forgot.' He ran down the stairs and handed me a piece of paper.

'What's this?'

'Your sister, Gracie. They found her in a hoodoo joint tonight.'

I read the address and crunched the paper into a ball in my hand.

'Take your time, Tommy. If it's something bad you're thinking, just count to twenty first. If it's still what you wanna do, then count another twenty. And another, till you change your mind.'

'Why are you saying this?'

'Because Carpentier is with her.'

I ran three blocks in the rain to the address Sammy had given me. The front was a grocery and behind it was a large gambling room where I could hear the clicking of *mah-jongg* and *pai gow* tiles.

Through a beaded curtain a woman sat at a small bar nursing a drink. She had a cute painted face and a head full of permanent waves that had recently splashed in from the ocean. There was a purple haze in the air and

I could smell the sweet scent of opium. A big guy, who was probably meant to be guarding the place, was way out of it, slumped in a deep sleep on the bar top. This joint was obviously paying good money to the Chinatown cops, unconcerned as everyone was at the possibility of being raided. I pushed past him and pulled back curtains to the small interior rooms.

I found Gracie lying on a raised, oblong couch, close to naked and hopped up to heaven. She was so full of dope she hardly noticed that I'd entered the room. Sitting in the dim shadows was Carpentier, also in the process of chasing a purple cloud to somewhere, but he wasn't as far gone as Gracie.

'Don't I know you?' he said.

'I'm a friend of Effie Kazarian. My name is Tommy Moran. I'm Gracie's brother.'

'Tommy?' said Gracie in a tired, slurred voice. 'Is that you?' She held out her hand like she was asking for a snowball cone outside Mr Rizzola's corner store, but she didn't look like my Gracie. The eyes were the same, distant and crazy, but now hidden in deep shadows. Her once perfect face was now sallow, crumpled and old, her lipstick smeared, her marcelled curls in disarray.

'Gracie has a brother?' said Carpentier. 'I thought she was Little Orphan Annie.'

'You abused her.'

'No, I fucked her. Have done for some time.'

'Like you fucked Rosa Abruzzinni.' His pencil moustache curled into a smile to immodestly indicate another conquest.

'So what?'

'You're a piece of shit. An animal.' Carpentier sat himself up and twitched back his rooster mane.

'We're all animals, Tommy. Especially when we're fucking. Just like your sister. Just like Rosa. Just like your Effie and that horny priest with the big dick.'

I took out the pistol and fired. Maybe I should have counted to twenty as Sammy had advised, but my thoughts were so full of hate, I didn't get past zero. The first bullet cut through the artery in his leg and the second lodged somewhere below his navel.

Carpentier wriggled on the floor, clutching his stomach and spilling blood like a cracked sump. Gracie started to cry and I dropped the pistol and cradled her in my arms. We both watched as he squirmed in his death throes, as if we were two kids watching a half-dead cockroach crawl across the kitchen floor in our old apartment on Filbert Street.

I sat there holding Gracie until Sammy and Willi Chu arrived. Sammy picked up the .45 on the floor and gave it to Willi who, without a second's hesitation, finished off Carpentier with two slugs to the heart. He was still and the rest was silence. Just like it said in Hoagie's book. A great, empty, hollow silence as we stared at Carpentier's silk-suited corpse. Willi handed the gun back to Sammy, who wiped it with his handkerchief. Flipping open Carpentier's jacket with the toe of his white buck shoe, Sammy took the knife sheathed at the dead man's hip. I watched as he weighed the knife in his hand and then, without warning, he slashed me down the side of the neck. I screamed and clutched my neck as the blood oozed through my fingers. Sammy once again calmly wiped the handle of the knife and put it into Carpentier's dead hand. The blood ran down my arms and Gracie sobbed like a three-year-old.

I stared at Sammy in total disbelief. 'Why? Why did you do that?' I pleaded.

'It's for the best, Tommy. Now you killed in self-defense. I'll get you some witnesses and a good lawyer.'

55

During the trial, Sammy and Effie were in court every day. Justifiable homicide was the verdict and I got ten years in Folsom Prison.

'You'll be out in six,' Sammy had predicted, and I was.

Effie and Mara visited me at Folsom every month for the first year, and after that I looked forward to the home-made Valentine card from Mara on my birthdays.

Gracie and Maeve came whenever they could. Gracie had spent a spell out at Agnew's Mental Hospital, as they now called the Insane Asylum, and, for no particular reason, had changed her name to Crescenza – she said it was Italian for Grace and that she preferred it.

Sammy's business took him to Los Angeles and so I didn't see him much, but he used to write a lot. He loved dictating long letters to his many secretaries. He even produced a few movies, all starring his new bride, Mona Fong. No one ever saw the films in America, but by all accounts they were really big in China. He even got a new car, a Duesenberg – just like Gary Cooper.

I looked out the bus window, nursing my bottle of wine in the brown bag.

'Oh, boy, this is some bridge,' said the guy next to me as we drove over the new Golden Gate Bridge.

'Sure is,' I agreed. The bridge had opened while I was in Folsom and it was just spectacular.

'One of the Seven Wonders of the World, they say.'

'Is that a fact?'

'Yep, up there with the pyramids and suchlike.'

I looked back at the bridge soaring upwards, its red towers and cables poking into the clouds, and the cityscape beyond. It wasn't going to last as long as the pyramids, but it was a good deal more useful and was truly magnificent.

'The Colossus of Roads,' said my companion. 'D'you get it?' he said, laughing at his own joke.

Sure, I got it. There were twenty-two religions, five senses, four thousand languages, seven deadly sins, sixty-six books in the bible, thirty-eight Shakespeare plays, a hundred and fifty-four sonnets, three musketeers, four deuces, twelve labors of Hercules, ten Commandments, nine planets and apparently now eight wonders of the world. I thought of Hoagie and his book: *There is no darkness but ignorance,* it said. In all the books in the Folsom Prison library, I never read anything smarter.

'Without a doubt,' I answered and smiled as the bus entered a dark tunnel, driven through the rock into Sausalito.

Sammy had been right about the Mob in New York. In April of 1931, Joe Masseria was assassinated by the Young

Turks – Vito Genovese, Albert Anastasia, Bugsy Siegel and Joe Adonis – while he was eating lunch with Charlie Luciano. Charlie was conveniently in the men's room at the time of the carnage, taking a very long leak, he told the press. Consequently Sal Maranzano did become the big boss, but it didn't last more than a heartbeat, because the same boys promptly stabbed and shot him the following month, and the Young Turks were happy to deal with Chinamen in San Francisco, just as Sammy had known all along.

Frankie Stutz was the forgotten man. He disappeared like the pea in the shell game. Some people said that he'd retired to Key West and had quit the rackets and most people believed it. Then, in 1936, a Boston terrier dug up Frankie's remains in the Presidio. The autopsy said that his body contained a pound of bullets, which my cellmate at Folsom said was about sixty slugs. Whoever killed him wanted to make sure he was dead.

Monsignor Jack Cathain went on to become a big shot in the Curia at the Vatican and Archbishop Meehan was 'retired' to a remote Carmelite convent of nuns in New Mexico, overseeing their confessions and breviary to ensure their 'perfect and perpetual' chastity. And probably his own as well.

The Abruzzinnis sold their store on Columbus and moved to Florida. Soapy Marx ran for Congress, Jack Dempsey opened a restaurant, and Rabbi Weissmuller's cousin Johnny, the Olympic swimming champ, became even more famous in all those Tarzan movies.

*　*　*

I walked up the hill to the Eichelberger vineyard. In San Francisco I had found a bottle of L.M. Numuth Cabernet – the one that Kaz said was the best ever. In the corner of the label someone had penciled '1906': a great year for wine, if not for the city of San Francisco. I imagined, as I had done a thousand times at night in my cell, uncorking it with Effie and Mara. I thought maybe we could talk about old times and, later perhaps, if all went well, Effie and I could sneak up to the workers' loft and . . . I stopped dead in my tracks. The yellow poppies were sprinkled across the hills like stardust, the late sun threw long shadows into the mustard-covered vine rows and I stood there, completely still, in the middle of the road. Who was I kidding? Why the hell was I there? Hadn't Effie sent me a postcard?

It takes six months to build a Pierce-Arrow, Tommy.
Sometimes the arrows don't always land where they are supposed to.
I've thought about this a lot. It's time to move on to a Dodge.
It's parked right outside.
Bye. I'm really sorry.
I loved you, Tommy.
Effie

There was also a drawing of a Wappo Indian and a man with a revolving head. Underneath it said, '*Love, Mara x*'. Maybe she finally got to Coney Island.

I looked again at the wine bottle and felt for the box of Zubelda Turkish cigarettes in my pocket – old Kaz's

favorites. But hadn't Sammy told me the old man had
died of emphysema in the winter of '34? Hadn't Sammy
also told me that Effie had married – a nice guy, Sammy
said – one of the smart ones who bought up all the good
acreage after Repeal? Mara, now a teenager, had been the
maid of honor. It must have been quite a wedding up
there on the Eichelberger hill. I looked across the fields
as the fog crept up the valley, throwing a horse blanket
of cotton mist over the hillsides. I called over to a field
hand who was tending the vines.

'Hey, fella!'

'*Qué?*'

'Hey, fella!'

'*Qué?*' He walked towards me.

'You want a bottle of wine?'

'*Qué?*' He took the bottle, looked at the label and his
eye went to the year penciled in the corner. He smiled.

'*Mil novecientos seis?*'

'Yeah, 1906. It's a very good wine,' I explained, but he
knew far more about grapes than I did.

He nodded. '*Bueno, gracias.*'

'*De nada.*'

In the distance I could see the old lava-stone house,
the sycamore and the California oak silhouetted on the
horizon. In the fields the vines crept over the hillside,
chasing their own shadows. I took out my handkerchief, brushed the dust from my jacket, pants and shoes,
turned around and walked back to the main road in
search of some new life for me, leaving Effie and Mara
to theirs.

I have to confess to feeling a little sorry for myself as I emptied the wad of dollar bills from the field hand's wallet. This guy was loaded. The Depression must be over.